Some nights a̲...

Hunter's Moon

continued . . .

PRAISE FOR

Dark Light

"Exciting . . . White captures the fear, frustration, and sorrow that settle in after a hurricane as well as the courage, friendship, and spirit that fuel the survivors' will to keep going . . . *Dark Light* excels with boundless energy, a cohesive plot, and richly drawn characters . . . White's aplomb with fascinating characters, unique setting, and revolving subplots make *Dark Light* one of his brightest novels."
— *South Florida Sun-Sentinel*

"A compelling, readable tale by one of this country's premiere crime novelists."
— *Booklist*

"A tale that reaches back and forth in time, remarkable for the duplicity of its cast and the diversity of its twisting and turning."
— *Kirkus Reviews*

"It's film noir all the way. If a book can be written and read in black and white, this is it."
— *The Miami Herald*

"Evocative writing that combines the sensibility of a traditional noir novel with the unearthly mood of a ghost story."
— The Associated Press

"The novel peaks in a . . . burst of satisfying action."
— *Publishers Weekly*

"A cataclysmic ending that seems ripped equally from the pages of history books and tomorrow's newspaper."
— *The Raleigh News & Observer*

Titles by Randy Wayne White

Sanibel Flats
The Heat Islands
The Man Who Invented Florida
Captiva
North of Havana
The Mangrove Coast
Ten Thousand Islands
Shark River
Twelve Mile Limit
Everglades
Tampa Burn
Dead of Night
Dark Light
Hunter's Moon

NONFICTION

Batfishing in the Rainforest
The Sharks of Lake Nicaragua
Last Flight Out
An American Traveler
Tarpon Fishing in Mexico and
Florida (An Introduction)
Randy Wayne White's Gulf Coast Cookbook
with Carlene Fredericka Brennen

Hunter's
MOON

Randy Wayne White

BERKLEY BOOKS • NEW YORK

THE BERKLEY PUBLISHING GROUP
Published by the Penguin Group
Penguin Group (USA) Inc.
375 Hudson Street, New York, New York 10014, USA
Penguin Group (Canada), 90 Eglinton Avenue East, Suite 700, Toronto, Ontario M4P 2Y3, Canada
(a division of Pearson Penguin Canada Inc.)
Penguin Books Ltd., 80 Strand, London WC2R 0RL, England
Penguin Group Ireland, 25 St. Stephen's Green, Dublin 2, Ireland (a division of Penguin Books Ltd.)
Penguin Group (Australia), 250 Camberwell Road, Camberwell, Victoria 3124, Australia
(a division of Pearson Australia Group Pty. Ltd.)
Penguin Books India Pvt. Ltd., 11 Community Centre, Panchsheel Park, New Delhi—110 017, India
Penguin Group (NZ), 67 Apollo Drive, Rosedale, North Shore 0632, New Zealand
(a division of Pearson New Zealand Ltd.)
Penguin Books (South Africa) (Pty.) Ltd., 24 Sturdee Avenue, Rosebank, Johannesburg 2196,
South Africa

Penguin Books Ltd., Registered Offices: 80 Strand, London WC2R 0RL, England

This is a work of fiction. Names, characters, places, and incidents either are the product of the author's imagination or are used fictitiously, and any resemblance to actual persons, living or dead, business establishments, events, or locales is entirely coincidental. The publisher does not have any control over and does not assume any responsibility for author or third-party websites or their content.

HUNTER'S MOON

A Berkley Book / published by arrangement with the author

PRINTING HISTORY
G. P. Putnam's Sons hardcover edition / March 2007
Berkley premium edition / March 2008

ISBN: 978-0-425-22037-5

BERKLEY®
Berkley Books are published by The Berkley Publishing Group,
a division of Penguin Group (USA) Inc.,
375 Hudson Street, New York, New York 10014.
BERKLEY® is a registered trademark of Penguin Group (USA) Inc.
The "B" design is a trademark belonging to Penguin Group (USA) Inc.

PRINTED IN THE UNITED STATES OF AMERICA

10 9 8 7 6 5 4 3 2 1

This book is for my mother, Georgia Wilson White,
of Richmond County, North Carolina

•

and for my aunts
Jewel, Johnsie, JoAnne, DellaSue, Vera,
Lucille, Authorine, and Judy.

•

and for my uncles
Levaugn, Kerney, Thomas, Mitchell,
Paul, Eugene, and Carl

AUTHOR'S NOTE

This book required extensive research, and the author is grateful to experts in many fields, while taking full blame, in advance, for any misunderstandings that have led to factual errors. Thanks to my dear friends, Dr. Brian Hummel, Dr. Thaddeus Kostrubala, Capt. Jimmy Johnson, David Thompson, Jerry Franks, Capt. Russ Mattson, Robert Macomber, Judge Tony Johnson, and all the folks at Cabbage Key, Useppa Island, and Doc Ford's Sanibel Rum Bar and Grille for their input, kindness, and forbearance.

Capt. Mark Futch, one of the world's finest amphib pilots, invested much time in helping me make the flight scene herein accurate, and not just by taking me on low-level flights. As I was finishing the book, Capt. Futch, with writer/filmmaker Krov Menuhin aboard, landed his Maule off the dock at Useppa Island, where I was holed up working. Even though they were returning from a two-week trip to Central America, these men sat patiently going over charts and answering questions.

The scenes in the Panama Canal Zone were carefully choreographed, and especially helpful was my friend Tom Pattison, although all of my Zonian friends contributed, because we have had so much fun in Panama over the years, so thanks to Capt. Bob Dollar and Mindy, Priscilla Hernandez, Legendary Vernon Scholey, Mimi and Lucho Azcarraga, Teresa Martinez, Priscilla and Jay Sieleman, now director of the Memphis-based Blues Foundation.

Thanks to my pal George Riggs, I had a solid table on which to write this book, and, thanks to my teammate Gary Terwilliger, my writing shed had electricity—useful for working after sunset.

Finally, I would like to thank my sons, Lee and Rogan White, for, once again, helping me finish a book.

Sanibel and Captiva are real places, faithfully described, but used fictitiously in this novel. The same is true of certain businesses, marinas, bars, and other places frequented by Doc Ford, Tomlinson, and pals.

In all other respects, however, this novel is a work of fiction. Names, characters, places, and incidents are either the product of the author's imagination or are used fictitiously. Any resemblance to actual persons, living or dead, or to actual events or locales is entirely coincidental.

All that is necessary for the triumph of evil
is that good men do nothing.

EDMUND BURKE

It's easier to be a genuinely humane person if you can
afford to hire your own personal son of a bitch.

S. M. TOMLINSON

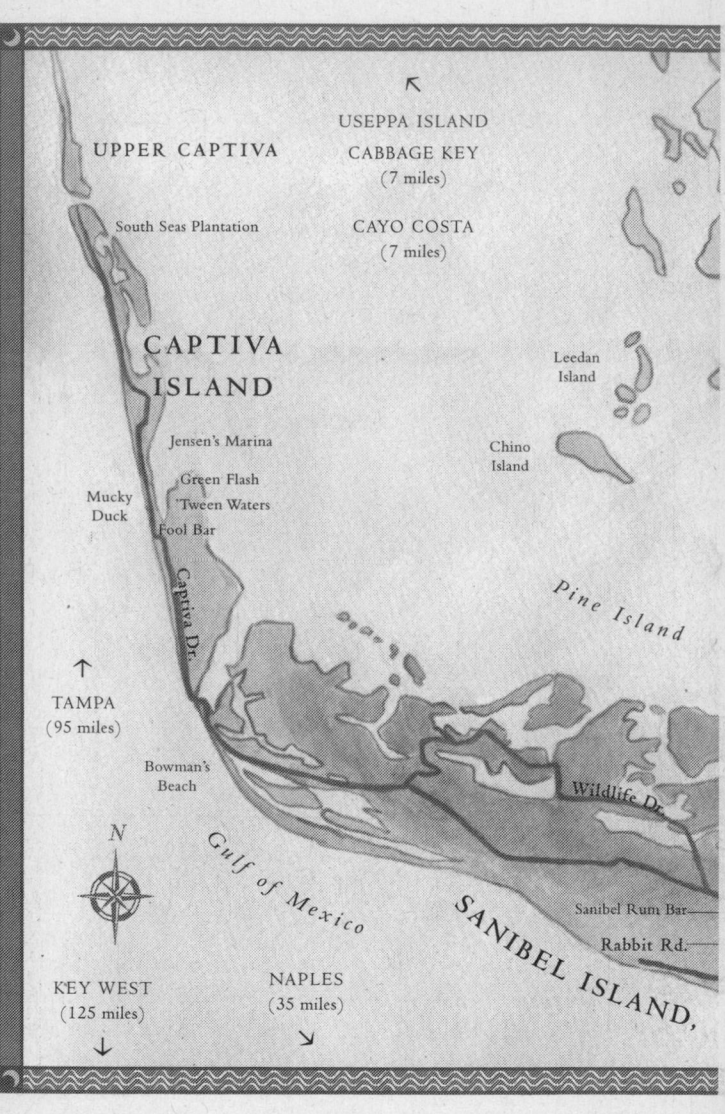

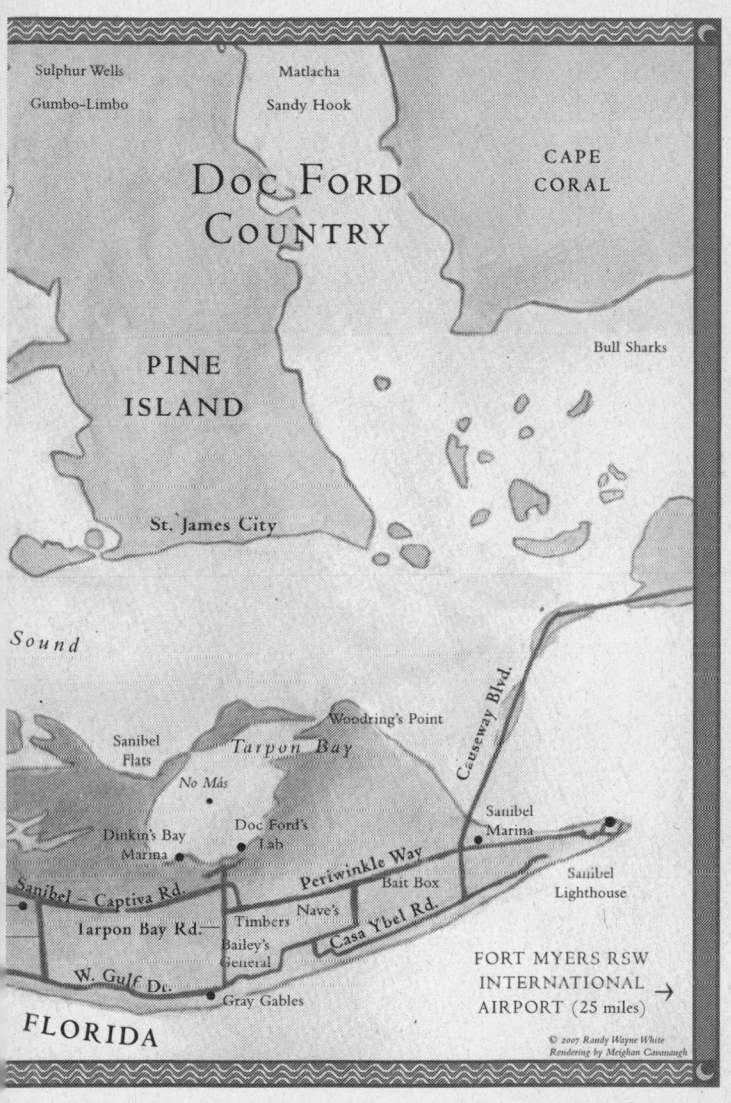

Sulphur Wells

Matlacha

Gumbo-Limbo

Sandy Hook

Doc Ford Country

CAPE CORAL

PINE ISLAND

Bull Sharks

St. James City

Sound

Woodring's Point

Sanibel Flats

Tarpon Bay

Causeway Blvd.

No Más

Doc Ford's Lab

Sanibel Marina

Dinkin's Bay Marina

Periwinkle Way

Bait Box

Sanibel Lighthouse

Sanibel – Captiva Rd.

Nave's

Casa Ybel Rd.

Tarpon Bay Rd.

Timbers

Bailey's General

W. Gulf Dr.

Gray Gables

FORT MYERS RSW INTERNATIONAL AIRPORT (25 miles) →

FLORIDA

© 2007 Randy Wayne White
Rendering by Meighan Cavanaugh

1

On a misty, tropic Halloween Eve, an hour before midnight, I stopped paddling when coconut palms poked through the fog ceiling, blue fronds crystalline in the moonlight.

An island lay ahead. Maybe the right island. Hard to be certain, because the fog had thickened as it stratified, and my sense of direction has never been great.

If it was the wrong island, I was lost. If it was the right island, there was a chance I'd soon be detained, arrested, or shot, maybe killed.

I'm human. I was hoping it was the wrong island.

I checked the time as I reached into the pack at my feet and opened a pocket GPS. The navigational display was phosphorous green, like numerals on my watch. It was 11:17 p.m., I discovered, and I wasn't lost. I'd arrived at my destination, Ligarto Island.

As I drifted, the tree canopy floated closer. Slow-motion fog cordoned off water and palms became brontosaurus silhouettes grazing in moonlight.

Fitting. *Ligarto* is Spanish for "lizard."

I've spent years on Florida's Gulf coast, exploring above and below the water. It's what self-employed marine biologists do and I am a marine biologist. Usually. In all those years, I'd never had reason to set foot on Ligarto. Until tonight. I was here because a powerful man had demanded a favor. Doctors had told him he was in the final weeks of remission, with a month at most before leukemia immobilized him. Would I help him escape?

"Escape to *where*?" I'd asked. We were in my lab, standing amid the aerator hum of saltwater tanks, the smell of formalin and chemicals. He'd surprised me, tapping on my screen door after midnight.

The man had nodded his approval. "Perceptive. Most would've asked, 'Escape from *what*?' Which is romantic nonsense."

His confidence was misplaced because I didn't understand the reference. Death? Afterlife? Nonexistence?

"No sentimental baloney, Dr. Ford. You nailed it. The question is, *where*? I have about four weeks to live, really *live,* before they hook me up to the tubes and monitors. I want to spend part of that time traveling—but freely. Incognito."

"Travel anonymously in this country? *You*?"

"Yes, this country . . . and others."

His wording seemed intentionally vague.

"No specific destination?"

"When I left the Navy, I traveled everywhere. Followed my instincts. What was I, twenty-five? Hitchhiked, worked on a freighter, even hopped a train. That's the way I want it to be."

An evasion. He didn't bother to conceal it so I didn't pretend to be convinced.

"Relive your youth. Put on jeans, a T-shirt, and blend in. Is that the idea?"

"You're saying I'll be recognized. I don't think so. People expect to see me on television, not the street."

"Take it from a guy who's never owned a TV. People know who you are . . . especially after"—I caught myself—"after the recent controversy."

Annoyed, he said, "I don't have time for diplomacy. Are you talking about my wife's death? Or the million-dollar bounty on my head?"

I knew that his wife had been killed in a plane mishap. I'd also read that he'd infuriated religious fundamentalists, Muslim and Christian, but I was unaware that a reward had been offered. I remained diplomatic.

"Both."

"That was five months ago—eternity, to the American public. Please stop second-guessing. You're like the so-called media experts who gave me a ration of crap for being a concept guy, called me a dope when it came to details. Believe me, I'm no dope, and this has nothing to do with revisiting my youth. I'd love to stick it up their butts one last time."

The media, or the fundamentalists? Either way, his bitterness was unexpected.

I'd been hunched over a microscope studying a sea urchin embryo—it was liquid green, round, and clouded like a miniature planet.

I stood. "Why are you telling me this?"

"Sharing personal information? Because you've proven you can be trusted. You know the incident I'm talking about. You refused to discuss it."

He was referring to something that happened eleven years earlier, in Cartagena, Colombia.

I replied, "You're giving me credit for something I didn't do."

"Wrong. I'm giving you credit for keeping your mouth shut. Remember who you're talking to, Dr. Ford. I trust you with my secret because I know your secrets. Or should I say, I know *enough*. Surprised?"

No, I wasn't surprised.

"Do the feds still call that 'coercion'?"

"Not in the executive branch. It's called 'doing business.' Something else that may interest you is information I have about a friend of yours. Mr. Tomlinson. Things I doubt even you are aware of."

Tomlinson is my neighbor at Dinkin's Bay Marina, Sanibel Island, Florida. He's part sailor, part saint, part goat. Picture a satyr, with salty dreadlocks, bony legs, wearing a sarong. Tomlinson and I are friends despite a convoluted history, and despite the fact that, as polar opposites, we sometimes clash. We'd clashed recently. I hadn't seen the man in two weeks.

I returned to the microscope and toyed with the focus. "Tomlinson has secrets worth knowing? I'm shocked."

He wasn't misled by my careful indifference. "You may be. When you learn the truth."

I looked up involuntarily.

The man's smile broadened.

"Yes. I can see you're interested."

FOG ISN'T MENTIONED IN GUIDEBOOKS ABOUT sunny Florida because tourists are seldom on the water at midnight, when a Caribbean low mingles with cool Gulf air.

The cloud now settling was as dense as any I'd seen. Gray whirlpools of vapor descended, condensed, then re-formed as moonlit veils. Water droplets created curtains of pearls, so visibility fluctuated. Each drifting cloud added to the illusion that the island was moving, not me, not the fog. Ligarto appeared to be a galleon adrift, floating on a random course and gaining speed. I had to start paddling soon if I hoped to keep up.

I did.

Took long, cautious strokes. Paddled so quietly I could hear water dripping from foliage, drops heavy as Gulf Stream rain. The reason I didn't want to make noise was because I knew a security team was guarding the island. Pros, the best in the world.

They would be carrying rocket launchers, exotic weapons systems, electronic gizmos designed to debilitate or kill, no telling what else. Probably five or six men and women, all bored—a little pissed-off, too—forced to work on a favorite adult party night: Halloween.

A dangerous combination for any misguided dimwit foolish enough to attempt to breach island security.

Dangerous for me, the occasional misguided dimwit.

Every few strokes, I paused. In fog, there's the illusion that sound is muffled. In fact, fog conducts sound more efficiently than air. If there was a boat patrolling the area, I would've heard it. Instead, I heard only an outboard motor far away—someone run aground, judging from the seesaw whine. I could also hear the turbo whistle of a jetliner settling into its landing approach, as invisible from sea level as I was invisible to passengers above.

Maybe the patrol boat was at anchor . . . or maybe a few yards away, hidden by mist.

If so, there was nothing I could do. I was alone, in a canoe, miles from my Sanibel home, in a chain of bays that links cities along the Gulf Coast. Tampa was some-where out there in the gloom, a hundred miles north. Naples, Marco, and Key West were south. Maps in airline magazines show bays but not the smaller islands between beaches and mainland, islands the size of Ligarto.

There are hundreds. Most are deserted mangrove swamp, bird rookeries of guano and muck. A few are pri-vately owned, havens for wealthy recluses. From a jet-liner, on a clear day, passengers may spot cottages among groves of citrus and bananas. They may covet the isola-tion, the quiet swimming pools, the docks—compound-sized islands rimmed by water.

They won't find them mentioned in tourist brochures. Admission is by invitation. Wealth is requisite, power im-plicit.

Ligarto Island is private. An industrialist tycoon bought the place during Prohibition and built an elegant fishing retreat. The industrialist's heirs still own the compound.

That was the rumor, anyway, and rumor is all locals ever heard about Ligarto.

Visitors came and went without interacting with neighboring islands—Gasparilla, Siesta Key, Useppa, Palm Island, Captiva. Silence is not always passive. The silence associated with Ligarto Island was hostile. It discouraged contact.

Ligarto was a place where the powerful enjoyed anonymity. Software moguls, international entrepreneurs, American political icons used it as a retreat—another popular local rumor.

Tonight it wasn't rumor.

When the celebrated man surprised me in the lab, tapping on the screen door, I'd said to him, "When you say 'escape,' you mean from your security team. You're serious when you say you want to travel alone."

"Yes . . . at times, on my own."

Another evasion.

"A security detail is with me around the clock, three shifts a day, seven days a week. It's been that way for more than thirteen years, and it got tighter when the bounty was offered."

I'd glanced beyond an aquarium alive with sea urchins toward the dark porch where ninety feet of boardwalk connects my stilt house with shore. A question.

"Relax, Dr. Ford, no one can hear. You met my bodyguard. He's watching from a safe distance."

It was difficult to be alone with this man and relax. He was referring to the United States Secret Service.

"Why don't you tell your agents the truth: You want time to yourself. You're . . . ill. They should understand."

"The issue isn't illness," he snapped. "I have a *measured* amount of time to live. Surely you understand the difference."

I appreciated his insistence on precise language and nodded.

"Besides, they don't know the latest prognosis. Even if they did, it's not that simple. They're federal employees, with standing orders. I won't compromise them as professionals by asking their permission."

"The same agents have been with you a long time?"

"Several. I also have my staff to think about— secretaries, schedulers, travel assistants. More than a dozen. When my wife was killed, some of them wept like children. Wray had that effect on people. Her decency, her humor, her . . . her"—the man's voice caught, he swallowed—"Wray's intellect, and sense of grace. Which means they can never know. They're like family. When I say escape, I mean *disappear*."

I don't follow politics, but even I was aware that he and his wife had been childhood friends, partners for life. Wray Wilson had been an inspiration to many. Born deaf, she'd earned a master's degree before most kids her age— her future husband included—had graduated from high school.

She'd been on a chartered flight, a humanitarian mission carrying medical supplies to Nicaragua. The plane had caught fire during an emergency landing near a volcano. Wray Wilson and six other people were killed.

Distraught, the great man had demanded an international investigation. Later, he made headlines by hinting that his wife's death wasn't accidental.

Grief is part of a complicated survival process, but it can also debilitate. I wondered if grief had unhinged the man. He was too young and vigorous to be senile. But mental illness might explain his behavior. What he was proposing was impractical, maybe irrational.

I became agreeable in the way people do when they are dealing with the impaired. "I can empathize, sir. If a doctor told me I had a month to live, I'd want to . . . well, escape. So I understand, and I'm honored, but—"

He interrupted. "What makes you so damn certain you don't have a month to live? Or two weeks?"

"Well . . . I don't know. You're right, of course, but we all assume—"

"No, Dr. Ford, we don't all assume. Your time may be more limited than you realize—that's not *necessarily* a threat. It's true of everyone, everywhere. And please don't use that patronizing tone with me again. Do you read me, *mister*?"

Only Academy graduates and ex–fighter jocks can make the word "mister" ring like a slap in the face. He was both.

The man might be nuts but he wasn't feeble.

I started over. "Look, I do empathize, but"—I gestured, indicating the room: wood ceiling, towels for curtains, rows of chemicals and specimen jars, books stacked on tables, fish magnified through aquarium glass—"but I'm a biologist. I don't see how I can help."

"I've done the research and I can't think of anyone more qualified."

"It's possible, sir, that you have the wrong man—"

"No. Don't waste my time pretending . . . or maybe denial is a conditioned response in people like you. I *know* Hal Harrington. He's your handler, isn't he?"

Harrington was a high-level U.S. State Department official and covert intelligence guru. I'd known him for many years.

I replied, "Harrington? With an *H*?" I pretended to think about it. "I'm not familiar with the name."

"Maybe if I remind you of a few details. Would that convince you?"

"I really don't know what you're—"

He held up a hand. "When I was in office, they said I had access to every classified document in the system. Baloney. After what happened in Cartagena, I asked for a dossier on you. Know what I got? Nothing. Or next to nothing. Later, I ran across other globe-trotting Ph.D.s with backgrounds just as murky as yours. Scientists, journalists, a couple of attorneys, even one or two politicians. That's when I began to suspect.

"I started digging. Insomniacs crave hobbies. I won't tell you how but I discovered documents that hinted at the existence of a secret organization. An *illegal* organization, funded by a previous administration. Something called the 'Negotiating and Systems Analysis Group.' Only thirteen plank members; very select. 'The Negotiators.' Sound familiar?"

I'd replaced the slide containing the sea urchin embryo

with another—a blank slide, I realized, but I pretended to concentrate.

"It was deep-cover intelligence. Members were deployed worldwide as something called 'zero signature specialists.' An unusual phrase, don't you agree? Zero signature. It suggests they were more than a special operations team. Just the opposite. It suggests that each man worked alone."

They weren't killers in the military sense, he said. They had a specialty.

"Their targets disappeared."

The celebrated man studied me as if to confirm I wouldn't react.

I didn't.

TO PADDLE A STRAIGHT COURSE, I FOCUSED ON the canopy of palms that punctured the mist. Their trunks were curved. Fronds drooped like sodden parrot feathers.

The breeze was southwesterly, warm on my face and left arm—another directional indicator—but the mist was autumnal. I should have been shivering. My clothes were soaked, but I was too focused to be cold.

I was dressed for a dinner party, not a canoe trip: dark slacks, dress shirt, a black silk sports jacket tailored years ago in Southeast Asia. I'd dressed for the role I would have to play if the Secret Service intercepted me. It could happen.

To get on and off the island undetected, I had to know how the Secret Service operated, so I did my homework.

I spent time at Sanibel's library and on the Internet. More valuable was a discussion I had with an old friend, Tony Stoverthson, who'd worked for the agency prior to passing the Florida bar.

I knew the island would be protected by a dozen or so agents working in three shifts. They would've created an on-site command post that would include liaison people from the local sheriff's department and the Coast Guard. The command post would maintain direct contact with the agency's intelligence division in Washington and also their main headquarters in Beltsville, Maryland. Unique code names would be assigned to the island, the protectee, members of the protectee's family (if any), even the protectee's boat.

Tony told me, "The agency's dealt with all types of celebrities and they're all assigned a name. Prince Charles was 'Unicorn.' Ted Kennedy, 'Sunburn.' Amy Carter was 'Dynamo'; Frank Sinatra, 'Napoleon.' A protectee's limo might be called 'Stagecoach.' An island might be called 'The Rock' or 'Fort Apache'—a name that's immediately understood but still maintains security."

The more I learned, the more I came to think of Ligarto Island as The Rock.

The agents would be armed with MP5 submachine guns and semiautomatic SIG-Sauer pistols, although some older members might still carry Smith & Wesson Model 19s. Other tools, such as night-vision goggles, Remington street-sweeper shotguns, and antiaircraft ordnance, would be included in their arsenal.

Security might include sharpshooters from the

uniformed division of the agency's countersniper team. The team would establish a shooting post on one of the island's highest points—a tree, maybe, or water tower. In agency slang, the sniper would be armed with a JAR (Just Another Rifle), which, in fact, was a high-tech weapon custom-designed for the Secret Service. The sniper team would be in radio contact with Beltsville, which would provide the shooter with sight adjustments, depending on the island's temperature and humidity.

I'd also learned there would be at least two boats. One would be smaller, capable of running onto the beach if necessary. The other would be a fast patrol boat.

Daunting. So I *planned* on being intercepted. Because I didn't want to be arrested or shot, I also planned on lying my ass off. A believable lie, I hoped.

I would tell agents I was on my way to the annual Halloween party at the friendliest of nearby islands: Cabbage Key, a popular bar and restaurant, accessible only by water. I'd have to do some acting. Pretend to be appropriately sloshed, tell agents I'd gotten lost in the fog.

If they contacted Cabbage Key's superb dining room, they would find my name on the guest list: Marion D. Ford, Dinkin's Bay Marina. Reservation for one, admission paid in advance.

Establishing plausible deniability is not a subject taught in college. The famous man was right: My past includes training in subjects other than marine biology.

Nearby, I heard a heron's reptilian growl. I was passing an oyster bar where wading birds had gathered—unusual for this time of night. Maybe they were grounded by fog.

Was that possible? Or maybe feeding in the light of this full moon.

I touched my paddle to the bottom. Felt shells crunch as the canoe pivoted with the current. Once again, I listened for the patrol boat. Nothing. Could still hear the distant outboard . . . could hear the river-rush of tide flushing seaward . . . then I was surprised to hear voices. Men's voices whispering: a few staccato fragments, words indecipherable.

Garbled by distance?

No. They were *close*.

I waited, using the paddle as a stake, my canoe pointing down-tide like a weather vane.

Water drizzled from leaves . . . yowl of raccoons . . . creak of trees . . . then another muffled exchange: two men, maybe three.

The island was to my right. The voices came from my left. The men had to be in a boat. Or wading. The syllabic patterns were exotic, not English, not Spanish. That's why it registered as garble. I didn't hear enough to guess at the language.

Fog is romantic in a cozy sort of way, but, in primitive lobes of our brain, it also keys primitive alarms. The alarms remind us that tribal enemies use fog as cover.

During thunderstorms, people retreat in clusters, voices hushed. The same is true of the slow, silent storm that is fog. Men were out there in the gloom. Foreigners in a Florida backwater. Why?

There were plausible explanations.

I didn't like any of them.

A million-dollar bounty had been offered for the celebrated man's head. My guess: They were here to collect it.

THE NIGHT THE CELEBRATED MAN APPEARED AT my door, I'd said to him, "If you travel outside the country, no security, what happens if the bad guys take you hostage, or worse? It could get some of our people killed, maybe even start a war. To be blunt, you'd be putting the nation at risk. Is that worth a couple weeks of personal freedom?"

I'd expected indignation. Instead, he became philosophical, which is an effective cloaking technique. "History's fickle. Small events have started wars. I suppose some minor event could also prevent war—who can predict? The only time I depend on men and nations to behave like they have any brains is when there's no other choice. I'm speaking theoretically, of course."

Was he?

"Who knows what I might stir up. The risks depend on where I go. And who you consider to be bad guys. It's far more likely someone will take a shot at me in the States instead of in a country I'm not scheduled to visit.

"That's another reason I'm eager to get on the road, Dr. Ford. Someone's going to take that shot—*soon*, I think. My enemies view me as unfinished business. What they don't suspect is, I have some unfinished business of my own."

He used his fighter pilot's voice—a combat vet on a mission.

"It sounds like you have a target in mind."

"Maybe."

"Something to do with your wife's death?" I knew the accident was still under investigation. It had only been a few months.

"Possibly. Her plane caught fire *after* it landed. Seven people killed, no survivors. Do you find that suggestive?"

I shook my head. "I don't know the details."

"I think you know more than you realize." The man was looking at me strangely.

"Are you suggesting something? Or am I missing something?"

"Maybe both." I watched his jaw muscles knot. "But I think I'll reserve the details until we come to an agreement. For now, let's just say there are several stops I'd like to make. I've lived a big life. I've called liars liars, frauds frauds, and I've stood toe-to-toe with every variety of despot and egotistical ass. When enemies visit my grave, it won't be to plant flowers."

"You have old scores to settle."

"You disapprove; it's in your tone. Good. Getting even is for amateurs. I want revenge." After a moment, he chuckled. "I'm joking. My plans aren't that dramatic."

It was disturbing. Witness a wounded beast stumble and most of us wince. I winced inwardly at his stumbling paranoia, his outdated bravado; his weak attempt to cover malice with humor. I was thinking *Yes, he's mentally ill.*

According to my pal Tomlinson, who turns into a newspaper junkie the instant his Birkenstocks touch soil, the man dropped from public view shortly after his wife's death. He retreated to a Franciscan monastery, then spent time with a famous Buddhist scholar on Long Island.

When he reappeared, he had changed. The man had always been dignified, under control, even when speaking his mind. In the last few months, though, his behavior had bordered on the outrageous.

"He's doing what no one in his position has ever done," Tomlinson told me. "If he's asked a question, he tells the truth—his version, anyway. He's managed to offend just about every political and religious organization in the world."

The million-dollar bounty was an example, Tomlinson explained. It started when the man called America's news media "cowards and fiducial incompetents" because they sidestepped reprinting an editorial cartoon from a Danish newspaper that sparked worldwide riots. The caricature depicted the prophet Muhammad with a lighted bomb fuse in his turban—mild by Western standards.

The man remained outspoken even when Islamic clerics issued an international *fatwa,* or religious decree, demanding his head. Literally. The reward was posted soon afterward.

"The media used to despise him," Tomlinson told me. "Then, for a while, he was their darling. But that's changing because he refuses to back down on the cartoon issue. 'When did the *New York Times* and *Wall Street Journal* start deferring decisions about free speech to religious fundamentalists?' That's the sort of thing he's been saying and he won't shut up.

"Ultimately, they'll crucify him. He knows it. He seems to be inviting it."

Standing in my lab that night, the man sounded in full control of his facilities, even while sharing a plan I dismissed as irrational.

"The group I mentioned, the Negotiators—they operated without oversight. Their victims were seldom found so there's very little proof they were licensed to kill. But there *is* proof. I have it. Ethically, I couldn't ask a law-abiding citizen to help me . . . That's why I'm asking you."

With an edge, I replied, "Very flattering."

"It's not meant to be. I'm explaining why I'm here. The illegalities my trip requires won't be a problem for someone with your expertise."

"You're asking me to break laws, too."

"None you haven't broken before."

His inflection conveyed subtext. Was he telling me he wanted someone killed?

I said, "You don't need me. You need a magician. The Secret Service will realize you're missing before you make it to an airport."

"Not the way I've set it up. We'll have enough time."

My expression read *We?*

"That's the deal. You're coming. Spring me loose, keep me alive, and get me back. Help me disappear and I'll make your past disappear."

He interpreted my unresponsiveness as mistrust.

"I'm not the first to offer, I know. But I'm the first who has the power to make it happen."

2

I let the canoe swing free, then drifted awhile before I ruddered toward the island.

I'd studied charts and aerial photos. Ligarto consisted of about seventy acres of high ground, most of it built by Florida's pre-Seminole inhabitants. They were a sophisticated people who constructed cities of shell. On Ligarto, they'd built courtyards, dug canals, and raised shell pyramids four stories high.

Archaeologists believe that royalty lived atop those pyramids. The equivalent of post-Columbian royalty still did: The celebrated man was staying in a cabin on the highest mound.

From the aerials, I knew the layout. I also knew that Ligarto's Prohibition-era docks were on the western shore along a private channel. That's why I was approaching from the east. To the east, water was seldom more

than chest-deep, scarred with reefs of oyster and rock—
okay for canoes, bad for powerboats. A fringe of mangrove swamp buffered the island so there was no easy
place to land.

Visitors, welcome or unwelcome, would not be expected from the east.

I paddled close to the mangroves, mist smoldering
out of the bushes as if the swamp was afire. I caught a
branch, slid a paddle beneath thwarts, and repositioned
my feet as the canoe swung under limbs. It was a cheap
canoe, green plastic hull, quieter than aluminum, with
ridged seats. I'd been paddling for an hour. I had to pee
and my feet were numb.

I sat rubbing my ankles and waited, straining to see
through the mist. I was hoping I wouldn't have to wait
long.

I didn't.

There were four men, not two. They were in an inflatable boat, all of them paddling, but the last guy, starboard aft side, also used his blade as a rudder. They came
directly at me. For a moment, I thought I'd been spotted.
But then the boat turned north, hugging the shore, passing within twenty feet of where I sat motionless, all
senses testing, as they paddled into mist.

Water-laden air molecules transport odor as efficiently
as they conduct sound. After a few seconds, the smell of
men and equipment arrived on foggy tendrils: military
canvas, rubber, machine oil, the stink of wet boots, the
stink of stale tobacco laced with an unexpected hint of
eucalyptus or clove.

Spiced tobacco. Distinctive.

An inflatable boat resembles an overinflated inner tube, pointed at the front, with rigid buoyancy chambers made of high-tech fabric. In military jargon, it's a "rubber boat," or an IBS (Inflatable Boat, Small). This one had an outboard engine mounted aft, but it was tilted upward and locked, so the vessel should have been difficult to control.

The four men made it look easy. Blades cut the water in synch; strokes short, efficient. This was a military unit, or paramilitary, a trained assault team: Two men had already pulled on ski mask balaclavas. All four had weapons slung over their inboard shoulders, ammo clips fixed. One of the rifles had the distinguishing banana clip of a Russian AK-47 or one of that weapon's myriad clones.

Weapons identification is something else not taught in college science labs. I maintain a working knowledge for a reason.

A Secret Service agent carrying a Russian assault rifle? No way. Nor do agents whisper in a foreign language or smoke clove tobacco—the odor reminded me of Kreteks, the cigarette of choice in Indonesia and some parts of the Middle East.

These weren't federal agents on maneuvers. It was *remotely* possible they were American friendlies assigned to test the island's security. Staging mock attacks is part of Secret Service training. In Maryland, the agency built a mock city to simulate attacks on motorcades. Agents participate in crisis scenarios known as AOPs, "Attacks on Principals."

But war games in this fog? At this hour?

No, I'd stumbled onto a hit team. The men were assassins with a plan and they were now only minutes from their target.

The celebrated man had told me he had enemies. He'd said he expected someone to take a shot. I'd dismissed the million-dollar bounty as media sensationalism, just as I'd dismissed his fears as an outdated sense of his own importance.

He was right. I was wrong.

"It's something you'll get used to," he'd told me the night I agreed to help him. I'd been pressing for details on what, exactly, he was offering me in exchange.

"Not that there's anything in my past that I regret," I'd added.

"Really? Then you're one of the few rational men I've met who can say that. Or maybe I've misjudged you."

"When I say 'regret,' I mean there's nothing that warrants records being destroyed."

"I'm not that stupid. The only thing destroyed when a man tries to erase the past is his own future. How many fools have marched off that cliff? What I can offer is clemency—in a legal sense. The same for other members of your little group . . . including your friend Tomlinson."

Long ago, Tomlinson had been a suspect in the bombing of a U.S. Naval base. There are men in high places who still believe he's guilty of murder. They want him dead.

"A pardon, you mean?"

"Yes. Retroactive."

It strengthened my impression that the man had an obsolete sense of importance.

"It's my understanding you lost that power when you left office . . . ten years ago?"

"Nine. It just seems longer because of all the screwups and bad luck the last two administrations have had." He was standing in my lab at the bookcase, hands on hips. "I don't suppose you have something on the subject?"

No, but I had Internet access. I'd moved the computer next door into my quarters because it wasted so much of my time in the lab.

I watched him put his wide farmer's hands on the keyboard. A few minutes later, he motioned to the screen. He said, "Do you see this name?" then went on to explain the significance.

He was right, I was wrong—if what he told me was true. That's when he said, "Don't feel bad. Me being right is something you'll get used to."

The man had also told me there were enemies who wanted to kill him.

Right again.

I watched the four men, with their masks and automatic weapons, paddle into fog and moonlight, their boat surging forward like a water spider.

I gave it a few seconds, then went after them. I used mangrove limbs to vault the canoe into open water and turned bow onto their course.

Keeping the man alive—that had seemed like the easy part.

* * *

I DUG HARD WITH THE PADDLE, FOUR ABBREVI-ated strokes on the left, three on the right, gathering speed. Then I stopped, thinking about it as I glided.

Fog is where mankind's first monsters were born. What awaited me on the other side of the veil? The coincidence of arriving at the same time as the hit squad was suspicious . . . or was it?

Halloween is the only night when military gear can be worn as costume. It's a night when gunshots may be dismissed as fireworks. Halloween provides natural cover for those who venture into the night with sinister intent.

Plausible deniability—that's why I was dressed for a party, not a wet night in a canoe. The assault team had chosen Halloween for the same reasons.

The timing wasn't coincidental. It was a professional choice.

Then why the hell was I pursuing armed professionals? It was *stupid*. I hadn't brought a gun—with the possibility of being intercepted by the Secret Service? Even if I had, it was idiotic to blunder ashore and take on four guys with automatic weapons.

No. The smart thing to do was go running and hollering to security agents, tail between my legs, and hope they didn't shoot before giving me a chance to explain. I could deal with the fallout later.

I swung the canoe around. Secret Service would have people guarding the channel on the other side of the island, so I began paddling toward Ligarto's southern tip with the same sprinter's rhythm: four strokes on port side, three strokes on starboard, ending with a slight rudder correction.

I wasn't worried about making noise now. Once I'd put some distance between the hit team and myself, I intended to start yelling, whistling, thumping my heels on the hull, calling out the alarm.

I didn't get a chance. The canoe was still gathering speed when there was a sharp *bang*. Not a big explosion; more like a dozen firecrackers with the same fuse. Even so, water conducted a mild vibration through the plastic hull. Above the tree line, a haloed incandescence flickered.

My brain was still trying to pinpoint the source of the noise when there was a second firecracker, *bam*.

On the water, most explosions are caused by sparks in unventilated boats, a sickening sound because passengers are usually aboard. But these twin detonations had the sharper, metal-on-metal report of military ordnance. My first impression was they were stun grenades or flash bangs, but the shock wave didn't carry the distinctive stink of nitro aromatics. Whatever had fueled the combustion was odorless.

I stopped paddling as I considered the significance. There are a bunch of odorless explosives, but only one stuck in memory—Semtex, a Czech-made plastique preferred by terrorist types, sold on black markets worldwide. More power than TNT and undetectable to conventional security devices. A firecracker-sized glob made a grenade-sized noise.

It fit: foreigners using black market ordnance.

The explosions were on the *western* side of the island. The men I'd seen were on the *eastern* side. It meant they had accomplices . . . or the explosives had been planted earlier and detonated by timers, or remotes.

I reconsidered my options. A western approach was now suicide. The Secret Service would be on a war footing. They'd shoot before I had a chance to identify myself. Even if they gave me a chance to talk, I would be too late. The assault team had landed by now, or soon would.

I had to intercept the killers, I decided, before they got into position. Find a way to slow them and give the feds time to regroup.

Once again, I turned and began trailing the inflatable, retracing my path along the mangroves. As I paddled, I heard muted shouts. Expected to hear automatic weapons fire but didn't. Not a shot fired. The silence told me there was no follow-up attack. It also told me there were no human targets visible to Secret Service. Anything that moved they would have shot.

The explosions were a diversion. Silence carried that message, too. Freeze the attention of security agents; make them focus on the island's western rim.

I began to paddle harder, the canoe lunging with each stroke.

I'd made the right decision. I knew something the Secret Service didn't. Assassins were approaching from the east.

* * *

BAM . . .

A third detonation sounded like a dud bottle rocket. Once again, I expected the clatter of small-arms fire. Once again, fog conveyed only the outrage of screaming night birds, then a drizzling, shadowed silence.

Weird. A tactical diversion is designed to create a hole in security. Move fast, it might work. Hesitate, it will not. The timing has to be tight or the hole slams shut.

If the fireworks were a diversion, why hadn't the assault team slipped through that hole, into the island's perimeter? Federal agents don't run from gunfights, yet there was nothing to indicate Ligarto Island was under attack.

I considered the possibilities. Maybe the assault team's timing was bad. The guys I was trailing hadn't had time to get into position prior to the feeble series of bangs and booms, so why detonate before they were ready?

They wouldn't—not intentionally. So . . . maybe the charges had gone off accidentally.

Terrorists use garage remotes and cell phones as detonators. Remove the phone's outer casing, solder a blasting cap to the ringer circuit, and wire it all to a chunk of explosives. Later, dial the number from anywhere in the world to ignite the blasting cap.

On a soggy, foggy night, how reliable was a cell phone? Detonators could be short-circuiting because of moisture. Even the timing between explosions seemed accidental.

Maybe these guys weren't so professional after all.

I paddled close enough to the mangrove fringe to see

under branches but focused on the contrail of bubbles that marked the inflatable's path. The fog was so dense that I risked rear-ending the other boat. Even so, I continued to push.

If the diversionary explosions *hadn't* gone off accidentally, I'd overlooked an explanation: The assault team had an accomplice already ashore . . . an insider waiting for his support team to arrive.

It meant the man I'd promised to help might already be bound and bagged for delivery. Or he could be standing quietly, awaiting my arrival, while a shooter focused crosshairs on his chest.

I couldn't let that happen. The doctors had already presented the man with a death sentence. He was so desperate to make the most of his final weeks, his vulnerability had been unmasked. I liked him better because of it.

When a great beast stumbles we not only wince, we also feel an indefinable dread as it falls. Our weaknesses are magnified, our fears confirmed.

This guy wanted to go down fighting. There was hope in his strength, strength in his survival.

SURVIVAL.

He'd brought up the subject five days earlier, the first time we met. The first time we met officially, anyway. I'd been invited to a party on Useppa Island, a classy Old Florida sanctuary isolated by water and time. It's not unusual for powerful politicos to vacation on Useppa, so I was only mildly surprised that the invitation's RSVP response card required a Social Security number.

Someone was doing background security checks.

I avoid the high-society party circuit, but the hostess was persistent. "You have to make an appearance, Doc. I can't tell you why, but you really *must*."

That's not the reason I went. I went because my new workout partner, Marlissa Kay Engle, is a musician and actress who's savvy enough to understand that entertainment is one of those rare industries that pretends to loathe wealth and power, but, in fact, is a courtesan to both. I didn't mind. Marlissa is hauntingly, heartbreakingly beautiful. It was reason enough for me to endure a social function that required shoes and slacks.

I arrived, prepared to make polite conversation with a visiting ambassador or two. Instead, I was surprised to see *him*. When he spotted me, he nodded as if he'd been waiting. Suddenly, I understood why I'd been invited.

"It's been a long time, Dr. Ford. The last time we spoke, you were stepping off a boat in Cartagena near the Old Walled City. And I was still a little numb from how close that rocket came to nailing my vehicle. Colombia, remember?"

I was aware of a Secret Service agent to his right, another on the Collier Inn's balcony. Both wore Hawaiian shirts, neatly pressed but baggy enough to conceal weapons. The agent on the balcony held a beach towel that probably hid a submachine gun.

"I think you've confused me with someone, sir. Colombia, as in South America?"

"I don't recollect any rocket attacks in South Carolina, do you? *Of course* I mean South America. Not that I'm surprised by your reaction. Selective memory is a survival device. I've heard you're an expert on the subject."

He emphasized the sentence in a way that forced me to struggle with the double meaning.

"Expert on *what* subject?"

I watched him exchange a knowing glance with the agent to his right—a stocky man of Mongol or Asiatic heritage who looked too old to be on active duty. His personal bodyguard, I discovered later. Also the celebrated man's friend and confidant.

"I'm talking about survival. The Darwinian theory. Your friend, Tomlinson, was just telling me about the paper you two are coauthoring on . . . what did he call it? Fatal Specialization something."

Tomlinson was at the party? Another surprise. Yes . . . there he was, standing beyond the pool where coconut palms framed the Gulf of Mexico. He was wearing white linen slacks, a linen jacket. He was also barefooted, and shirtless, to the delight of the women around him. Marlissa included.

Not a surprise.

Marlissa was the reason we'd argued a few weeks earlier, though we never referred to her by name. Tomlinson and I both embrace the conceit that we are chivalrous men and therefore equitable.

"I'd like to take a look at your research, Dr. Ford. Sounds like it might support what I've been preaching for the last few months. Would you mind?"

I was flustered by our unexpected meeting. I also didn't know what he was talking about. Aside from the plane crash, and an occasional headline, I hadn't read much about him for many months, maybe years. He interpreted my expression accurately.

"Don't worry, you're one of millions who hasn't been getting my message. Which really pisses me off."

He enjoyed my reaction. "That's right, once a sailor, always a sailor. I'm mad because no one takes what I'm saying seriously—a disaster waiting to happen. 'Apocalyptic,' although I seldom use the word. It makes people nervous." He waited through my bland silence before adding. "But it's happening. *Now.*"

I said, "Apocalyptic, as in 'catastrophe'? Or the Bible story?"

"That's the first time I've heard someone refer to Revelations as a Bible story." He was still having fun. "You've read it?"

Yes, and I thought it a bizarre mix of myth and wistful psychosis—it was disappointing that a man of his accomplishments considered it worthy of discussion.

"You don't take it seriously?"

"I wouldn't want to impose on someone's religious beliefs, sir—"

"Speak freely, Dr. Ford. I've got big shoulders, and so does God, I suspect, if there is one."

"All right. I put Revelations in the same category as astrology and palm readers. Nostradamus, conspiracy theories, and visitors from outer space—the same. Sorry."

"No need to apologize. You're a realist."

"I'd like to think so."

"In that case, you should take Revelations *very* seriously. Because it doesn't matter what you think or what I think. There are powerful people who believe—really believe—that the Apocalypse is divine prophesy. Leaders who not only welcome the end of the world, they're determined to make it happen. The scary thing is, these people are gaining political clout in both hemispheres.

"Their followers are devoted, educated, and absolutely secure in their righteousness—the most dangerous of all human trinities. Destabilize the United States, lure us and our allies into Armageddon, and the doors to heaven will open. That's what they believe. That's their goal. And we're making it easy for them."

The man had a speech on the subject. It had to do with a connection he perceived between prophecy and technology. He was worried about the country's reliance on fragile essentials, or "blind horses," as he called them—an old horse traders' term for unreliable equipment. Internet. Cell phones. Satellites and oil.

He was an articulate speaker, but I was more interested in his intent. It was no accident I'd been invited to this party. The same might be true of Tomlinson. *Why?*

"The First World has created a techno-environment that's unrelated to the natural world. It's a manufactured reality. But it has become America's *national* reality.

"What happens if zealots scramble the Internet? Or interrupt the oil supply? The impact would be similar to environmental cataclysm on a primitive community—volcanic eruption, a meteor strike. Disrupt a society's *perceived* reality and you've destabilized its foundation. Panic would roll across this country like a wave. The perfect setup for World War Three."

His fervor reminded me of the driven men you sometimes hear preaching doom on busy street corners. I commented that he spoke of panic as if it were a weapon.

"In terms of bang for the buck, panic's the most lethal weapon around because we're not prepared. Think about what's going on right now in Central America. I understand you're currently doing work there?"

I nodded, surprised he knew. I'd made several trips in the last few months. An international consortium was proposing to build a canal across Nicaragua. Unlike the nearby Panama Canal, it wouldn't use locks to raise and lower sea level. Two oceans would, for the first time in many millions of years, be connected. What would be the impact when sea creatures from the Pacific Ocean, Caribbean, and Atlantic Ocean intermingled? I was one of several biologists hired as a consultant.

"I assume you've been following the conflict there?"

I nodded. "Along with the rest of the world."

The conflict had to do with the Panama Canal. In 1979, after the U.S. transferred control to Panama, Panama leased the canal's operational rights to a Hong Kong company. When the Hong Kong company's multidecade lease expired, Panama awarded the contract to an Indonesian firm, Indonesia Shipping & Petroleum Ltd (IS&P).

Indonesia is the world's most populous Muslim country.

The CEO of Indonesia Shipping & Petroleum was Dr. Thomas Bashir Farrish, heir to an oil fortune, who lived a playboy life as "Tommy Raker" in Europe and the United States until he became a follower of Ustaz Abu Bakar Bashir.

Farrish's mentor was sent to prison after a café bombing in Bali that killed 202 people, but Bashir continued to preach that "the Western world will crumble when Indonesia joins in Jihad."

Awarding operational control of the Panama Canal to a company owned by Thomas Farrish was controversial—and critics were soon proven right.

Within months, owners of Western-owned vessels were complaining of a lack of security and unfair treatment while in the Canal Zone. Three crewmen on a Canadian containership had been beaten to death. The captain and cook of a Texas oil freighter were abducted and beheaded.

Recently, when the U.S., in protest, imposed economic sanctions on the countries of Panama and Indonesia, IS&P announced it would turn away all U.S.-owned ships until the conflict was resolved.

So far, the Panamanian government and the League of Latin Nations had refused to intercede.

"Dangerous," I said.

"Worse than dangerous. I think Thomas Farrish is the most dangerous man on earth. Panama is like Noah's Ark, the population's so varied. You've *been* there, you know. It could potentially signal Arma—" He almost used the term again but caught himself. "It could start global war. That's why I'm trying to get the message out. Dependency equals vulnerability. Fragility invites attack. Hook your wagon to a blind horse and sooner or later it'll pull you off a cliff.

"Mr. Tomlinson was telling me your paper has to do with plants and animals that go extinct because of over-specialization. Our country has become too specialized. Do you see the connection?"

I nodded. Our paper's working title was "Fatal Tracks of Adaptive Specialization."

But I didn't believe for a minute that he contrived this meeting because of a research paper. What did the man want? If it had something to do with the assassination attempt in Colombia, why was he lecturing me on the dangers of technology?

He continued talking about parallel dynamics, biological and social, but he was suddenly more formal. I realized that people were gravitating toward him, drinks in hand, munching hors d'oeuvres, as they eavesdropped. Private conversation over. Local power brokers present. Their courteous attention told me they didn't take the man seriously.

I stole a glance at Tomlinson. He smiled, sleepy-eyed, already pleasantly stoned, and flashed me the peace sign. Apparently, he'd forgotten our argument and the chilly civility that had followed. I'd heard he'd been living alone on a barrier island. Staying on his sailboat some nights, but also beach-camping. "Spiritual Bootcamp," he told one of the fishing guides. I was glad to see him.

I listened to the famous man say, "Reporters treat me

like a circus act. *Humoring* me. Know why? Because I've called for mandatory drills—a couple of days a year, ban all but emergency use of cell phones and the Internet. Make citizens learn how to communicate by mail or, God forbid, face-to-face, like human beings. Same with personal transportation. Our people should know what to do during a gas crunch so they don't panic when the inevitable happens. 'The only thing we have to fear is fear itself.' Everyone knows the quote but no one *thinks* about what FDR meant."

Anticipate the fear, that was his point. The economic depression of the 1930s, he said, wasn't caused by the stock market collapse. It was caused by a *panic* sparked by the stock market collapse.

"Schools have fire drills, ships have lifeboat drills. Is that crazy? But my colleagues in D.C., and the press, react like I've gone off my rocker. Tell me, do I look old enough to be senile?"

He had the politician's gift for self-deprecation. He chuckled as he combed fingers through his silver hair. I watched the power brokers mirror his smile, but their cheery condescension said yes, they thought he was irrational.

Half an hour later, as the man left the party, he motioned me to a private corner. "I'll be in Florida awhile. Would you mind if I came to Sanibel some night to discuss your research? Maybe get Vue to help me slip away." He indicated his bodyguard. "I'll bring a bottle of wine or a six-pack—or give you a signed picture for your son. It's the least I can do for a man who maybe saved my life."

Later, when Tomlinson and I compared notes, I didn't mention the incident in Colombia, but I told him the man wanted to visit the lab.

Tomlinson already knew.

I said, "You saw him after I left the party?"

"Yeah. And we talked earlier, too. He's entered what he calls his 'redemption phase.' He told me he spent a month at a Franciscan monastery studying the Bible and the Quran. Now he's interested in meditation. Wanted to know if I could take him through the basics, 'Zen Beginner's Mind.'"

"Why you?"

Some of the chilliness of the previous weeks returned. "I'm sure that surprises you—me being such a *flake* and all. Isn't that what you called me? No, wait . . . you said I was a 'weirdo flake.'"

He was mistaken. During the argument, I'd called him a "flaky weirdo," but I now shrugged as if I couldn't remember. "*How* did he know you're an ordained Buddhist monk? That's what I'm asking."

"Oh. He's read my book."

Tomlinson has published several books, but his little volume *One Fathom Above Sea Level* is considered a classic on spirituality by New Age mystic types. It's the man's own guide to life and the universe as seen through his eyes, six feet—or one fathom—above the water's surface.

"He sounded serious about studying Zen. But I think he's got a secret agenda."

I said, "You don't trust him?"

"How can I tell? Politicians aren't real. They're not

even actors. They're characters in an opera. I voted for him the first election. Second time, no way. But I was still disappointed when he didn't run.

"When his wife was killed, though, he dropped all the party-line bullshit. Some things he says, he rages like a spiritual warrior. But then he'll spout crap so outrageous, so offensive, it triggers my gag reflex. Which makes him ... . human, I guess."

I've never heard Tomlinson, a spiritual warrior himself, sound starstruck. He did now, adding, "Even so, he's one of those rare, rare beings. A true un-shallow dude, man. *Very* heavy. How can you say no to a guy like Kal Wilson? The man was *president of the United States.*"

3

I knew the location of the president's cabin. Did his assassins . . . ?

I thought about dragging the canoe into the bushes and charging cross-country to his quarters. But the direct route was through swamp and it's impossible to charge through mangroves. Or even walk. They are rubbery, salt-tolerant trees elevated above water on interlaced roots. The roots resemble fingers of a creeping hand or hoops in an obstacle course. You have to climb, duck, hurdle, and shimmy your way through mangroves.

Maybe the assault team was discovering that now. Or maybe they were bound for the island's northern point, where, according to aerial photos, there was a shell ridge—an easier place to go ashore.

I hoped not. The shell ridge was where the president said he'd be waiting for me. Midnight sharp.

I checked my watch. 11:32 p.m.

The man had probably already left his cabin. If the hit team landed on the ridge, he'd walk into their arms. The president might even mistake one of his killers for me. I pictured him approaching with his hand outstretched. An easy target. I imagined his transitioning facial expressions—confusion, surprise, realization . . . then anger. The man was a fighter.

Would his last thought be that I'd betrayed him? Yes, the logical conclusion. His brain might spend its final microseconds racing a bullet's furrow, trying to make sense of my treachery.

I paddled harder.

I've known patriots and I am no patriot, but communal allegiance is deep-wired—dates to the Paleolithic. We are predisposed to sacrifice for the greater good. The greater good for what—a nation, a sports team, a street gang, a religion, a murderous cult, a pal—varies with our backgrounds.

The possibility that an American president might die believing I'd betrayed him was repugnant. But how could I stop four guys with automatic weapons?

I had no idea. Maybe catch them in the swamp. Slip up from behind, and . . . then what?

Not a clue.

I'd have to manufacture opportunities. Not unfamiliar. Before restarting life in Florida, I'd spent years in small, vulnerable countries gathering data, ingratiating myself to locals, dealing with dangerous men, impossible situations, making up the moves as I went.

I'd think of something.

Right.

I went through my list of makeshift weapons: emergency gear, mosquito spray, pocketknife, flashlights, a shaving kit, fire starter, lighter, flares, and a half-empty fifth of vodka—a prop to convince Secret Service I was drunk. There were also two wooden paddles, and a third made of aluminum and plastic.

I pictured myself swinging a paddle like a broadsword. Attach a burning flare and I had . . . nothing. They'd shoot me the moment I was in range.

I had flashlights that might be useful. Not the Maglite junk commonly carried. Some guys buy expensive golf clubs. I buy serious flashlights, and the best lab equipment I can afford. It's a reaction to dealing with hurricanes and small wars.

I had three palm-sized LEDs. One, a high-tech marvel made by Blackhawk, was powerful enough to cause retina damage. It also had a strobe that caused blinding dizziness, according to the literature. Useful, if true.

I thought about how to work it: Come up from behind with a paddle, then with my unusual flashlight, and then . . . ? Well . . . hope my survival instincts kicked in.

There was that word again.

I paddled through pockets of sulfur-warm air, then bubbles of cooler air, the density of mist varying with each advection exchange. For a few minutes, it seemed as if the fog might be lifting. Then, abruptly, three strong strokes sent the canoe gliding into a cloud so thick that I couldn't see beyond my knees.

Disorienting. I drifted, expecting visibility to improve. It didn't.

There was no visual reference. I took a couple of experimental strokes and it felt as if the canoe veered wildly to the left. I used the paddle as a brake, applying back pressure, but it only magnified the sensation. I tried to touch bottom, couldn't.

I sat motionless for a moment, yet it still felt as if the canoe was rotating at the same cauldroning speed as the fog. With a couple of sweep strokes, I attempted to compensate but made it worse. I became more confused.

I couldn't see the island, didn't know its direction. If I'd been flying an airplane, I would have panicked. Instead, I was just peeved at my incompetence. The only choice was to sit patiently until visibility improved.

I placed the paddle across my knees and reached into the pack for another look at the GPS. That's when I heard it: the spring-ratchet clatter of someone trying to start a motor. A pull starter with a rope. I heard it again . . . then again.

A lawn mower makes a similar sound when it's out of fuel: spark plugs firing into dry cylinders. But this was no lawn mower. It was an outboard . . . probably the outboard motor on the assault team's rubber boat.

I couldn't see the inflatable, but it was no more than a few dozen yards away. The starter cord was being pulled with enough force to create small waves that reached me seconds after the ratcheting sound. I fought the urge to escape blindly into the fog. Instead, I sat immobile. I touched one hand to a paddle . . . then began to search inside my bag with the other, feeling for a flashlight. I found one, put it in my jacket pocket. Found another, then found the lighter, too.

As I drifted, water molecules moved inside my inner ear, bursting as if carbonated. The silence amplified a nearby exchange: men whispering, strident, frustrated. The language was unfamiliar. Complicated syllabics, vowels harsh, rhythmic. There was a momentary silence . . . then, much closer, I heard the outboard's starter gear clatter four times in quick succession.

The motor wouldn't start.

I felt a balmy gust of wind. Fog stirred. My canoe pivoted as if under sail. I drifted in silence for several seconds, removed my glasses and cleaned them as I waited. I thought I was staring in the direction of the inflatable when, from behind, I felt something bump the canoe . . . something elastic, springy, no sensation of weight.

I turned, expecting to discover I'd drifted into mangrove limbs. No. I'd collided with the rubber boat.

THE MOON WAS HIGH, SILVER AS AN ARCTIC SUN. Enough light to cast shadows but not enough to reveal detail. I couldn't see facial expressions but the men in the inflatable had to be stunned. We stared at each other dumbly as our vessels revolved, then bumped again.

That roused them. They lunged for their weapons; I threw my hands out as if to fend them off. It's a reflexive, defensive posture, and why most people shot in the face at close range are also missing fingers. That's what came into my mind as they stabbed rifles at me — I'd be missing fingers when my body was found. An odd, final vanity for a man who was about to die.

I lowered my hands to hide them . . . or perhaps because, even as a victim, I remained a determined disciple of the clean kill. I released my breath, curious, at some remote level, how my brain would signal the intrusion of a bullet. Darkness or a shattering light? If these men were pros, they wouldn't hesitate . . . but they did hesitate.

Why?

I realized that my eyes were closed. I opened them. I gulped for air and voiced the first finesse that came to mind. "Don't shoot. You need me. I can start your engine." My voice was improbably calm.

The men replied with threatening gestures that I interpreted as commands. I raised my hands again, still expecting the killers to fire. They didn't. I became more confident when a voice asked, "Who are *you*?"

The man was whispering for a reason. He didn't want to give away their position.

From the distance came the rumble of engines: a patrol boat, Coast Guard probably. The hunters were now being hunted and here they were with a motor that wouldn't start.

My confidence grew.

A red beam drilled a smoky conduit through the mist. The flashlight panned across my face, the canoe's deck, my backpack, my clothes duffel. "You are Secret Service?"

I laughed, careful not to force it. "Me? I'm a . . . *mechanic*."

The man's English was spotty. I had to repeat the word twice.

"Why you then following us?"

He kept his voice low. I raised mine as if we were a hundred yards apart.

"Following you? In this fog? I couldn't follow you if we were in the same boat and your ass was on fire."

They didn't laugh. But they didn't shoot, either. That was the way to play it, I decided. Stay aggressive.

"Not so loud. Not necessary to be shouting."

"I'll speak any damn way I want. I paddled over trying to be a nice guy, help you start that engine. And this is the thanks I get?"

There was a pause of reconsideration. They were desperate, I realized. Escape mode.

The man doing the talking was next to the throttle—their leader. I watched him focus for a moment on the patrol boat. It sounded closer.

He began to hurry . . . turned and pulled the outboard's starter cord. Nothing. He adjusted the choke, then pulled again, three times fast—it wouldn't start. He made a blowing sound.

"If you are mechanic, why this boat for rowing?"

"Because I don't want to go to jail for drunk driving. *That's* why."

I reached toward my feet, found the vodka bottle, and held it up. At the same time, I palmed a flare from my open bag and slid it into my pocket. "I figured you were cops. But that can't be. So why you got those guns in my face?"

In the silence that followed, I wondered if I'd pushed too far. I was relieved when a man with better English interceded.

"We are soldiers. Guests of your military—but this is secret. You know war games? But we can't get goddamn engine started. We are supposed to be at a certain location by midnight but now we have this goddamn trouble."

He used slang like an ornament, profanity learned from a book. I couldn't place the accent or his static progressive verbs. Indonesian or Middle Eastern. It meshed with the million-dollar reward.

"You're foreigners."

"Yes . . . Singapore. America's friends."

He sounded friendly, but I didn't buy it. I'd worked with Singapore's Special Operations Forces. Pros, very tough, and they didn't carry AK-47s.

"If you're friends, lower those goddamn guns."

The friendly terrorist thought for a moment, then pretended not to understand. "We must find location named 'Palm Island Resort.'"

"In this fog? Palm Island's six or seven miles of thin water and oyster bars. Good luck."

"Yes, good luck. Already too much bad. You know way?"

He'd missed my meaning, but I replied, "Palm Island? Sure." I nodded, and made a vague gesture with the vodka bottle, maybe pointing east toward the mainland or west toward the Gulf of Mexico. I didn't have a clue. "It's not far. I could run it blindfolded."

The men were getting impatient. One of them held

my canoe's forward thwart. The boat rocked precariously as he reached beneath his seat. "Engine. You fix?" He was holding an object vertically. A small knife.

"They haven't made the engine I can't fix."

He touched the blade to his neck. "Then *fix*." I pretended to take a gulp of vodka, then thrust the bottle toward him. He was so surprised he nearly dropped the knife. "Have a drink. You're not mad, you're just thirsty. But move your ass first. I need room to work."

I LIVE NEXT TO A MARINA AND IT'S A RARE WEEK that I don't help some newcomer start his boat. The problems are typically minor because small outboards require only three essentials: fuel, air, spark. It simplifies troubleshooting.

The plastic gas tank was full, fuel hose connected. I removed the hose from the engine and sniffed. The smell of gasoline should have been strong. It wasn't.

As I said, "I need a screwdriver or a knife," I felt the boat shift. I turned. Knife guy had moved behind me, close enough that his knee brushed my back. He had a full, black beard, heavy glasses.

He was positioning himself to cut my throat— probably as soon as I got the engine going.

"Perfect," I said. "Thanks."

The man didn't react for a moment when I reached to take his knife. Then he knocked my hand away.

"Hey, you want your motor fixed or not? I need a *knife*."

The friendly terrorist was listening to the patrol boat, trying to gauge its heading—not easy because of the fog, but also because the diesel engines now blended with a familiar, rhythmic thumping. It was the sound of an approaching helicopter.

Tampa Coast Guard was joining the hunt. Or maybe a military chopper from nearby MacDill Air Base.

The man snapped, "Folano!" then added a few anxious words I didn't understand.

Folano slapped the weapon flat-bladed into my palm, then was silent, letting his anger fill the boat. The knife had a polished handle and a short, curved blade. Nice. I touched a finger to the edge—sharp. No wonder he didn't want to loan it.

I said, "Appreciate it, Folano," then turned and removed the engine cowling.

Once again, I found the fuel hose. It had a standard quick-clip connector with an inset brass bearing. The bearing functioned as a valve. I squeezed the primer bulb, then used the tip of the knife to push the valve open. Gas should have squirted. It didn't.

I unscrewed the gas tank's plastic cap and heard a vacuum rush. Open a fresh jar of pickles and the sound's similar.

A vacuum. That was the problem. They hadn't opened the air vent, so gas couldn't flow. A common oversight.

I opened the vent, replaced the cap.

The engine would start. But I wasn't done.

"Hand me that red flashlight."

I was working on a forty-horsepower outboard, an older

OMC, with the throttle and gearshift built into the tiller. A lot of power for a small boat. I searched until I found the internal safety switch. It had distinctive wiring, yellow and red. Bypass the safety switch and an engine will start in gear.

Dangerous.

I cut the wires, then twisted them together, bypassing the safety switch.

I found the carburetor, inserted the knife, and bent the butterfly plate wide open. The engine would now get maximum fuel delivery no matter how the throttle was manipulated. There was no way to stop the gas flow without cutting the fuel hose.

The engine was now rigged to start in forward gear, at full speed.

Very dangerous.

It'd taken me less than two minutes. With my back to the men, I locked the engine cowling in place, then pretended to lunge after something I dropped.

"Damn."

"What now has happened wrong?"

I stared into the water for a moment before I sat up and took the vodka from the bearded man. This time, I really did have a drink.

The friendly terrorist asked, "Why have you stopped working on the engine?"

"It's fixed."

"How can you be certain? You haven't started it."

The patrol boat was still cruising the island's west side, maybe confused in the fog, but the helicopter was closing in.

"Trust me, it'll start." I patted the seat next to me. "Give it a try."

I made room as the bearded man said something, then tried English. "Where knife?"

I jabbed my finger at the water. "Down there, knife." I was looking at the bad knot they'd used to tie my canoe to the inflatable. If the rope didn't break, I'd have to cut it free—which is why I'd wedged his knife securely into the back of my belt after pretending to drop it.

The bearded man growled a reply as I took the special strobe flashlight from my pocket and braced myself. The friendly terrorist's hand was on the throttle.

I watched him lean toward the starter cord. The man put all his frustration into that first pull . . .

4

Ignite a rocket on the rear of a small boat and the results would have been similar. When the engine fired, the inflatable catapulted into the fog like a dragster. Men in front were thrown backward. The bearded man landed face-first in the bilge. The friendly terrorist would have been launched over the engine if I hadn't grabbed him by the belt.

I was going overboard myself soon. I didn't want his company.

Over the engine noise, he shouted, "This goddamn thing! How to stop my crazy motor?" The man wrestled with the tiller handle. He couldn't reduce speed and the transmission wouldn't allow him shift to neutral without decelerating. "*Son of a beech. What bad shit is now happening?*"

My canoe, still tied to the inflatable, became a wild,

swinging rudder. It caused the little boat to veer left, then right, as we tunneled an accelerating arc through the mist. Fog sailed past my face as if driven by a twenty-knot wind. It was inevitable that we'd soon hit something—an island, an oyster bar, rocks. I didn't want to be aboard when it happened.

I had the high-tech flashlight in my hand. When I punched the switch, it began to strobe with a dizzying, irregular rhythm. Each starburst was intensified by fog, each microsecond of darkness magnified the boat's speed. My brain was unable to process the chaos and I had to blink to stem the sudden vertigo. The terrorists felt it, too: four faces frozen, wide-eyed, with each explosion of white.

"Idiot! You blind us!"

That was the plan and I wasn't done.

I looped the flashlight's lanyard over the tiller and pulled the flare from my pocket. I pictured me popping the gas tank, flare burning, as I cut the canoe free and rolled overboard. These guys liked bombs—let them experience what it was like to ride a floating incendiary. The inflatable would blaze like a torch.

But then, out of nowhere, a dazzling incandescence appeared overhead. It was brighter than my strobe and so unexpected that we all ducked. The circle of light swept past our little boat, touched the water ahead, then found us again.

I turned. The fog was so dense my eyes registered only vaporous glare. Where the hell was the light coming from? Then I felt a faint seismic vibration. It moved through the boat's hull and into my chest, increasing incrementally. The cadence was familiar.

A moment later, a thudding sound accompanied the vibration, the flexing *whomp-ah-whomp-ah-whomp* of rotating blades, and I knew the source of the light. A helicopter was tracking us, flying low off our stern.

"Goddamn! What bad luck is here now?"

Maybe bad luck for all of us, depending on the helicopter. Coast Guard helicopters are equipped for rescues at sea. Military helicopters are equipped with machine guns and rockets. Which had the Secret Service called?

"Mechanic. You take!" Panicking, the friendly terrorist shoved the tiller toward me and lunged for his assault rifle. The boat turned so violently that I almost went overboard with the bearded guy. It also snapped the rope holding my canoe. The loss of drag caused an abrupt increase in speed that almost flipped us.

I pushed the man off me and climbed back into my seat. The friendly terrorist was on his knees trying to shoulder his assault rifle. The other men were also struggling to get to their weapons.

I put my hand on the tiller arm, straightened our course, then moved to the inflatable's port side. Coast Guard or not, if the friendly terrorist started shooting, the chopper would return fire. I didn't want to get much farther from my canoe, but I also didn't want the terrorists to get a clean shot.

I shielded my eyes and glanced behind. I guessed the chopper was a few hundred yards out. The pilot had waited until he was almost over us to toggle his megawattage searchlight. It told me something. Visibility was zero yet he knew where we were.

Some kind of high-tech radar? Older infrared systems don't work well in fog. But this aircraft's electronics had nailed us. A thermal image sensor system maybe. Or thermal FLIR goggles. Whatever it was kept the chopper latched to our stern. The pilot seemed to be keeping his distance intentionally.

I took another quick look, then concentrated on driving. The chopper's military searchlight illuminated the mist without piercing it; my strobe added blinding starbursts. The combination screwed up my depth perception, which was nil to begin with. I'd straightened our course but couldn't tell if I was focusing on a veil of fog fifty yards ahead or five feet ahead. It was like rocketing underwater through radiant bubbles.

Two men remained hunched low in the inflatable, gripping the outboard safety line. But the friendly terrorist and Folano had managed to balance themselves between the middle seat and deck, both with automatic rifles. In a moment, they'd open fire.

I waited. Kept our course steady, expecting to slam into a reef at any moment . . . or take a bullet in the back. The boat's top speed couldn't have been more than thirty knots, but it felt like fifty. When Folano touched his cheek to the rifle's stock, taking aim, I jammed the tiller hard to port—a threshold turn that almost jettisoned him into the water.

"Goddamn *mechanic*."

From his belly, the friendly terrorist pointed his rifle at

me. I ducked low and pulled the tiller hard to starboard, then shoved it away. The boat skidded for a moment, then heeled at an impossible angle. He tumbled onto his side and lost control of the weapon.

In rapid succession, I rocked the steering arm back and forth. With each wild turn, the boat careened on its edge, so the four men could do nothing but stay low and hang on to the outboard safety line.

Behind us, I suspected the chopper's crew interpreted our zigzagging as evasive action. They'd been on our tail for less than a minute, but it was enough time for their weapons systems to lock. The pilot was probably on the radio with his superiors, maybe asking permission to fire. Stick a rocket into our engine's exhaust. Could that happen?

Yes.

I continued zigzagging, eyes forward, as I looped the fuel hose around the tiller arm to prevent the boat from circling. Then I found the gas tank with my right hand and twisted the cap off. Gas sloshed. The fog had wicked fumes; the two vapors melded into a petroleum cloud. Striking a flare now would've been insane, so I lobbed the stick over my shoulder. Then I felt around in my pocket for the lighter—a search that was hampered by my own misgivings. In a cloud of gas fumes, I knew what would happen if spark was added.

I did it anyway . . . took a deep breath . . . released the tiller so I could cup my left hand over my eyes, then flicked the plastic lighter and . . .

Whoof!

A sphere of pressurized heat blasted me backward. I used the momentum to somersault overboard, my left hand now covering my nose, my right hand over my nuts.

Impact: I skipped once on the hard surface, then water settled around me, the bay warmer than air. I stayed under for a moment, then surfaced. I'd worried about landing on an oyster bar, but the depth here was waist-deep, the bottom soft beneath my shoes.

I crouched low in the water, expecting the boat to be in flames. It wasn't. Maybe the explosion had consumed oxygen so abruptly that it had extinguished itself. Whatever the reason, the inflatable wasn't ablaze but the strobe I'd left aboard was still firing.

The helicopter rocketed past at tree level and I ducked again . . . then stayed low, thinking the terrorists might manage to fire a shot. They didn't. Maybe they'd gone overboard, too, when I'd ignited the gas.

I waited, listened. I heard no voices, saw no movement ahead. They were still on the boat.

After a few moments, I stood, my eyes tracking the course of the inflatable by the strobe's irregular starbursts, feeling relieved but also dumb. The chopper pilot didn't need thermal imaging to find the boat. All he had to do was follow the blinking light.

The noise of the engines faded but the fogbank continued to flare. It reminded me of a storm cloud filled with lightning. I was surprised the boat hadn't hit something. I was also surprised that the chopper hadn't opened fire.

I turned . . . and got another surprise.

Towering above me, closing in fast, was a red light and a green light, aligned like glowing eyes—a boat's running lights. The patrol boat was bearing down on me at high speed in pursuit of the inflatable.

It was like stepping off a sidewalk into the path of a cement truck. The pilot couldn't see me, I didn't have time to get out of the way, and there were only a few inches of clearance between the boat's churning propellers and the soft bottom.

I reacted instinctively and dove to the right, trying to dolphin out of harm's way. But too late . . .

The vessel was on me . . . then over me. Its forward displacement wake lifted me off the bottom when I tried to submerge. I felt the boat's port chine graze my thigh and I balled up into a fetal position, expecting the props to chop my feet off. I released air from my lungs, trying to get deeper, then all that displaced water slammed me hard into the bottom as engines screamed past overhead . . . slammed me so hard that I threw my hands out, anticipating impact.

If I hadn't, I would've broken my neck. Instead, when I hit bottom my left arm buried itself up to the elbow in muck.

Underwater, I waited for a few seconds to be sure the boat was gone, then I tried to pull my arm free. Surprise! My fist had created a suction pocket. It wouldn't budge.

I got one foot on the bottom and tried to stand. I still couldn't break the mud's hold.

Impossible.

Calmly, I tried again . . . and felt muck constrict around my forearm.

I opened my eyes. Darkness accentuated a darker realization: I might die this way. Ironic. It was also absurd. Die on a calm night, in waist-deep water, because I'd gotten one hand stuck in the mud—after the life I'd lived?

Funny, Ford. *Fun-n-n-ny.*

I stopped struggling. Told myself not to panic; to stop fighting and think. I did . . . which instantly reduced the pressure around my forearm. I could feel the hole collapsing into rivulets of sand around my fist, as water trickled in and breached the vacuum. I gave a gentle pull . . . and my hand came free.

I surfaced, blowing water from my nose and gasping for air but alert: a second boat might be following in the wake of the vessel that had nearly crushed me.

I stood, waited . . . Silence.

I turned. The patrol boat's course was marked by a contrail of bubbles but its lights had been swallowed by fog. I could still hear its engines, an eerie demarcation between sight and sound: A six-ton boat had vanished into a void of infinite gray.

I took a few careful steps, still shaken by the series of close calls. Bad luck has its own momentum. It's not conditional or personal, but misfortune does seem to gain energy from panic. Time to move purposefully.

I did.

If the patrol boat's wake was still visible, the inflatable's narrower track should be visible, too. I made a slow search and found the residue of exhaust oil and disturbed water.

I backtracked, following the rubber boat's course, walking, sometimes swimming. The knife with the curved blade, and the extra flashlight I'd slipped into my pants, had both survived, and I used the flashlight. After several minutes, there it was, a ghost ship, awash in fog but still afloat: my canoe. I was afraid the patrol boat had crushed it.

Before I vaulted aboard, I allowed myself a blissful minute to pee.

My watch read 12:15 a.m.

5

I used the GPS to get my bearings, then paddled. A few minutes later, blue topography materialized in the moonlight: Indian mounds elevated above mangroves.

I traveled along Ligarto's rim. As I did, I heard the diesel rumble of another vessel. It was on the western side of the island. Occasionally, its searchlight breached the fog canopy. The boat was headed north, its engines fading.

Why north? Why not back up the helicopter and patrol boat?

I thought about it as I paddled. Decided there could be only one reason: The former president was aboard. Secret Service agents were taking him to safety. The Special Operations Center at MacDill Air Base was in Tampa, and so was the Coast Guard's regional headquarters.

What other explanation could there be? The inflatable

would've been easy to find. The explosion hadn't damaged the gas tank much because I could still hear the engine—the overrevved scream of an outboard plowing bottom. The boat had finally hit something, and its engine was killing itself; probably kicking up a geyser of mud and grass as it buried the rubber boat on a sandbar.

Less than ten minutes had passed since I'd flicked the lighter and jumped, but they'd been long, long minutes for the four foreigners. They'd spent them careening through fog, out of control, with a helicopter on their tail. With the inflatable grounded, the men would either have to fight or wade. I hadn't heard any shots, so maybe they weren't the martyr types . . . or maybe they'd found the bottle of vodka I'd left aboard.

I pictured the guy with the bushy black beard, Folano, guzzling from the bottle and smiled. He could have the liquor—I had his knife. I hadn't looked at it closely but the heft and balance suggested superb craftsmanship. Consoling. The Blackhawk flashlight I'd sacrificed was expensive.

I continued paddling but not fast. The more I thought about it, the more likely it seemed the Secret Service had hustled Kal Wilson aboard the northbound boat. If he was no longer on Ligarto, there was no reason for me to hurry. Even so, I decided to land on the shell ridge as planned.

Maybe I'd learn something. Secret Service agents wouldn't be as quick to open fire, and they might be talkative if I had information to trade. I'd use a spare flashlight to draw attention and tell the first person I met to notify the cops about four crazy foreigners with guns. That would get a conversation started.

Wait . . . only four foreigners? I remembered the unlikely timing of the explosions, then reminded myself there could be a fifth terrorist already on the island, an insider.

Adrenaline is a chemical accelerant and I felt supercharged. If the Secret Service hadn't found the fifth terrorist, I might . . . or he might find me.

That was okay.

In fact, I hoped it happened.

WIND STILLED; MOON FLOATED BEHIND HALloween clouds. Fog became rain—an ascending, silver weight.

Good. My clothes were soaked but visibility was improving. Steam seeped from the tree line, then was vented upward by the bay's cool surface. Moonlight was chameleon. It mimicked a night sky that was charcoal, then copper.

Ahead, I could see an elevated darkness that, according to the GPS, marked the shell ridge. The ridge crossed the island—a foot highway built a thousand years ago by contemporaries of the Maya. Florida was home to an ancient people. Visitors to Disney World and South Beach never suspect.

I approached cautiously: two strokes, glide . . . two strokes, glide. The elevated darkness assumed form. A break in the tree line appeared as a ravine of white. I turned the canoe toward the island and gave a final stroke. Shells grated beneath the boat's hull as the bow lifted itself onto the bank.

I waited: tree canopy sifting rain ... *bee-WAH* groan of catfish ... vertibraeic pop of pistol shrimp. A separate, living universe intermingled below, indifferent to my vigilance or to the absurd world above the water's surface.

Was I alone?

I leaned my weight to port, swung one leg, then the other, out of the canoe and stood in knee-deep water. On the island, fog strata created a tunnel; the ridge, made of seashells, glowed like bone. I pulled the canoe onto the ridge. Hid it in a mangrove thicket that was several feet above the tide line, but I tied off to a limb, anyway—the rituals of a compulsive man.

I was undecided about carrying Folano's knife. The Secret Service would ask questions if they found it. But what if there was a fifth assassin? He would be armed.

I took the knife. Slid it through my belt, over my hip. I was still wearing my black sports jacket, an incongruous combination—dressed for a dinner party, soaking wet, and armed to kill.

I carried a flashlight but didn't use it as I started up the ridge. At the first clearing, I stepped into the open, faced the island's interior, and waved my arms overhead—a maritime distress signal. If there was a sniper team positioned on Ligarto's highest point, I wanted to give them a chance to hit me with a spotlight before they hit me with a bullet.

The only response was the twittering of midnight birds and the faraway boom of an owl: *Hoo-ah . . . Hoo-ah-hoo . . . Hoo-ah . . .*

I stepped back into shadows and hugged the tree line as I walked, shells resonate beneath shoes. Every few yards, I stopped; checked behind, then searched the corridor of mist ahead.

It was now half past midnight; no sign of the president. I began to feel sure he'd been evacuated. I also began to feel an unexpected disappointment. Outwardly, I'd bristled at being coerced by the celebrated man. *"Help me disappear,"* he'd said, *"and I'll make your past disappear."*

So why the sudden regret? Weird.

Or was it?

It wasn't a time for reflection, so I told myself to drop the subject—*Concentrate, Ford. Focus!*—and continued along the ridge. But my mind kept drifting back to the question, inspecting the paradox consciously, then subconsciously.

Unusual. I seldom waste time reviewing the past or fretting over future consequences, yet the interplay continued. It produced a slow clarity.

Kal Wilson, I realized, didn't have as much leverage over me as he believed. I cared more about securing a pardon for Tomlinson. Unlike me, the poor guy wrestles with moral shadings of guilt. He believes in the concepts of sin and redemption.

There are so-called hipsters who use the persona to cloak their laziness and arrogance. Tomlinson, though, is without device. He is one of those rare, transcendent souls who lives ravenously, celebrating life in equal portions of bliss and despair. Tomlinson can be a pious pain in the ass, but he is also a man, and a good one. There aren't many and the good ones are worth saving.

But nobody reacts favorably to blackmail. So I'd balked at the president's offer. On a subconscious level, though, I'd been curious about how the trip would go. Maybe even looked forward to it. As a biologist, it was an unusual opportunity: Kal Wilson had occupied the loftiest tier of this planet's social hierarchy. For a time, he'd been the most powerful man on earth. How was he different? How would he handle himself now that his end was near . . . ?

I stopped for a moment, my concentration intense as I checked my perimeter. All clear. Then I paused to stare at the moon. Wilson had one lunar cycle left to live. If his doctors were right, this moon would wane, then wax full again, before cancer dragged him down. Twenty-eight days—a unit of time as fundamental as sunrise, menses, ocean tides.

What was the appeal of spending those last days with a man of his accomplishments?

The allure was complicated. I continued walking, senses alert. My brain continued to probe, but subconsciously.

Concentrate, Ford. Focus!

Focused or not, I *was* disappointed. But I felt worse for the former president. He would not spend his last days traveling as a free man. Four or more assassins had come to end his life. In a way, they'd succeeded, even though they'd botched the job.

At least, I hoped they'd botched the job . . .

I would find out sooner than expected.

At the top of the ridge, I stopped when I perceived movement within a grove of gumbo-limbo trees. I squatted . . . waited . . . watched long enough to confirm the movement wasn't wind shadow. No . . . something was there. Man-sized, twenty yards away.

I touched fingers to the knife and drew it. With my left hand, I felt around on the ground until I found a conch shell—Indians had used big conchs to build this ridge. It was the size of a glove, pointed at both ends. I slipped my hand into the shell.

The silhouette of a man became visible. He turned and walked in my direction. A second man appeared. He followed.

The fifth terrorist and an accomplice?

I crouched lower, trying to time it right as the men neared. I hoped they would walk past, give me a chance to get a look at them. Instead, the two silhouettes stopped within a few yards. I relaxed a little when I heard a familiar voice say, "Why the hell are you kneeling? Do you really think a man your size can hide when the moon's this bright?"

As I stood, I dropped the conch shell and tried to slip the knife into my belt without them noticing. I felt like a stupid kid.

"I hope you don't make a habit of being late, Dr. Ford. Forty minutes? My God! Mr. Vue and I were about to give up."

Even though he whispered, the president's tone told me *Don't ever be late again.*

WE WERE ALREADY WALKING TOWARD THE canoe, both men in a hurry. When I tried to speak, the president's bodyguard touched a finger to his lips, clapped his hand on my shoulder, and urged me toward the water.

"Later, later. Not much time."

"But what about the—"

"We go *now.*"

Mr. Vue moved his hand to the small of my back and began to push. He was about five-nine, weighed over two-fifty. When I tried to resist, my feet skidded over the shell path like a car being towed.

"*Wait.* I have information your people need. I intercepted a hit team. Four men, heavily armed, Middle Eastern, I think—"

"*Hit team?* You've got to be kidding." Wilson kept walking—he didn't want to believe it.

How could he not know?

"There's a helicopter and a patrol boat on them right now. An assault team with automatic weapons and ski masks. You weren't told?"

Finally, he paused. His bodyguard allowed me to jolt to a stop.

"You saw them?"

"Up close."

He looked at Vue. "Security said we might have a problem. But I think Ford's wrong. I think he saw some of our guys." His tone was hopeful. "But check."

The bodyguard touched a finger to the transceiver in his ear and said, "Shadow One to Moonraker. Need weather update." He leaned to listen, head down. After several seconds, he said, "Thanks. We waiting to hear disposition." Vue spoke the articulate English of an immigrant from Indochina, unnecessary articles dropped, *r*s blurred.

He removed the finger from his ear and said to Wilson, "The boat spotted on radar? It has aboard four men, as Dr. Ford said."

Wilson made a sound of frustration.

"But they are not yet sure if they bandits or friendlies. That was Apache we heard from MacDill—a boat crew from SEAL Team Four happened to be standing by. So the situation is copacetic, no worries. We just waiting to find out if they good guys or bad. Coast Guard will get back."

"Did they say they were armed?"

As Vue said, "They haven't seen weapons so far," I said, "Trust me, they're loaded for bear. Four men with assault rifles or submachine guns, and there could be a fifth or sixth guy already on the island. Someone planted those charges."

Wilson said, "You mean the three gunshot-sounding bangs?"

They didn't sound like gunshots to me but I nodded.

He looked to his bodyguard, using silence to delegate.

Vue took over. "That's what got security guys excited. They have scanner that transmits on random frequencies. Preemptive. It detonates covert ordnance. When we hear *bang-bang-bang,* they call in cavalry. Then radar picked up a small boat—"

Wilson interrupted, "But, Vue, it sounded like *firecrackers.* Halloween night, I figured. I thought the guys were overreacting. Secret Service always overreacts. Hell, at first they tried to make me get on a boat and leave for Tampa. But Ford's telling me—"

I said, "Judging from the accents, four men of Middle Eastern, maybe Indonesian, descent—I'm not sure; there're hundreds of dialects. But *Muslim* regions. They're wearing tactical gear and armed. They came to collect the bounty on your head. It's possible they got spooked when their ordnance detonated early."

"*Damn it.* Why'd they have to choose tonight of all nights?" He sounded unconcerned about the assassination attempt but furious about the timing.

Vue pulled at his lip, thinking. "What do you mean 'intercepted them'?"

I started to summarize. Got as far as taking the bearded man's knife and futzing the outboard when Vue held up a finger—"Hold moment"—then touched the same finger to his ear and bowed his head to listen. He punctuated long silences, saying, "I copy . . . Copy that . . . Are you sure? . . . Heard and understood."

Then he said, "Uh-huh, Moonraker will contact Smallville, run background checks. We maintain level-four alert. Hunter, yes . . . he on station. Eyeball not necessary." Vue turned to look at the former president. "But, no way, not going to interrupt man in his cabin unless bandits verified. No . . . FIGMO to that, Moonraker. You heard Hunter's briefing. I'm clear . . ."

FIGMO—an old and profane military acronym: Fuck You I've Got My Orders.

Vue turned. "Four men. Three Indonesian passports, one British, all Muslim surnames. But no weapons. They carrying green cards and Florida driver's licenses . . ."

I said, "Then they dumped the weapons during the chase," as Vue continued, "They say they work in the Sarasota area. They here on vacation, staying at place called Palm Island Resort. They claim they on way to party. Party at some local island, but got lost in fog—"

As I said, "What about the tactical gear? The ski masks?" Vue said, "It is Halloween party. They say they think it funny, dressing up like soldiers, a joke. Coast Guard says they might be drunk."

I was shaking my head, anticipating what came next as he added, "No weapons, but they found bottle of vodka aboard. Half empty."

When I said, "Your people aren't going to fall for a bullshit story like that," Wilson touched the sleeve of my sodden sports jacket as if admiring the material. "Yes, dressed up for a party. They'd have to be idiots to come up with something so transparent."

The man could be a ballbuster.

I said, "For a local guy, it's a *reasonable* story. But foreigners? That's why I need to speak to security—"

"You're not talking to anyone without my authorization. Secret Service will figure it out. But if these four guys aren't carrying weapons, and they have all their papers"—Wilson was speaking to Vue now—"what's illegal about dressing up on Halloween? Shooting off a couple of firecrackers? What do you think, Vue? I think it gives me enough wiggle room to stick with my plan."

The stocky man was shaking his head. "They'll want to ship you out. Tonight. If there's any chance of risk—"

"Well, what Secret Service wants and what *I* want may be two different things. I can tell you who's gonna win that debate."

"Mr. President . . . *Kal,* I think it better you wait. We go back cabin, let other agents eyeball. They know you okay, then. Dr. Ford, he wait here three, maybe four hours. Leave oh-dark-thirty. Safer then—"

I was thinking: *Sit in a mangrove swamp until 5 a.m., October, no breeze. Mosquitoes would drain me dry.*

"Can't do it. I've got this trip *scheduled.* I can't spare three hours." Wilson began walking toward the bay again, taking long strides for a man his height. He had a knapsack slung over one shoulder. Vue was carrying his duffel bag.

The smell of military olive drab is distinctive. It was like the former president was twenty again, field-packed and headed off to war.

6

When we got to the water, I used my flashlight to indicate where the canoe was hidden, then moved away to give the two men privacy. Over the last few days, I'd read a lot about the former president. I knew that Le Huy Vue had been his personal assistant and bodyguard for more than fifteen years. The media liked the storybook irony: Vue and Wilson had fought in the same war but on opposing sides. After the war, Vue was one of thousands who fled Indochina, seeking refuge in America. "Inseparable" had become the cliché used to describe their relationship.

Even if I was unaware of the history, I would've noticed their visual exchanges, the intensity of the silences they shared. Wilson was terminally ill. This might be the last time they saw each other.

As I waited, Vue did a lot of throat clearing. The former

president made soothing sounds, laughed, maybe cracking jokes. I couldn't make out what they said. I didn't try.

It was 12:50. Tide would be high around one, the moon would set at sunrise. We had good water and plenty of light. I felt wakeful, energized, confidence growing. I didn't know where Wilson wanted to go but that was okay. Some of my best trips have had destinations so vague that the trip itself became the destination.

My blue Chevy pickup was loaded and ready. Wilson had told me to park someplace private, so I'd left it at a friend's house on Pine Island, just a couple of miles away. The gas tank was full, oil changed, tires good, and there was a cooler in back filled with ice, beer, and food. The truck is more than twenty years old, but any vehicle packed for a road trip handles like it's new.

The only other instruction Wilson gave me was to clear my calendar for two weeks. That wasn't easy. I had research projects under way and orders to fill. The University of Iowa's medical school needed three liters of shark blood. Colorado College wanted several dozen ivory barnacles and assorted sea tunicates, all shipped live. Duke needed horseshoe crabs—their blood is sensitive to endotoxins and valuable as a diagnostic tool in cancer research.

My personal life was just as demanding, and even more complicated than usual. I like independent, strong-willed women, but those very qualities can also be a monumental pain in the ass when friendship crosses the dangerous line into romance. Marlissa Kay Engle was an example. Dewey Nye, my former girlfriend, was another.

In the last couple of weeks, I'd come to the conclusion that actresses and female tennis pros should have warning tags wired to their bra snaps.

A more pressing concern was my teenage son, Laken. More than a year ago, he'd been abducted and held captive by a sociopath and professional killer. Because Laken's a tough kid, and because I'd had some very good luck, the man went to prison, and Laken had returned home to Central America, where he lives with his mother, Pilar. Laken was untouched, not a scratch.

He is a bright and rational young man in every way except one—he's taken what he considers to be an academic interest in his abductor's "mental illness." He refuses to terminate contact. The killer writes rambling letters describing his "symptoms" and detailing his unhappy childhood. My son frequents medical libraries and is now well-versed in brain chemistry and behavioral anomalies caused by injury and birth defects.

The killer also has a savant's gift for computers and electronic gizmos. He has used that gift to trick victims more than once.

The man's name is Lourdes. Praxcedes Lourdes. Lourdes is a convincing liar because, like most psychopaths, he has no conscience. He's had a lifetime to perfect the social camouflage necessary to hide the truth—he is a monster.

I can't stop the correspondence between my son and his abductor because, several months ago, the man was extradited to Nicaragua to stand trial for murder. Seventeen counts. Lourdes is a serial killer. His fetish is setting people on fire—ultimate control. The peasants speak of him in whispers. "Man Burner," they call him. *Incendiario*.

But the Nicaraguan judicial system doesn't care about the fatherly concerns of a U.S. citizen, so I've spent a lot of time on the phone talking to attorneys in Managua. It's the main reason I accepted the consulting job in nearby Panama. It's also the reason why, after months of my badgering, Pilar took Laken to live in San Diego until I convinced the courts to act. I had friends on Coronado who would keep watch.

I was much too busy to disappear for two weeks. But I cleared my calendar, anyway—and I was secretly relieved.

So I was ready. And cautiously optimistic. As Vue had said, the cavalry was here, Coast Guard and military, but they were busy dealing with the four assassins. Secret Service radar hadn't picked up my plastic canoe as I approached. Presumably, it wouldn't track me as we returned to my truck. And if agents did swoop down, guns drawn? Kal Wilson was my willing passenger. He could do the explaining—which might be interesting. See how the great man handled it.

So I stood facing the water, waiting while the two men loaded gear and said their good-byes. Luckily, I turned to look when Vue said something loud enough for me to understand: "If this hurts, Kal, tell me and I'll . . ."

I was surprised to see that the president had his sleeve rolled up. Vue was using a penlight, concentrating on the man's shoulder as if inspecting a wound. Why?

I was considering explanations when I noticed a third person approaching. A man. The moon was so bright his shadow glided with him along the white shell ridge. Vue and the president were oblivious.

I whispered the only warning I could—*"Pssst! On your six!"*—and ducked into the mangroves. A fighter pilot would understand.

Wilson did.

CALMLY, THE FORMER PRESIDENT TURNED. AT THE same time, he hurried to get his sleeve down. Vue took a couple steps forward, placing himself between the approaching figure and Wilson. I hid in the bushes, listening.

"Identify yourself."

A flashlight went on. A man in slacks and sports jacket used the light to show himself. "It's me, Mr. President. Agent Wren." Short man, styled hair, eye sockets in shadow because the light angled from below his chin. He switched off the flashlight and continued walking.

"You're looking for me?"

"Yes, Mr. President. I was worried, sir. Am I intruding?"

"Yep, Adrian. You're intruding. I didn't make myself clear at the briefing? As of an hour ago—midnight—I began my retreat. My wedding anniversary is today. First day of November—it would've been our fortieth. Or maybe you forgot."

"Of course I didn't forget. You and the late Mrs. Wilson, a very special day. But what you don't understand is, the security situation has become serious. Coast

Guard has detained four men, foreign nationals, all Muslims—"

"Islamicists or Muslims?"

"I don't understand the distinction—"

"Then you need to do some reading."

I knew the distinction, but only because of recent research I'd done. I listened to the president say, "What you should understand is that no one, and I mean *no one*, is supposed to bother me for the next fourteen days. It's a spiritual matter, Adrian, which means it's private. In an emergency, you contact Mr. Vue. He brings my meals and delivers messages too important to wait."

The agent had stopped a few yards away. Vue moved to Wilson's left—a mobile wall. I got the impression Vue didn't like Agent Wren. Same with the president.

"I'm very sorry, sir. Our understanding was that sequestering yourself meant you weren't going to leave your cabin. Two weeks of solitary meditation. Very healing, I'm sure. But here you are *outside* your cabin." The man had the infuriating ability to sound compliant but with a subtle, superior edge.

"*Our* understanding, Adrian? I missed the evening news. Were you named director, Secret Service?"

"Of course not, sir—"

"Then maybe you have something in your pocket. A special little friend? My guess is, it's the GPS tracker."

Tracker?

Wren reached into his jacket and produced something the size of a TV remote. When I saw green lights blinking, I knew what it was.

"Sorry, Mr. President, but I took extra precautions tonight for obvious reasons. The tracker indicated you'd left your cabin. I thought it was a false reading, so I tried to find Vue. When Vue didn't respond, I knocked on your cabin door—"

"You *what?*"

Vue took it as a cue. "He did right thing, Mr. President. That's procedure."

"Bullshit. I gave orders not to be disturbed. Period."

"He was just doing his job, sir."

"His job, my ass. Agent Wren's job is to follow orders. Don't take his side in this, Vue—"

Good cop, bad cop, Wilson and his bodyguard knew their roles.

"Vue's right, Mr. President. I wouldn't risk disturbing you unless agency protocol required—"

Like heat, Wilson's voice began to rise. "Agent Wren, for the next two weeks I want you to *pretend* like agency protocol requires you to follow my orders. *Pretend* as if I'm the man in charge, not you. Do you read me, *mister?*"

"I understand, sir, but—"

". . . Because, Agent Wren, if I'd known a GPS chip in my shoulder gave you permission to stick your nose into my personal business I'd've had the doctors stick it up my ass instead of sewing it into my arm!"

"If you got the impression I'm snooping, sir, I want to reassure you—"

"I don't want to be reassured. I want to be obeyed. For your information, Agent Wren, we are on *an island*. Do you know the sailor's definition of an island? An island is a navigational hazard inhabited by drunks, whores, farmers, thieves, and other sons of bitches who were dumb enough to get off the fucking boat . . ."

"Really. That's quite amusing, sir—"

". . . which is why I *strongly* suggest that unless that electronic gizmo you're holding, the whatchamacallit, 'Angel Tracker,' indicates I'm swimming out to sea, or drifting toward Mars, you'd better mind your own god-damn business. Or you will find yourself on a boat headed for an assignment that includes icebergs and sex-starved polar bears. Not palm trees and moonlit beaches. Am I getting through to you, *mister*?"

"Well . . . of course, sir. When you put it that way. And it really is such a beautiful tropical night . . ."

I continued listening, impressed by Wilson's gift for seagoing profanity. But I was also picturing the president with his sleeve rolled up, Vue concentrating.

Angel Tracker.

Suddenly, I understood.

I've done a lot of fish-tagging projects. Worldwide, the electronic fish tag of choice is made by Applied Digi-tal Solutions, a Florida-based company. Because I'm on their mailing list, I knew that the company had patented an implantable microchip for humans. The chip is the size of a rice grain and transmits its location, along with a unique verification number, via satellite. The system is called "Digital Angel."

Kal Wilson had a locator microchip in his shoulder. Vue had been in the process of removing the Digital An-gel when Agent Wren interrupted them. Smart.

The president was leaving with me. The microchip was staying in his cabin.

Something else smart: Wilson had established the precedent of spending long periods of time alone— Tomlinson had mentioned his month at a Franciscan monastery. Maybe it *was* possible that the former president could sneak out for a week or two without Secret Service missing him.

Maybe.

But I didn't believe it. I doubted if Kal Wilson believed it.

7

The former president told me, "Stop calling me 'Mr. President.' Same with 'sir.' Even when we're alone. Break the habit before we go public." Ligarto Island was two miles behind us but he kept his voice low. Something about being in a canoe in darkness causes people to whisper.

I said, "I'll try. But it'll seem strange."

"Not as strange as it'll seem to me. Vue's one of the few who calls me by name. And my wife, of course. It's not because I'm a prick—though I *can be*. It's because the office demands that degree of respect."

"Then I should call you by your real first name?" I knew that Kal, although his legal first name, was an acronym made up of his given name and two middle names.

Because I wasn't sure of the pronunciation, I was

relieved when he said, "No. For now, use something impersonal. Military. Nautical, maybe."

I said, "What about your Secret Service code name?" Vue had used it a couple of times on the radio.

Wilson shook his head.

I tried again. "Captain?" I waited through his silence, then said, "Skipper?"

"'Skipper' . . . yes, that works. Use it. Drop all the other formal baloney. No, wait . . ." He thought about it for a moment. "I spent June on Long Island. Seaside mansions, and about half the people there were named Skipper. Skipper's too old money. I grew up on a farm."

"Well, how about—"

"How about 'Chief.' I left the Navy as a lieutenant commander so it's a bump in rank. But it's better than Skipper." There was a smile in his voice. The man had known some chief petty officers.

I said, "It fits." I was thinking *chief executive, commander in chief*.

"Hold it. No . . . Chief's too pushy. If we run into strangers, they'll start asking questions if you call me Chief. It needs to be bland. I don't want to attract attention."

I remembered Vue using the military acronym FIGMO, and said, "Why not 'Sam.' That's as simple as it gets." It was short for Samson bit, the cleat on the bow of a ship. It was also an acronym with a couple of meanings. One was profane, and stood for 'Shit Awful Mess'; the other, a type of missile.

Wilson laughed when I reminded him of SAM's three

meanings. He thought about it for a few minutes before saying, "I *like* that. For now, that's what you call me. Sam. Try to treat me like I'm just a regular guy."

"Okay. You're making it easier for me. Sam."

"Making what easier?"

"Talking about the way you handle a canoe. You've got us zigzagging like drunks. It's going to take forever to make land unless we switch places."

The paddler in the stern controls the boat and Wilson had insisted on taking that seat.

"But I want to steer."

"I'm aware of that . . . but it's not working out. I should be in the back."

"You're saying I'm not competent?"

"I'm saying I'll get us there faster."

"Come on, Ford. What's the problem? I prefer honesty to—"

"Okay, okay, you're not competent. In fact, you're worse than not competent. You bang the hull, and you splash me about every third stroke. You *suck* at the helm."

"I didn't say to be crude—"

"Don't be offended. I have more experience. That's why I should be steering."

In a flat voice, he replied, "But you don't know where we're going."

I was aware of that, too. When we left Ligarto, I'd told him my truck was two miles east, loaded and ready, as he had ordered. The former president replied, "There's been a change of plans. We're not using your truck."

Instead of east he was steering us west—*trying,*

anyway—toward the chain of barrier islands that separates mainland Florida from the Gulf of Mexico.

"It's time to trust me. Tell me where you want to go. We'll find shallow water and trade places."

"I share my plans on a need-to-know basis. I've already explained that. A few details at a time, that's all. It's a standard security measure."

With exaggerated patience, I said, "I need to know the boat's destination because I will soon be sitting where you're sitting and I will be steering, not you. Which means we will be going in a straight line, not zigzagging, or making little tiny circles on the great big ocean. So why not tell me the destination now, before we switch places? Give me something to aim for . . . Sam."

The man softened. "Am I that bad? Or are you in a pissy mood?"

I said, "Both."

He laughed. "Know what? You've got a point. I try to pick the best people available and let them do their jobs. No second-guessing, ever. Out here, Doc, you're the expert. And you've had a long night."

He said it so amiably, I felt bad for snapping at him. But I also realized that by challenging me, then deferring, he'd created a sense of indebtedness—the precursor to loyalty. The man knew how to leverage, pushing, then backing off.

But he was right. I'd had a long night.

* * *

ON LIGARTO, AGENT WREN HAD INSISTED ON escorting the former president to his cabin. That left me alone, waiting in swamp and mosquitoes, unsure what to do. Leave or stay?

I stayed . . . stayed for two miserable hours before Vue returned. "President be here soon," he said, then surprised me by adding, "He is sick. How sick is he?"

Vue didn't know—my first revelation of how private and stubborn Wilson could be.

I evaded, telling him I knew nothing about Wilson's health.

Vue's reaction was strange. He sounded pleased. "Already, you are lying for him. Good. I lie for him many times. I would die for President Wilson, he is such a friend. That how I know he must be very sick or he would not be determined to do this thing."

I said, "Determined to do what?"

It was Vue's turn to lie. "How would I know? I am his bodyguard. If I could travel, he maybe tell me. For all these years, I go *everywhere* with him. That's why I must stay here. It is the only way to fool Secret Service. But there's something I want to ask *you*." He was eager to change subjects. "Where that knife you say you take from those men?"

I found the knife and handed it to him. He used his penlight to inspect it, then shook his head solemnly. "I believed what you tell us before, but I believe more now. This is knife, very rare. It called a '*badek*,' some places; Indonesia. Or a '*khyber*' in Burma and the Himalayas." He touched the knife's edge. "Very best steel, hand-forged, and sharp. It curved for this"—Vue swiped a finger across his throat. "You don't have weapons. How you take this knife from a man?"

He seemed impressed when I told him, but it didn't make him any more talkative. He shrugged when I pressed for details about Wilson's travel plans. When I asked for an update on the men in the inflatable, his answers were vague; he seemed preoccupied. He kept returning to the subject of President Kal Wilson.

"This very hard for me 'cause I used to taking care of the man. Dr. Ford, you must be his bodyguard now. When you return safe with the president, you and me, we meet privately. I expect you give me full report."

He spoke unemotionally, but there was an implicit threat.

Less veiled was Vue's interest in the electronics I was carrying, or had aboard. I told him I had a GPS, and a cell phone, adding, "My VHF radio's broken and the cell phone's worthless. I can't get a signal out here."

I was lying about the VHF—I'd dropped the damn thing overboard when I was loading the canoe. But the man's interest wasn't conversational, I discovered.

"You very sure that all you have?"

"Yep. Very sure."

Without warning, he took my wrist. "What about your watch? They lots of electronic watches now." I was wearing my old stainless Rolex Submariner, something I rarely do, but it seemed to fit the situation.

He inspected both sides of the watch, then said, "No laptop? iPod? No personal data file?"

"In a canoe? Nope. Canoes and electronics don't mix. Plus, I don't own any of that crap, anyway."

Vue didn't see the humor. He held out his hand. "You give me GPS and cell phone. President be here soon and you go."

That made no sense. "Why would I leave the GPS? There's still fog out there. And it's my personal cell phone."

His hand didn't waver, nor did his tone. "You give me all electronics. President's orders. I keep them safe 'til you get back."

"But *why*?"

Vue shrugged, another lie. "I dunno. He call these things blind horses. Maybe he want you to use your own eyes."

I felt like telling him to spare me the aphorisms. Instead, I said, "He's worried about being tracked. Why don't you just say so?" I handed him my phone and little GPS, finally grasping why Wilson had refused to let me use my twenty-one-foot Maverick flats boat. I could have poled in just as quietly, and the skiff was specially rigged for night travel—tactical LED lights mounted beneath the poling platform; a spotlight, with an infrared lens, mounted above. The Maverick will do fifty knots in a foot of water—*only* a helicopter could have caught us.

But Wilson had demanded I come by canoe. Less chance of hidden electronics, I realized.

Before Vue left me, he loaded the president's bags into the canoe, saying, "I am from the snow mountains, Burma, near the Chinese border. There are men in my village who think they know of you. You had many friends, some with green faces. And yet, our men say, you always traveled alone."

I waited. He was talking about Indochina.

"You not traveling alone now. Understand? You never leave the president alone. Not for a minute, because he die soon, I think. In my village, when a great man dies we place his body on a platform where the wind can take it. President Wilson, he is a great man, and he must not die alone."

Vue, I was guessing, came from one of the many tribes that inhabit mountainous regions from Afghanistan to Nepal, from Burma into Southeast Asia. Like Great Britain's infamous mercenaries the Gurkhas, the tribesmen are known for their loyalty and their fearlessness. According to legend, they are the descendants of mountain gods, but the ethnic majorities of Burma, Cambodia, and Vietnam refer to them as *"Mois"*—a racial slur that means "savages."

I said, "I've been in those border areas. I attended a funeral like you're describing. It was for the father of a friend, a member of the Hmong tribe. You call it a 'wind burial'?"

"Yes. Put the body high among the trees, so the spirit flies."

As he added, "*Mong,* that word mean 'brave,'" I was remembering a line of mourners in colorful dress, winding up a hill with a red coffin, and chanting as vultures cauldroned overhead. There was the smell of incense and ox dung.

"The burial ceremony is important. But it more important how a great man dies. Do you understand? There must be wind and light so the sky can take him."

I shook my head. "No. I don't understand."

Vue shrugged his massive shoulders, then turned, done with it. I watched him disappear into the darkness of the shell ridge.

The former president arrived an hour later, carrying a backpack. "Secret Service thinks I'm locked in my cabin," he whispered. "Let's get our feet wet."

AT 4 A.M., WIND FRESHENED OFF THE GULF OF Mexico; heat radiating from the Everglades was siphoning weather from the open sea. I was in the stern, paddling toward the Gulf, using the October moon as a beacon. It was desert yellow, gaseous. It cast a column of light broad as a highway.

When we'd traded seats, Wilson finally revealed our destination. We were bound for the southern point of Cayo Costa, an isolated barrier island three miles southwest of Ligarto. There was a settlement of shacks and beach houses on the point that were only occasionally inhabited by the eclectic mix of beach bums, hermit entrepreneurs, and hippie dropouts who owned them. There were no roads on the island, no landing strips.

When I asked why he wanted to go to Cayo Costa, the former president told me I'd find out when we got there. It was the answer I expected.

Cayo Costa was now an undulant darkness less than a

mile away, ridged like a sea serpent floating on the Gulf's rim. The moon was over the island, its reflection linked to our canoe like a tractor beam, drawing us away from mainland Florida, leaving sleeping tourist resorts and city lights behind.

Wilson noticed.

"The way the moon hits the water . . . it's like a passageway. Almost like the deck of an aircraft carrier opening up." After a pause, he asked, "Do you believe in omens?"

"Umm . . . no."

"Would you admit it if you did?"

I smiled. "Probably not."

"Me, neither. Which makes us both a couple of superstitious liars. There was a moon like this the first time I landed on the *Kennedy.* It turned out to be good luck, so I take this as a good omen. Did you ever make a night landing on a carrier, Ford?"

"No. Well . . . in a helicopter once. But not what you're talking about."

I expected him to add something, tell me how terrifying it was. He was a Naval pilot. He'd experienced it. But all he did was nod. It was another of his techniques: Say little, imply much. You had to listen or you might miss something.

I continued paddling as Wilson opened his backpack. His back was to me, a precise silhouette in the liquid light. I watched him roll his sleeve and wipe his shoulder. Disinfectant. The Angel Tracker had been just under the skin, he told me. Easy for Vue to make a tiny incision and remove it.

Wilson patted a fresh bandage in place and then swallowed a couple of pills. For the first time, I noticed that his profile lacked a familiar contour. His stylish hair had been buzz-cut.

I assumed he'd figured out some kind of disguise. Was that it?

"I've got all my medicines, vitamins, and things in here." He was talking about the backpack. "I can't lose this. Or get it soaked. I hate taking pills, but they buy me time."

Lightning flickered on the horizon, revealing distant cumulous towers. I waited through a minute of silence before saying, "That storm's ten, twenty miles out to sea. You're okay. But if we travel by canoe tomorrow, you'll need a waterproof bag, plus flotation." I paddled a couple of strokes before adding, "*Are* we going by canoe?"

He rolled down his sleeve and closed the backpack. "When it's time for you to know, I'll tell you."

As expected.

Useppa Island and Cabbage Key were behind us. Windows of sleeping households twinkled through trees, and Cabbage Key's water tower was a solitary star above mangroves, bright as a religious icon. To the south, lights of Captiva Island and Sanibel were a melded blue aura; Cape Coral was an asphalt fluorescence to the east.

Separating us from Cayo Costa was the Intracoastal Waterway where navigational markers blinked in four-second bursts: white . . . red . . . green. The Intracoastal is a federally maintained sea highway that runs from Texas to New Jersey. Big boats depend on it. I avoid it.

The water would be rougher there because its deep channel accelerated an outgoing tide like a faucet.

I told Wilson, "You can stop paddling. We'll let the tide do the work. Get some rest—but secure your life jacket first." I explained why.

"I wondered why you were bearing north. You being such an expert paddler, there *had* to be a reason."

The man didn't miss anything

I said, "The channel's going to be running fast, like a river. If we get swept too far south, we'll have to wait for the tide to change, then work our way back."

"We can't wait," he said. "I don't have time. So stay as far north as you need to be."

I nearly responded, "Aye, aye, sir."

For the last half an hour, I'd been watching a light on Cayo Costa. A yellow light that brightened, then dimmed—a fire, I realized, on the island's point. There was pink sand there, where the water of Captiva Pass swept past, fast and deep, into open sea.

"Are we meeting someone?"

He realized I was talking about the fire. "Yes. A friend."

I knew better than to ask who.

"Did you tell him to do that?"

"No. I've been wondering about the fire myself. It's the last thing I'd want."

"Maybe he has camp pitched and breakfast cooking. That would be okay. We both need sleep and I didn't pack a tent."

"Don't worry about details. But there wasn't supposed

to be a fire." His puzzled inflection read *Why draw attention?*

"It's not a private island. Maybe he has company."

The former president replied, "That would not be surprising."

The way he said it, it sounded like his friend might be an interesting character. I wondered if it was Vue. Vue could've hopped a boat and beat us to the island by an hour. But why?

I could feel the running tide beneath us now, the canoe beginning to hobbyhorse among black waves. I adjusted our course, got my paddle rhythm set, before I said, "Give me twenty, twenty-five minutes and we'll find out."

8

I concentrated on paddling while Wilson sat with his forehead in his hands, resting, I hoped. He had such a powerful personality it was easy to forget he was sick.

Leukemia contributed to the illusion. I'd lost a friend to the disease recently so I had a layman's knowledge. It's a progressive cancer in which the abnormal production of white blood cells destroys red blood cells. In the final stages, a person can appear healthy even while a microscopic war is being waged within. Anemia and bruising are the first symptoms. Death can be the next.

Even the word carries a chill. Like many cancers, leukemia seems inexplicably random and is therefore more frightening. Without clear cause and effect, the disease hints that life itself is random and without design. My friend Roberta Petish had a bright spirit, a huge heart, and she lived big up until a few days before her internal war was lost. I understood Wilson better because of her.

I liked the man's aggressiveness. Instead of lying back waiting for death, he was determined to race the bastard to the finish line. I was glad to be with him. For now . . .

Paddling rough water kept my hands busy and allowed my mind to drift. Wilson's silhouette at rest was an amorphous gray. He sat as silently as the battle raging inside his circulatory system. The man had survived his share of battles and prevailed in many. The research I'd done reminded me that my traveling partner was an unusual example of the species, *sapiens*.

Kal Wilson was a man of contradictions and one of those rare people who was stronger for them. He'd been born and spent the early part of his life in the village of Hamlet, North Carolina, but his family had moved to Janesville, Minnesota, when he was an adolescent. Having roots in the Deep South and Bedrock North was an unusual political asset.

Wilson was a decorated combat pilot who, as a midwestern congressman, became known as his party's steadiest antiwar voice. He was a conservative on some issues, liberal on others, but refused to be typecast as either.

Criticized by his party for refusing to join the rank and file, he ran as an Independent and won three more terms in the House and then a seat in the U.S. Senate. Wilson switched parties yet again when he ran for the presidency. Even his campaign platform bucked Democratic and Republican stereotypes with unorthodox positions on gun control, abortion, the death penalty, and drugs.

Wedge issues that defined lesser politicians set Wilson apart as a freethinking maverick. He was passionate about stem cell research but pushed hard for returning the Pledge of Allegiance and prayer to public schools. He was an environmental hawk who railed against the hypocrisy of not relying on our own oil preserves. He was an antiwar dove, although he warned of a "global fascist awakening."

Voters have an affection for maverick outsiders that's almost as strong as the contempt felt for mavericks by Washington insiders. Things did not go smoothly for Kal Wilson when he and his renegade administration arrived inside the Beltway.

By the fourth year of his term, the man's star was flickering. "Unorthodox" had been redefined as "inept." His administration had brokered a cease-fire in the Middle East but been blamed for Central America's instability, particularly the countries bordering the Panama Canal.

Wilson's main adversary had been Juan Rivera, a man I came to know well during my years in the region. Rivera was a Fidel Castro–style revolutionary who publicly, and repeatedly, outmaneuvered the American president, contributing to the perception that Wilson was weak.

When Wilson changed the phrase "global fascist awakening" to "global fascist fundamentalism," it was perceived as a ploy to boost his approval rating. When he stopped referring to terrorists as "Muslim extremists," insisting that "Islamicist killers" was more accurate, he drew fire from both parties in our politically correct Congress.

It got worse when a reporter from Al Jazeera television asked him to explain the difference between "Islamicist killers" and "Zionist killers"—an impossible question because of the way it was couched, but Wilson answered, anyway.

Zionists, he said, believe a Jewish state should exist in the world. Islamicists, he continued, believe that the world should exist as an Islamic state.

"Are they both killers?" the reporter pressed.

Wilson bulled ahead. "An interesting distinction. Killing women and children at a bus stop or in a Nazi concentration camp—or at the federal building in Oklahoma City, for that matter—should be referred to as 'murder.' They aren't acts of war. They're acts of cowardice.

"So 'fascist fundamentalism' would be a more accurate term when used generally. 'Islamicists' would be the specific that describes murderers who use religion as a shield."

Kal Wilson, the "freethinking dove," was vilified as a bigot and a warmonger, and he effectively alienated fundamentalists of all faiths.

It had something to do with a bounty being offered for his head.

THE SILHOUETTE DOZING IN THE FRONT OF THE canoe was the president of the United States . . .

As my mind lingered on the complex personality that was Kal Wilson, I sometimes paused to remind myself what the man had achieved, trying to counterbalance his unpresidential snoring.

Why wouldn't he snore? He was human . . . one of six billion members of our species who, at that very instant, were inhaling or exhaling, making respiratory noises, as the earth orbited through the silent universe that blazed above our canoe.

He was flesh and finite; an ordinary man. As a man, though, he had lived an extraordinary life.

Wilson was among the youngest men ever elected to the presidency. He'd upset an incumbent, served one turbulent term, then shocked the country by not running for a second.

"Our reasons," he said, "are personal"—the plural "our" referring to his wife, who, he often said, was the smarter half of their two-person presidency.

At a news conference, a famous anchorman referenced Wilson's fifty-seven percent approval rating, before pressing, "Is it because you and the First Lady fear that you've polarized the American people?"

Wilson's reply was measured and presidential—he never lost his poise in public.

Offstage, though, an unseen microphone caught what he whispered to his wife: "What I fear is polarizing the American press by smacking one of those pompous assholes in the face. Most of them are spoiled brats born with silver spoons up their asses. That's why feeding people a line of crap comes so natural."

Like most presidents, Wilson had run-ins with the media. But his "spoiled brat" line so endeared him to the public that the media retaliated by attacking as a pack. "Personal reasons" wasn't explanation enough for not running, so the press speculated. Theories made headlines based on shock value, not fact, and they ranged from the offensive to the grotesque.

Wilson never fired back, though. A distant descendant of Woodrow Wilson, he'd become an expert on the office long before he held it, and he was fond of stiff-arming reporters by quoting his predecessors instead of allowing his own words to be twisted. He remained in the background, refusing comment on world affairs, and taking pains not to second-guess the current administration.

An example: Wilson, a track star and boxer at the Naval Academy, made headlines by winning his over-fifty age group in a Chicago triathlon, but then quit the sport. Characteristically, he offered no explanation, but friends said it was because he felt it wasn't in the nation's best interest to divert the spotlight from a sitting president.

Even out of office, Kal Wilson remained presidential. He stayed cool—*cold*, some said. The exception was when he denounced the media for not running the Danish editorial cartoons that sparked riots.

Tomlinson was wrong when he told me the incident was after Wray Wilson's plane had crashed but right about the former president becoming more outspoken in the weeks after her death.

Wilson began using the term "Islamicists" and "Nazis" as synonyms.

He referred to the Islamic cleric who offered a bounty for his head as a "failed paperhanger" who didn't have the courage to look an enemy in the eye—an obvious comparison to Adolf Hitler.

In an interview with BBC television, Wilson warned that the United Kingdom, Holland, France, and Germany, through their policies of appeasement, were "providing the knife and whetstone" that Islamicists would use to cut Europe's throat.

He said, through the "dangerous charade" called "political correctness," the United States was doing the same.

Both political parties began a subtle process of distancing themselves from Wilson. Newspaper editorials hinted that his thinking had become "unsound" as a way of explaining why they now refused to quote the man.

"Even former presidents sometimes need editing," an editorial suggested.

"Censorship through intimidation," Wilson responded, "is the first objective of tyranny. Once accomplished, the truth is easily perverted to serve the tyrant's goals."

For the first time in his career, Kal Wilson was criticized for behavior that was unpresidential.

DID WILSON BELIEVE THERE WAS A LINK BEtween the million-dollar bounty and the former First Lady's death? In the next few days, I would find out.

That was one reason I'd felt disappointed when I thought the trip was canceled. Another was that it was my chance to find out how Wilson was *different*. It interested me as a biologist and as a man. Extreme environments catalyze extreme adaptive mechanisms. By virtue of having inhabited the White House, Wilson was unlike other men.

But how?

I thought about it as I banged the canoe through the Intracoastal's rough water into the slick, moon blue shallows. It was a question made more interesting because the man was a few feet away, motionless but no longer snoring.

Had the office elevated him? Or only isolated him?

Both, I guessed.

All U.S. presidents are awarded a place in history, but the spatial corridor is limited—eight years or less. What happened before is historical context. What happens afterward is postscript. A president's life is defined by the office, then cast in bronze, often long before the man's death. Typically, the life of a former president consists of a long, polite silence that ends with a bugler's farewell.

Did ex-presidents chafe at inactivity? At the perception they are the walking dead?

Maybe that's why Wilson was determined to spend his final days as a free man. He was a cool one, sometimes cold. But history's bronze statue still had a beating heart, a warrior's soul. A river flowed beneath the ice.

I liked that.

But he wasn't an easy man to get along with, as I was learning.

"You could've cut off five, maybe ten minutes if you'd pointed us a few more degrees south. Get sloppy like that in an F-14, you could end up in Austin instead of

Boston—if the pencil pushers hadn't retired that beautiful machine."

Wilson hadn't spoken for half an hour. I thought he was still asleep.

I continued paddling, the island now so close I could smell the salt pan musk of cactus and sea oats. "I played it safe. We're only a couple hundred yards north of where you told me to land."

"A quarter mile, is more like it. But that's okay. That must be the cabin—do you see it?" As he stretched, he used his paddle to point at a shadowed geometric set back from the water. Its tin roof was ivory, the windows glazed. "We can lay in close to shore and no one will see us take our gear inside."

He was concerned for a reason. A few hundred yards down the beach, the bonfire was encircled by a cluster of men and women, their shadows huge. Some were dancing; others sat shoulder to shoulder, their faces golden masks.

I said, "Are you sure you want to risk landing where there're so many people?"

"I told you before, I don't think the public'll recognize me. And if they do? Well . . . it's better I find out now." He tilted his head for a moment. "Why the hell are they doing that, you think? Banging away at this hour?"

The beach people were pounding drums . . . tin cans . . . plastic buckets, too, judging from the noise. They maintained a steady, low-resonance rhythm that, for a while, I'd mistaken for the rumble of ocean waves. It was 5:45 a.m. Sunrise was in an hour.

I said, "It's called a 'drum circle.' A fad. People who normally wouldn't give each other the time of day meet to play drums, usually on a beach around sunset. But this time of morning? It's weird." I paused, surprised by a sudden word association. Tomlinson's face had jumped into my mind. "This friend of yours," I said slowly, "how long have you known him?"

In the chiding manner of a football coach, Wilson said, "You're an expert navigator who ignores shortcuts and a marine biologist who makes assumptions. I'm worried about you. Those are unexpected flaws in a man of your accomplishments."

"Huh?"

"You made an assumption, Dr. Ford. When I said we were meeting a friend, you assumed it was *my* friend."

He began to snub his backpack, getting ready to land, communicating the obvious through his aloof silence. It was worse than him saying it.

You assumed wrong.

EVEN THOUGH HE WAS DOWN THE BEACH, I RECognized Tomlinson's scarecrow dancing as he juked his way to the center of the circle and took a seat on a log— Ray Bolger from *The Wizard of Oz*. He was barefoot, shirtless, wearing a pirate's bandanna. The muscle cordage of his arms moved at languid angles as he slapped at an ebony drum angled between his knees.

A couple dozen people danced free-form around the fire to the beat of tambourines, cowbells, congas, Jamaican steel drums, water bottles, a surfboard, beer bottles, and at least one frying pan.

The former president seemed fascinated. "The reason they're dressed like that . . . it's because of Halloween?"

I said, "They're Tomlinson's friends, so I don't think it would matter."

Some wore full body paint: jaguars with breasts for eyes, or flowers, rainbow streaks, and bizarre tribal designs. A few were naked, others wore shorts and bikini tops. Those who weren't painted wore costumes. It was a popular year for angels, demons, and *Gilligan's Island*.

"I expected the place to be deserted. When he told me about Cayo Costa, I got the impression it hadn't changed much in the last forty years. That it was still unpopulated."

It was Tomlinson who'd also told the former president that he had friends who owned a cabin, that the cabin was empty, and where the keys were hidden.

"This isn't typical. Except for weekends, Cayo Costa's quiet." Because Wilson had said *still* unpopulated, I thought about it for a moment. "You've been on this island before, sir?"

We were carrying our bags from the canoe to the cabin. He slowed. "A long time ago. Our first trip together, Wray and me. I'd graduated from the Academy the previous spring. We took the train from Maryland to Tampa, borrowed a buddy's car, and drove to the Naval air base in Key West. Sanibel was on the way, so we spent a couple nights on the islands. We honeymooned on Useppa, the Barron Collier Room."

That explained why he'd attended a party there.

It was too dark in the shadows to read his watch, but he glanced at it anyway. "It was exactly forty-one years ago to the day that Wray and I came ashore here. Cayo Costa Island . . . only, back then, I'm certain it was called 'La Costa.' Palm trees and sand; not a human soul for miles. Pretty exciting for two hick kids just starting out. It was forty-one years ago, and"—he looked at his watch again—"forty-one years, plus . . . plus about an hour, that I . . . that we . . ." He caught himself; his pace quickened—getting too personal.

I let him move ahead. He was about to tell me that something important had occurred on this island between him and his late wife. They'd made a sunrise visit, probably shelling or picnicking. Today, November 1st, was their fortieth wedding anniversary, he'd told Agent Wren. Perhaps Wilson had chosen the same date, a year earlier, to propose. Here. On this island.

While he waited on the porch, I pushed the door open, then used my flashlight to hunt for lanterns and matches. "Did you tell Tomlinson you'd be arriving this morning?" I was as uncomfortable discussing personal matters as the former president. I was also anticipating being pissed off at Tomlinson for not having the cabin ready. I saw no food, no ice, and the generator wasn't running. Typical.

But I was premature.

Wilson said, "No, he'll be surprised. When he told me he knew of a secluded place, that it was available, I told him if I *did* show up it would be around the first of the month. He said his sailboat's anchored somewhere nearby. We'd been discussing Zen meditation. I suggested that if things worked out, maybe we could go for a cruise."

I'd seen Tomlinson's old Morgan, *No Más,* anchored off the beach, its hull pale as a mushroom in the moonlight, bow pointing water light into the tide.

"A cruise," I said. "Meaning his boat's ready, provisioned with food and supplies."

"I assume so."

"You told me to do the same thing. Have my truck ready."

Wilson placed his duffel bag on a table as I filled a Coleman lantern with fuel. "It's good to have options. We may need your truck before we're done."

"Did you tell him to bring a passport and block out a week or two, just in case?"

The president said, "Tomlinson doesn't strike me as the type who keeps a calendar."

"I think you know what I'm getting at, sir. You said you knew things about Tomlinson that would surprise me. Did you offer him the same deal you offered me?"

Wilson was unpacking a shaving kit, a towel, a photograph in a brass frame, positioning them neatly. He didn't reply.

I struck a match. The lantern hissed, filling the room with stark light. "Am I allowed to read between the lines, Mr. President? Or maybe it would be easier if you just came out and told me what's going on."

"You're supposed to call me 'Sam.' A slip like that with people around could cause problems."

"Sorry, *Sam*. We're taking Tomlinson's boat, aren't we? That's not hard to figure out. But where? Tampa? Key West? You mentioned both. Is this some kind of farewell, sentimental journey? If it is, I understand. I'll stick with you. But why involve Tomlinson?"

"You're a perceptive man, Ford. I *would* like to revisit some places important to my wife and me. But I don't have time. In fact, if we could press on right now"—he looked at the exposed beach, the falling water, his expression impatient—"I'd say let's get going. Wray and I loved this part of Florida. It's true. We had a lot of fun here. But you say the word 'sentimental' like it's sweet. There is nothing sweet about what I intend to do"—he looked at me sharply—"or what I intend to ask you to do."

"Then this *is* about your wife's death. You believe she was murdered."

"I believe it's *probable*. Wray and six other good and decent people. One of her best friends was aboard that plane. A fellow we'd known since grade school who became a very fine plastic surgeon."

"Do you have evidence?"

"It's my opinion. My wife's death wasn't an accident."

There was an intensity to his silence and something suggestive about the way he busied himself neatening his gear. Customs agents and cops learn to watch the hands. People who feel guilty use busywork to dissemble.

"You were supposed to be on that plane, weren't you, sir?"

His hand came to rest on the photograph. It was face-down on the table. "That's right."

"It wasn't mentioned in the news accounts."

"No one knew. No one was supposed to know, anyway, and the media still hasn't found out. I told the FBI, of course. They're working on the investigation with an international team. It's important for them to understand there was a motive."

"Why would someone in your position risk traveling to Central America in a small plane?"

"It was a private plane, but it wasn't a small plane. It was a Cessna Conquest. A dream to fly; we used it several times. It was part of what we did—*help* people. Anonymously. There'd been an earthquake that wiped out a village in western Nicaragua. They are common in that part of the world. We were taking supplies and a medical team. Our friend was a gifted surgeon."

I had personal experience with the earthquakes and volcanoes of the region but said nothing.

Flying supplies to people in trouble, the president explained, wasn't an unusual thing for him and his wife to do.

"When we began work on the Wilson Library, we also created the Wilson Center to stay involved with issues important to Wray and me. It was her idea to establish a response team that could get help to disaster victims fast. We are small, we're privately funded, so we're already on scene while the big bureaucracies are still dealing with red tape. It's a hands-on project. We work hard, and always anonymously."

Because of his schedule, the president said, he could

only occasionally join the Wilson Center's volunteers. He'd cleared the decks, though, for Nicaragua.

"But Secret Service talked me into canceling because of that damn death threat. The day after my wife was killed, I told my security people, and the director, that I would never again allow them to overrule me."

"Someone targeted the plane because they thought you were aboard."

His finger tapped at the back of the photo. "I'm convinced that's true."

"An incendiary rocket?"

He shrugged. His finger, I noticed, was tapping in synch with the distant drums.

"How many people knew you planned to make the trip?"

"Dozens. The Wilson Center has a full-time staff, plus many volunteers who have administrative responsibilities."

"How many knew you canceled?"

"Fewer, but still a sizeable number."

"You told me the plane made a scheduled landing. But newspaper accounts said the plane crashed while making an emergency landing. Are you sure you're right?"

He nodded. "Wray and her group got a message that a pregnant woman was in desperate need of medical attention. The woman and her son were to meet the plane at the airstrip."

"You must have someone feeding you solid information."

"Smart executives put together first-rate intelligence

networks or they're not smart executives. Even nine years after leaving office, it's not an exaggeration to say that my sources are beyond the comprehension of most. Many of the world leaders I dealt with have also retired, but we stay in contact, advise each other, and share information— even some of my old adversaries. No one in power wants our input anymore. In a strange way, we're like a secret and exclusive little club."

"Are you telling me you *know* who did it?" I waited through a long silence. "I would assume it was the same group that came after you tonight. Muslim fanatics."

The former president's hand stilled. "*Islamicists,* you mean? It's true they'd love to have my head on a platter. Literally." Abruptly, he resumed neatening his gear. I had the feeling I'd missed something.

"Maybe Hal Harrington can provide more informa-tion," he said. Wilson was good at that—dodging ques-tions by putting you on the defensive. "Or are you still pretending you don't know the man?"

Why was he asking about the covert intelligence guru again? Harrington was a member of the deep-cover oper-ations team the president had discovered: Negotiating and Systems Analysis. To give members legitimate cover while operating in foreign lands, the agency provided them legitimate and mobile professions.

Harrington, trained as a computer software program-mer, later founded his own company. He's now listed among the wealthiest men in the country. Did that have something to do with it?

I had no choice but to reply, "You've mentioned Harrington before. Sorry, I don't know the man."

"You didn't contact him after our meeting in your laboratory?"

"Even if I knew who you're talking about, the answer would be no." True. Harrington was still with the team. The head of it now. But I no longer trusted him.

"You're good, Ford. If you're proving you can keep a secret, it's working. But I'm tired. We can talk about this later. Otherwise, I'll give you information as you need to know."

He *sounded* tired. My eyes had adjusted to the light and I saw that his face was the same mushroom gray as *No Más's* hull. His hair had been shaved boot camp close but he looked monkish, not military. In every photo I'd ever seen, he had the silver, sculpted hair typical of politicians and anchormen. The change in his appearance was remarkable.

I said, "There's something that can't wait. You told me to pack a passport and enough clothes for a week. But if we're going after Mrs. Wilson's killers"—I made eye contact, trying to communicate my meaning without risking details—"I need more than socks and a shaving kit. There are some items at my lab that might be useful."

He was unaccustomed to being pushed. It was in his face.

"That's something we'll discuss. But not now." Blinking, Wilson leaned forward, removed his contact lenses.

Then he pulled a bottle of pills from his backpack and tapped two into his hand. "Is there water around here?"

I wanted more answers. If we were hunting professional killers, I *had* to stop at the lab. And there was no reason to bring Tomlinson. It wasn't coincidental that he'd been at the party on Useppa and was now on this remote island.

Tomlinson is my trusted friend, a solid travel partner, and possibly the most intelligent person I know—when he's not stoned or word-slurring drunk. But the man doesn't have the skills or the stomach for the variety of violence Wilson was hinting at. On this trip, he would be a liability.

But I didn't push because the former president was a sick man—for the first time, I could see the disease in his hollow, knowing eyes.

I hurried to the canoe and returned with water.

9

The former president was asleep. Finally. And Tomlinson still didn't know we were on the island. As I headed down the beach to say hello, I realized that I, too, was moving in rhythm with the drums.

I'd changed into a khaki shirt and shorts and was carrying a Sage fly rod I'd found in a storage room. I'd broken the angler's rule about borrowing equipment, rationalizing that I would return it in better shape than I found it. The reel needed oiling, and its sink-tip line was moldy.

As I walked, I made a hasty leader using spider hitches and surgeon's knots, then tied on a streamer fly of chartreuse and silver. Still walking, I began false casting, stripping out line. It was the last hour of a falling tide. The beach was stained pink at the high-water mark. Below was exposed sand, sculpted by current, smooth as wind-blown snow. Its surface was crusted. It collapsed beneath my weight.

I made a cast uptide, waited until the line matched the speed of the current, then began to strip the lure toward the beach. Water was freighting out faster than I could walk. Whirlpools formed at my feet, and swirled over dark water at the drop-off's edge. It was an intersection where predators would lie—saltwater snipers, awaiting bait that was overpowered by the lunar draw.

As I fished, I noted a buoyant darkness to the east separating itself from a velvet horizon. Soon, the sun would begin diluting shadow with rays of color. The moon had disappeared behind the tree line, but it would be visible from the island's southern point, where Tomlinson and his painted friends were drumming and dancing.

They hadn't noticed us land. I was now close enough to feel the percussion of the drums through my ribs, but there was still no indication they saw me. Fishermen, like joggers, are invisible to the uninitiated. And to the unsober, in this case.

Drum circles attract mystic types, big on celestial rhythms. On full moons, sunrise and moonset are simultaneous, balancing for a moment on opposite horizons. My guess was, they'd keep playing until the moon disappeared into the sea. Especially if Tomlinson was in charge. The man sought balance in everything but the excesses of his own life.

In that way, at least, Tomlinson and Kal Wilson had something in common. The president had refused to lie down until he'd gone exploring. The place we were staying wasn't just one cabin, it was a camp comprised of several one-room buildings—a kitchen and eating area in one, shower and toilet in another, and a bunkhouse set beneath trees next to the storage shed where I found a little Honda generator.

Nice place. Friendly, too, with its laid-back touches. DON AND JOAN WELCOME YOU, read a sign above the outdoor shower.

The former president insisted on helping me get the generator running before he settled himself in the bunkhouse. He was snoring when I checked a few minutes later. The photograph he carried was on the nightstand, its glass panel flickering with the reflection of ceiling fans overhead.

The last thing he said was, "If the fish are hitting, call me. I haven't had a morning alone with a rod in my hand since I ran for the Senate."

Stories I read described him as an "avid angler"—a term used so often that I'd dismissed it as the invention of some PR firm. "Image management," political consultants call it. The ideal presidential candidate attends church, fishes, wears a rubber watch, and owns a retriever. But there is no contriving the authentic inflections of fishermen. I hear them every morning around the docks at the marina.

Wilson had had almost no sleep, though, so I wasn't going to disturb the man even if fish were hitting. Which they were. My third cast, I hooked an immature snook. As I led it ashore, a pod of larger snook surfaced behind, including a couple of yard-long females.

Next cast, I came up tight on what felt like a snag's

deadweight, but then I discerned the muscular ruddering of a fish as it turned laterally to the current. I locked fingers over the line, lifted . . . then lifted again before the fish reacted, accelerating cross-tide so fast that line sizzled as it ruptured the water's surface.

As the fish moved, I glanced at my feet—the line was clearing while the reel ratcheted. The handle banged skin off my knuckles as I slipped my hand beneath the spool, fingertips creating heat as they touched the line experimentally: Too much pressure, the leader would break; too little, the fish might take all my line.

The fish was fifty yards into the backing before it turned, then stripped another fifty yards, running seaward. I began following it down the beach, trying to recover line. I was almost to the drum circle—they still hadn't noticed me, Tomlinson included—when the fish turned and angled cross-tide again . . . then began to fight its way uptide.

Until that moment, I'd thought it was one of the big female snook. This behavior, though, was unusual.

I turned and retraced my footprints up the beach, leashed to the fish, my hands sensitive to vibrations transmitted through the line. I could feel the steady oscillation of connective tissue as the fish angled into the current, using its body mass to resist as I leveraged with the fly rod, steering it toward the shallows.

It turned . . . sounded . . . then ascended. More unusual behavior. I pumped and reeled, the morning breeze keening through the line I gained.

I didn't care about landing and killing the fish, although

I would if it was breakfast-worthy. I wanted to find out what it was. Swimming against the tide, its erratic descents, didn't mesh with the behavior of familiar species. I at least wanted to get a look at the thing. So I waded waist-deep to the edge of the drop-off, trying to narrow the point of intersection. The tide was running so hard it eroded the sand beneath my feet, and I had to keep moving or I would have been swept away.

Then, abruptly, the line went slack. It didn't break; there was no elastic recoil. It collapsed, like a balloon deflating.

The fish was gone . . . I thought.

But it wasn't gone.

The line, I realized, hadn't broken. The line was moving toward me . . . no, it was torpedoing toward me at high speed . . . hissing now as it ripped the water's surface.

The fish I'd hooked wasn't alone, either. Its erratic behavior was explained. A shark's dorsal fin, two feet high and gray, was tracking the line, closing in so fast that it pushed a bulbous wake like a submarine.

I turned my side to the shark, watching the line as I tried to hurry into shallower water. But the sand was like snow and collapsed under pressure. I could walk but I couldn't run.

There was no escape. So I stopped and just let it happen, resigned but also fascinated.

The shark was a great hammerhead, as long as our canoe but triple the girth. It had to weigh a half ton. The dorsal was back-lit by the dawn horizon; its bizarre head was a transient shadow wider than my shoulders. I lifted my feet from the bottom and let the tide move me as the fish I'd hooked shot past my legs. The shark's wake followed, close enough that I felt its bulk graze my thigh.

An instant later, water imploded. The hammerhead breached. In its jaws was a barracuda, my chartreuse fly pinned neatly to the hinge of its mouth. Plasticine flakes glittered as the shark twisted and crashed into the water— barracuda scales. Then it swirled massively, so close I could feel the suction created by the hammerhead's tail stroke.

My feet had found the bottom. I walked and crawled until I was on the beach, the fly rod still in hand.

"An interesting fishing technique, Dr. Ford. But shouldn't you have a large hook strapped to your butt?"

The president had been watching. He looked fit in running shorts and a T-shirt. He was also wearing owlish, wire-rimmed glasses with tinted lenses—even in photographs I'd never seen the man wear glasses. It had been less than half an hour since I'd left him.

I was laughing, adrenaline wired. "Did you see the size of that bastard?"

"Yeah. You'd look nice in his trophy case."

I was searching the water. No fin. "It wasn't after me. It was locked onto the fish I was fighting. Probably didn't even notice I was there."

"You're the expert. But I think I'll give it a few minutes before taking a swim." He was a dry one—irony as understatement, a trait common in people comfortable under pressure.

"I thought I told you to call me if fish were hitting." Wilson put his hand out, not joking now. I realized he wanted the fly rod. He took it, looking around, seeing the sunrise, the painted dancers, then he smiled, touching an index finger to the bridge of his glasses. "God, I've missed this. Mind if I see what's on the other end?"

He reeled in the line. Nothing left but the barracuda's head.

"Five-footer, you think?" Wilson had done some salt-water fishing.

"A little over four maybe. Big."

I showed him the drop-off where I'd caught the snook.

"The barracuda was using it as an ambush point. The shark was doing the same thing. It's possible the barracuda didn't know."

"One predator using another predator as bait."

"Yeah."

That meant something to Wilson. I wasn't sure why but I could guess.

"Good," he said. "*Another* good omen."

As the man turned down the beach, though, I noticed a purple hematoma on his thigh and a smaller bruise on his calf.

Bad omens.

I STOOD AT THE EDGE OF THE DRUM CIRCLE OB-serving as a lone drummer started, offering a baseline rhythm. Others joined. As the noise grew, some added solo riffs and counterbeats. After a few minutes, the chorus broke down and a new tempo emerged.

The objective, Tomlinson once explained, was to connect with the Tribal Mind. If you found that magic zone, he said, you vanished into the sensation that your *body* was being played by the drum circle, not your drum.

Tomlinson looked as if he'd found the zone.

As I approached the circle, I saw people I recognized. There was a fishing guide, a couple of nurses, several restaurant people, even a Sanibel cop. Mizzen, the nautical setter, was there with Dr. Bill and Sherry Welch. We exchanged waves. But Tomlinson was too lost in drumming to notice. He didn't recognize my voice, either, when I came up behind him and said, "Do you take requests? Or only original material?"

The man's eyes weren't just dreamy, they were glassy, but opened wide, like miniature TVs reflecting images of painted figures dancing by the fire.

Without looking, he replied, "I can't take verbal requests, man. But if you feel what you want, I might tune to the vibe. *Comprendo?*" His head bobbed, hands blurred, as he added a triple-time riff. "Reason I don't take requests is . . . *rhythm*, it's the mother tongue. Earth's first language. Words, man"—he motioned vaguely, somehow without missing a beat—"they're pointless here. You gotta feel it to communicate. So far, though"— he inserted another flourish—"you're not putting out a signal. It's like you got no *soul*, dude."

I didn't answer. Stood looking over his shoulder until he got curious and turned. "Why . . . it's *you*, Doc?" His expression was theatrical. "*That* explains it."

When he grinned, I realized I'd been set up.

"How long have you known we're here?"

"Since before you landed, man."

"Uh-huh."

His hands slowed on the drum, then stopped, but he continued keeping time with his left hand. "Seriously. I went down the beach to take a whiz and saw you riding that track of moonlight. You're the only guy I know who paddles a canoe like he's harvesting potatoes. And *he's* with you."

"Surprised?"

"Nope. I was expecting him."

"I bet your friends are excited."

"No need to test me, Doc. The man gave me orders. It's top secret."

I looked toward the cabin. Wilson was a solitary figure in the dawn light. He was fishing: smooth backcast, a tight loop; double-hauling and making it look easy. Impressive.

I said, "Do you have any idea where we're going?"

"Going? You mean we're taking a trip? The *three* of us? That's cool . . . I guess . . . *despite* several troubling issues. Some of his outrageous political positions, for example. Which means I must anticipate conflict. I'll have to tread lightly to avoid ugly scenes. Unless—" Troubled, Tomlinson paused, now talking to himself. "Unless I'm just *imagining* this. Which is very possible with a snoot full of hooch, and a head full of conga. Yes, this could be another one of Señor Tequila's little mind fucks. A potential downer."

I said softly, "Tomlinson?"

"Yes, Marion."

"What the hell are you talking about?"

He focused. "Doc? I'm not imagining you, am I, Doc?" Fire crackled, sparks cometed across his eyes, as he sought reassurance by touching my arm.

I gave his hand a friendly whack. "Knock it off. I'm not Dorothy and you're no Wizard. We need to talk."

I searched his expression to see if he was acting. Tough to read. "Are you as drunk as you look?"

He stared at the palm of his hand. I realized he was using it as a mirror. *"Drunker,"* he said after a moment. "I stopped dancing when I started to slosh. That was about six margaritas ago. But I still look pretty damn good . . . except for those weird stripes above my eyes."

Joking. But also drunk. Or stoned. Or both.

"When you're done with orchestra practice, can you sober up enough to talk?"

"Not a problem. I always back off the accelerator a notch or two come dawn. Besides"—he looked west, where the moon was dissolving into a blue and animated darkness—"it's time to split. Tradition, man. We gotta dance the moon into the sea."

Huh?

He motioned with his head—*Follow me*—as he stood. "Drumming ends at sunrise, man. All Hallows' Eve becomes All Saints' Day. The ceremony dates back to the Druids, so it's gotta be done right." He held up a bony finger. "Just one more bit of business before I can grab my lunch bucket and punch the clock. Be patient, okay?"

Before I could respond, he turned, calling, "Conga

line! Conga time! Listen up, heathens." Yelled it a few more times, adding, "Keep in mind, kiddies, we didn't come here to have *fun*."

I have watched Tomlinson rally many conga lines. The jokes don't vary much, but the results often do. I stepped back to watch.

He tucked the drum under his arm and looped the strap over his shoulder, waiting as others stood, dusting sand off their butts. Then he began to drum, as he instructed, "We must play the sacred hymn. Find the beat, comrades. *Be* the drum. The ancient mantra passed down to us from on high . . . from the king's men of king's men. Please join me in this grooviest of liturgies."

Drummers parroted Tomlinson's tempo: *Boom-boom-boom . . . boom-boom. Boom-boom-boom . . . boom-boom.*

It was distinctive. Simple. Oddly familiar.

"Feel the love, brothers and sisters, as we march to the Holy Church of Waves Without Walls. There we will wash our sins away. Afterward, I suggest we retreat to whatever bedrooms are available . . . in groups of two . . . *or three* . . . where I beseech ye to go—go and sin some more."

There were bawdy hoots as a loose line formed behind Tomlinson. Hands on hips or drumming, they began a snaking dance toward the Gulf.

Boom-boom-boom . . . boom-boom. Boom-boom-boom . . . boom-boom.

Catchy. I was tempted to join when two waitresses from the Sanibel Rum Bar and Grille, Milita and Liz, tried to pull me into the line. Both were dressed as angels, although they'd jettisoned their wings.

Milita pleaded, "Come on, Doc. Relax a little . . . shallow up, man."

Shallow up. A new Tomlinson line. It meant stop being serious; leave the burdens of depth behind.

I respect Tomlinson's spirituality, but I don't envy the emotional toll of its uncertainties. There are times, though, when I wish I could just let go, the way Tomlinson does. Like now.

Drums throbbed as dancers created a moving wave, some bowing while others stood.

Boom-boom-boom . . . boom-boom. Boom-boom-boom . . . boom-boom.

When they began to sing, I understood why the beat was familiar: "Louie Louie . . . oh no . . . Me gotta go . . ." *Boom-boom-boom . . . boom-boom.* "Louie Louie . . . oh no . . ."

Tomlinson had said, "Kingsmen," not "king's men."

"Please, Doc?" Liz was pulling at my elbow.

Milita said, "We don't have to be at work until four. And we have that big house rented. There're lots of rooms."

But I have forever been, and will always be, an observer. And focus requires distance. As with a microscope, the degree of distance varies, but spatial separations, like walls, always stand between.

I gently disentangled myself from the ladies, promising to meet them later. Then I watched them hurry to join the conga line, dancing toward the Gulf of Mexico, where, I assumed, the unpainted members of the circle would strip naked and swim.

Swim?

I'd just been charged by a half-ton hammerhead. It was unlikely the shark would cruise the beach, seeking human prey, but I had to at least let them know it was in the area. Didn't I?

Yes, I decided.

I should probably also offer to stand watch. Wait until they were all safely out of the water and even dressed, Milita and Liz included. That was the responsible thing to do, wasn't it?

Yes, I decided.

Sand, like glass, is siliceous based, and the beach was vibrating like a window with the circle's sacred mantra:

"Louie Louie . . . oh no . . . Me gotta go . . ." *Boom-boom-boom . . . boom-boom.* "Louie Louie . . . oh no . . ."

Near the drop-off, where I'd hooked the barracuda, the president was landing a small snook. He was also moving in flow with the music, enjoying his first unpresidential morning, doing juke steps that mimicked the conga line's wave, his rhythm perfect but subtle, keeping it to himself.

The man could dance, too?

I tried a few juke steps myself as I followed the drum circle to the Gulf—an effort, at least, to shallow up.

Soon, though, I turned my attention to the sky. If the Secret Service discovered Wilson was missing, helicopter traffic would be the first indicator.

10

When I left Tomlinson, I slept for two hours, then strapped on shoes and ran the beach, pushing myself, alternating between hard sand at the water's edge and sugar sand on the upper beach. To make it tougher, I varied the pace, sprinting ten seconds out of every minute. Brutal. But I've come to realize that travel is the natural enemy of fitness. You have to improvise on the road or you're condemned to a roller-coaster ride of fitness decline.

I was in good shape. No, I was in *great* shape. For the last six months, I'd been living a Spartan life that, for me, has become a periodic necessity since slipping into my forties. It means swimming at least three times a week. Pull-ups and abs, every morning and evening, on the crossbeam beneath my house. Daily kick-ass runs, lots and lots of water, lean protein, few starches, and absolutely no beer or margaritas.

Tomlinson says I have a monastic side. That's why I do it. He may be right, but it's not the only reason.

For American males, our forties should be advertised as "The Most Dangerous Decade" because so few of us realize it's true. It's during our forties that most men die of heart attacks, smoke themselves across a cancerous border, or drink themselves into unambiguous alcoholism. It's during our forties that most of us experience panic attacks, nervous breakdowns, depression, and a gradual, invidious weight gain that we will take to the grave. Men in their forties are also more likely to have affairs, divorce, and make asses of themselves by dating women twenty years younger, who, twenty years earlier, they wouldn't have given a second look. It is during our forties that we lie awake at night, wrestling with decisions, and our own frail heartbeats, investing much thought and worry before deciding to go ahead and fuck up our lives, anyway.

I punish myself not only because fitness requires it but because I'm in my forties. I deserve it.

When I finished my run, I had a saltwater bath and returned to the cabin to find Wilson browning corned beef hash over a propane stove. He was pacing as he cooked.

"What time does the tide start falling?"

He'd seen the tide chart but often asked questions when he knew the answer. I said, "It's late, around sunset. The wind's out of the southwest so it could be after nine before it gets running."

"Damn it, we need to get *moving*. Aren't there usually two tides?"

"The Gulf of Mexico's unusual. It happens."

"I don't understand why we have to wait."

He was talking about Tomlinson's sailboat, I realized. *No Más* was solid but not nimble.

I said, "Maybe we don't. Depends on where you want to go. And how much time Tomlinson needs to sober up."

"Does he often drink too much?"

"Tomlinson's drinking habits are like the tides. He misses a day occasionally."

"Then he's used to functioning with a hangover. I want to get into open water as soon as possible."

"It's your trip. Where we headed?"

Wilson flipped the hash with a spatula, then stirred in a glop of pepper sauce. "When we're a couple miles out in the Gulf, I'll brief you."

I said, "I can't offer advice without information," then explained that incoming current moved through Captiva Pass at six or seven knots. *No Más* had only a small Yanmar engine. We couldn't exit the pass until the tide changed. Under power, though, we could avoid the pass by traveling north or south on the Intracoastal Waterway.

He thought about that, not eager to tip his hand. "I don't want to wait around here until sunset. We both need sleep, but we can do that once we're under way."

Like me, he'd been watching the sky, anticipating helicopters.

"Then we'll have to use the motor. Head north and use another pass when the tide turns. Or head south to Sanibel and cut to the Gulf at Lighthouse Point."

"Those are our choices?"

"Unless Tomlinson has another idea."

"It's settled, then. That's what we'll do."

I hesitated. "But . . . what about that other matter we discussed? There's equipment at my lab I need."

"How do you propose to get it? We're leaving in a few hours."

"If we're going south, Dinkin's Bay Marina is on the way. If we're not, I could hitch a ride in a powerboat, then arrange a rendezvous by radio."

Wilson shook his head. "Impossible."

"Mr. President," I said, seeing his eyes over the lenses of his glasses, "you told me you pick good people and let them do their jobs. If you are serious about . . . about resolving the matter you alluded to, trust my judgment, sir. I know what's needed to . . . to dispose of unresolved issues."

Wilson had green farmer's eyes, commonplace but for their intensity. "When I say I don't doubt your expertise, Dr. Ford, I'm not confirming your insinuation. But I've made my decision. Have your gear ready by . . . let's say three p.m. That'll give us another few hours to rest"—he moved his shoulders, working out kinks—"and I want to get some more fishing in."

"Have you spoken to Tomlinson? It's his boat. His decision."

"No. But it's time I said hello. I've been putting it off. I'm curious about how his friends will react."

Meaning would he be recognized. He didn't sound as confident now as he did in my lab. He stepped back as if I were a full-length mirror. "What do you think?"

With the shaved head, the owlish glasses, I wouldn't have recognized the man if I'd seen him on the street. But if someone took a close look?

"Risky," I said.

"Suggestions?"

On the bookcase, someone had left sunglasses with a white plastic nose shield attached. "Hand me your glasses." I clipped the shield to the bridge, used a towel to clean the tinted lenses, and handed them back. "Try these."

He slid them on. "Any better?"

"You look like you should be playing shuffleboard. Waxing the RV for a vacation from the retirement village."

The president's response was profane but good-natured, then he added, "There's something I haven't shown you." He put the skillet on the stove, pulled a leather case from his duffel, and opened it. "You ever see one of these before?" He began removing items.

It was a kit assembled by the CIA's Headquarters Disguise Unit.

"No," I lied. "Never."

"Then I can't tell you where it came from. But have a look."

The agency employed Hollywood makeup artist John Chambers, who won an Academy Award for *Planet of the Apes,* as designer and consultant. The containers varied, and some of the contents, but the basics were there: facial hair, dental caps, uncorrected contact lenses, theatrical makeup and glue, synthetic skin, scars, moles, birthmarks. It wasn't the crap sold in novelty shops. The kit was designed for operatives who had to escape from countries in which they were well known. Up close, the effects were more convincing than anything used on Broadway because they *had* to be.

"Have you tried any of this stuff?"

Wilson said, "A couple of things." He pointed. "That . . . that . . . that. But I felt ridiculous. Like a kid playing dress-up."

I pointed. "What about this?"

He shook his head.

"It could work. And it's simple."

"Do you know something about disguise?"

I lied again. "No. Just a feeling. Give it a try."

The president took the item, held it up for a moment. "Okay," he said. "I will."

IN THE INTELLIGENCE BUSINESS, AGENTS WHO rely on disguises are called "ragpickers"—a term that dates back to the days when spies dressed like bums so they could stand innocuously on busy streets. I'd been through an agency's two-day disguise evolution because it was part of the required tradecraft. I'd felt ridiculous, just as the president described it. But the course probably saved my life a couple of years ago when, for the first and only time, I had to improvise a disguise to get across the border from Venezuela into Colombia. It was only a day after Rodrigo Granda, a FARC "revolutionary," was kidnapped by "an unknown group" and spirited back to Bogotá to stand trial.

A poor disguise invites scrutiny. Wigs, fake beards, rubber noses, dark glasses, scarves jar the human eye. They *feel* wrong. A good disguise is neutral, cloaking or repelling, without surprise. Joggers, tourist photographers, construction workers, fishermen are stereotypes so common that the eye sweeps past without alerting the brain. People with deformities or facial scars are invisible for a different reason: Our eyes dart away instinctively. The scar may register on the brain, but other details do not.

Near the stove was a sink with a mirror. Wilson stood with his back to me, applying surgical adhesive to his face, as he asked, "Will this thing stay on if I get it wet?"

I was reading the directions that came with the kit. "It's supposed to. Once it dries, the only way to get it off is with this special solvent."

"It's ironic you chose this. I hope it works."

I said, "The worst that can happen is Tomlinson's friends realize it's fake. A lot of them are *painted,* so it'll be no big deal. Which reminds me: Tomlinson's not going to like the idea of using his engine. He's a purist. Especially with a bunch of locals watching."

Still looking into the mirror, Wilson said, "We'll find out how much of a purist he really is." Hinting at something, the way he said it. Then he turned so I could see his face, his expression asking *What do you think?*

I moved around the table and took a closer look. "Put your glasses on."

He did.

I looked at his face from several angles. "Is it comfortable?"

"I can't even feel it."

"Amazing. Leave the nose shield on your glasses if you want, but you don't need it. Not now."

"It looks real?"

"It's *incredible*."

He didn't seem convinced as he returned to the stove, slid the hash onto a plate, and nodded toward the table. Breakfast was for me, I realized. "Eat. I'm having *fish* for breakfast." He sounded very sure of himself.

Wilson stood at the mirror briefly before he took the pan to the sink, scrubbed it clean. Then he went out the door, carrying the fly rod.

I CHOSE A BUNK, LAID DOWN TO READ, BUT ALSO listened to the news on the cabin's clock radio. No mention of terrorists. No mention of a missing ex-president. But more trouble in Panama.

Outraged by a speech given by the pope, IS&P's CEO said he would "not be surprised" if Jihadists brought Holy War to Central America. "I am not inviting them," Dr. Thomas Bashir Farrish added, "but we will not turn them away, either."

Farrish was the most dangerous man on earth, Wilson had told me. Right again.

I awoke an hour later with Tomlinson shaking my shoulder.

"We got trouble, Doc. The water cops are out there talking to Kerney."

I said, "Who?"

"Kerney."

"*Who?*"

"You know—Kal Wilson. The president."

It took me a moment to recall that Kerney Amos Levaugn Wilson was his full name.

I was wearing nothing but running shorts. As I ducked into a shirt, I said, "Were they looking for him?" I hadn't heard helicopters. If one passes within a mile, I wake up.

"I don't know. I was asleep myself when one of the tribe got me."

"Did they *recognize* him?"

"Man, I didn't even recognize him for the first couple of minutes. His face—when I saw him, I thought *What the hell happened?* It's so damn . . . real." I was tying my shoes as he added, "Oh—Ginger Love's involved, too. The cops are questioning them both."

"Wilson and Ginger?" Maybe I was dreaming. "How did he hook up with *her*?"

Tomlinson lifted his eyebrows, a disclaimer.

"What's *that* woman doing here? Please tell me you didn't invite her."

"Drum circle's wide open. I let karma handle all my detail work, man."

Ginger Love and Kal Wilson? If I was dreaming, it was a nightmare.

Ginger Love is a self-described political activist. The islands attract them. Name an ideology or a cause. Ginger's less motivated by political ideals, though, than by a lust for attention and her craving for a stage to vent hysterical rants. A few months back, she came to the lab and tried to enlist me in some project. Her perfume and rage filled the room. Ginger Love was a spooky, overmedicated pain in the ass.

Tomlinson followed me out the door, then north along the shore. Where the beach ended and mangroves began, I could see the gray hull of a Florida marine patrol vessel—Florida Fish and Wildlife, officially. Two uniformed officers were talking to the former president while a half dozen of Tomlinson's group looked on—a couple of them painted but at least clothed. Ginger Love was there, with her Kool-Aid orange hair and signature straw hat.

Wilson was standing next to our plastic canoe. He'd been fishing from it, apparently. When I mentioned it to Tomlinson, he said, "I bet he doesn't have a fishing license. Maybe that's what this is about."

In Florida, a saltwater license is required if you fish from a boat.

"Even if he does, he can't show it. Or his ID."

I said, "I hope you're wrong." I was imagining the president resisting, then news footage of Wilson and Love handcuffed. Humiliating.

Before we got much closer, though, the officers gave farewell nods, pushed their boat into deeper water, and fired the engine as the little group splintered. Some returned in our direction, a few remained with the former president, Ginger among them.

When Mike Westhoff, one of Tomlinson's few jock pals, got close enough, I called, "What's the problem?"

Coach Mike smiled. "That woman's nuttier than a

bucket of loons. If it wasn't for your uncle, she'd be on her way to jail 'bout now."

Tomlinson and I exchanged looks. "Whose uncle?"

"*Your* uncle, Doc. He's right there." Mike used his linebacker chin to point. "Your Uncle Sam. He was great, the way he handled the water cops."

I was thinking *Uncle Sam?* The former president's alias had just gotten better.

Ginger, Coach Mike explained, had gotten into an altercation with the Fish and Wildlife officers. "The water cops were on the beach for some reason and she started bitchin' at them. Who knows why. But it attracted a crowd. Ginger has the rare ability to alienate *everyone*. But then Sam paddles in. He got everybody calmed down."

I said, "What did he do?"

Coach Mike thought for a moment. The man's a football coach, and he also has a Ph.D. in psychology. Even so, he was puzzled. "Damned if I can say. Just started talking. Asking questions, mostly. Very polite, but not faking it. Usually, when someone butts into a fight, they're the first ones cops put on the ground. But Sam, he's cool. You know"—Coach Mike was still digesting the scene—"he reminds me of *someone*. I can't put my finger on it. He looks a *little* like that actor, the older guy who plays a pilot, or a senator. Except for the scar, of course—no offense, Doc."

I said quickly, "None taken."

"He get a bad burn or something when he was a kid?"

"Burned, yeah. A long time ago."

"That'll make a person strong. It shows. Your uncle's

not wimpy, like the actor, and he doesn't have the TV hair. But in the face, you know what I mean? Around the eyes, and the way he smiles." Coach Mike was nodding. "Bring him to a Jets game sometime. You always have the most interesting relatives. I'd like to get to know Sam better."

I replied honestly, "Some people say that my uncle's unforgettable."

AS WE APPROACHED, THE WAITRESSES FROM THE rum bar, Liz and Milita, were watching as Ginger Love talked, rapid-fire, moving her hands as if conducting a symphony. Wilson faced her, expression patient. When he saw us, though, he held up a palm, telling us to stop where we were. "Sorry I'm late, guys. I'll be right with you." Setting up his escape.

Pretending we couldn't hear, Ginger said, "Sam, it's such a shame that Doc didn't inherit your charm. Or your sense of civic responsibility. Some men, though"—her laughter was weighted with forbearance—"never grow up. He and Tomlinson are so alike in that way."

I noticed that her eyes never lingered on the president's face. It's impolite to stare at scars, which is why I'd suggested it.

The Rum Bar waitresses were walking toward us as Wilson replied, "Very insightful to recognize the similarities, Ginger. But I don't agree with your assessment. You should get to know the guys better."

What was different about his voice? Had he added a

slight Southern accent? I was paying closer attention as Ginger replied, "Oh, I've tried and tried with those two, my friend. They're both terrified of strong women. Poor Doc, he scampers into his little world of fish and chemicals and experiments. Know why I think he's not politically involved? He's so naïve. If the man was somehow magically transported to a foreign country? A place where life is *hard*—places *we've* experienced, Sam—I think he'd be as helpless as a child."

I heard Wilson say, "Well, I hope you're wrong about *that*," as Milita and Liz stopped with their backs to Ginger Love, close enough for Liz to whisper, *"Bitch."*

Both women grinned.

"We tried to rescue the poor man. But Ginger pretended like we were invisible."

"Typical," Milita added. She turned to look at Wilson. "We really like your uncle, Doc. I wish he wasn't wearing that wedding ring—a man like Sam, a woman doesn't care about age. Why isn't his wife with him?"

Tomlinson and I exchanged looks. "She transitioned to the next Dharma," he said. "It was less than a year ago."

"Dah-harma?"

I translated. "She's dead."

"Oh no! That's so sad! Geez, poor Sam, I bet he was married to a good one. You can just tell, can't you, Liz? He's so . . . solid."

Liz was nodding but also listening. She timed it so she interrupted Ginger in midsentence when she called, "Sam? Sam! We need your advice about something. *Personal,* if you don't mind us borrowing him, *ma'am.*"

Ginger didn't like being called "ma'am." It's something I've noticed in women of a certain age. She stood glaring as Wilson joined us. She was still glaring as we turned down the beach toward our cabin, Milita saying, "If you're going to be in the area for a while, Sam, why don't you stop by the Rum Bar for a drink?"

WHEN WILSON, TOMLINSON, AND I WERE ALONE, the former president said, "Nobody recognized me." He was delighted. "Know what I worried about most? Someone recognizing my voice."

I was right about the Southern accent.

"It comes natural," he explained. "I spent the first part of my life in a little piney-woods village. I worked hard at getting rid of the drawl. But it's always right there if I want. Just a hint—actors always overdo it."

Tomlinson leaned to get a close look at Wilson's face. "Did you have a professional makeup artist create that?"

"In a way. But not for me."

"It's artistry, man. Even from here, it looks real. Such a small thing—but what a difference."

"So far, so good, but the fewer people I meet, the better. I was nervous, at first, the way the woman with the hat was looking at me."

The president had given us a condensed version of what had happened between Ginger Love and the water cops. Something to do with her being questioned about a loggerhead turtle shell she'd found. He was more interested in how strangers had reacted to him.

"Most people averted their eyes, pretending not to notice. One of the deputies said I looked familiar, but even he wouldn't look at my face. The woman asked if I'd ever thought about going into politics."

I said, "What did you tell her?"

"Told her I was flattered. But I came too damn close to using a Richard Nixon line—I have to stop quoting presidents. It's become automatic. But I was right. They didn't make the connection."

There was a boyish quality in his tone.

"What's the Nixon line?"

I'd omitted the prefix, which irritated Wilson. "*President* Nixon said that politics would be a helluva good business if it wasn't for the goddamn press." He looked at his watch, then at Tomlinson. "Can we leave in an hour?"

Tomlinson said, "Sam, we can leave now if you want," celebrating, his inflection saying *You did it, man. You're free.*

11

Three miles off Redfish Pass, wind out of the southwest, *No Más* on a starboard tack, Tomlinson said softly, "He used the same leverage on me."

"How?" I kept my voice low. Kal Wilson was be-lowdecks, reading.

"He said I don't really know who you are. That there are things about *myself* I don't know. And that he could get me pardoned. Because the president owes him."

Meaning the current president. During Wilson's last days in office, Tomlinson explained, he signed nine exec-utive pardons as a personal favor for the man who would succeed him two terms later.

I said, "I know. He showed me the list. It checks out—if you believe he'll do it."

Tomlinson said, "Yeah. If." He thought about it a mo-ment as I checked my watch. It was a few minutes before

6 p.m. The Gulf of Mexico was gradually encircling us as we moved off shore. Waves slid past, gray buoyant ridges that lifted *No Más*, zeppelin-like, inflating then deflating the fiberglass hull.

"Doc?"

"Yeah?"

"The man didn't have to threaten me. Hell, I still don't know exactly where we're going. But I wouldn't've missed taking a trip like this, unless . . . unless he's on some kind of destructive mission—"

I held up a warning finger as Wilson's head appeared in the companionway. He came up the steps carrying a nautical chart.

"I feel like I'm interrupting, gentlemen. Comparing notes?"

I said, "Tomlinson's worried you're planning something destructive. He was telling me he would've come along even without the coercion. I probably would've, too."

Wilson appeared pleased by my honesty. "The definition of coercion varies. Didn't we talk about that? I'm offering you both something of value in return."

Tomlinson said, "If I committed a crime, man, I have a moral obligation to pay. Reciprocity, man. That's what karma's all about."

Wilson looked at him sharply. He said, "*If* you committed a crime. You really don't remember—?"

"I *do* remember. That's what I'm saying. I helped build a bomb. A man died and I'm guilty. For me, there's no such thing as a pardon. It doesn't matter that it happened twenty years ago."

The former president was paying attention, no longer impatient. "Then why did you say 'if'?"

Tomlinson was lounging shirtless, using his toes to steady the wheel. He straightened, thinking about it. He'd been institutionalized after the bombing. Weeks of electroshock therapy had scrambled his memory synapses. "I . . . don't know. You're right. I've admitted that I'm guilty. There isn't a day goes by that I don't expect the cops to come banging on my door"—he glanced at me—"or worse. A bullet through the old coconut, maybe." He reflected for a few seconds more. "I don't know why I said 'if.' It just came out."

Wilson was studying him, nodding, as he took a seat beside me on the starboard side and unrolled the chart. "Think about it. If you don't care about a pardon, maybe you care about the truth."

Tomlinson sat back and his toes found the ship's wheel. "The truth, man, absolutely."

I was tempted to say the definition of "truth" is even trickier than the definition of "coercion," but the former president had taken charge. I listened to him say, "The truth is part of our bargain, too. I'll give you the information I have. You two have a lot in common. I think you'll find it . . . interesting."

"When?"

"When it's time, Doc. That'll have to do." He had the chart on his lap, holding it with both hands so the breeze didn't take it. "There's a more pressing matter. Our destination."

"I've been wondering, man. For the last half hour, I've

been taking it slow, just like you told me. Letting *No Más* have her head."

Wilson touched an index finger to the bridge of his glasses. "Then let's make a decision."

IT WAS ONE OF THE BIG NOAA CHARTS THAT showed the Gulf of Mexico and bordering land regions. The former president unfolded it, then folded it to narrow the aspect. He placed it on his lap so we both could see, before asking, "How long would it take us to sail to Tampa Bay?"

Tomlinson answered, "Depends on where in Tampa Bay you want to go. It's ten or twelve hours to the sea channel—that's the easy part. After that, it's twenty-five miles or so to the port. But lots of narrow channels."

Wilson nodded. "The Bahamas?"

"Two full days at least, no matter which way we go."

"What about Key West?"

"Twenty-four hours, plus an hour or two—if this breeze holds."

"You've made the trip?"

Tomlinson removed his toe from the wheel and knocked a knuckle on the oiled teak. "If this lady leaked asphalt, there'd be a highway between Dinkin's Bay and the patio bar at Louie's Backyard."

"What about Big Torch Key?"

Big Torch Key was only a few miles from Key West, but Tomlinson said, "Add a couple more hours, because we draw too much water to go in through Florida Bay.

There's a good anchorage at Key West, then we'd sail out and around. Come in from the Atlantic side."

"I see." The president moved his hand west, across the chart. "What about Mexico? How long to sail to the Yucatán?"

The Yucatán Peninsula extends almost to Cuba, forming the southwestern rim of the Gulf basin.

Tomlinson looked at me, his expression saying *Far out* as he replied, "Cozumel's three hundred ninety nautical miles from Sanibel. From Key West, it's three hundred ten miles. That's on a rhomb line, of course. So . . . depending on weather, it would takes us about three days."

"You're very quick with the data. I take it you've made that crossing, too."

I wondered if Tomlinson would change the asphalt analogy to bales of marijuana.

"Sure. Usually from Key West, but I've done both. It can be a dream trip, or a nightmare. Depends on how hilly it gets. Either way, we'd have lots of time for private study. We can start your introduction to meditation."

Tomlinson had referred to the former president's interest in Zen Buddhism a couple of times since we'd been aboard. Now, as before, Wilson ignored him.

The president rolled the chart. "Take us to Key West, Mr. Tomlinson." He went down the steps into the cabin.

I was putting the destinations together; events, too. Thinking: *We're going to Panama . . .*

* * *

ONLY A FEW MINUTES LATER, THOUGH, WILSON reappeared, his face stern. "Gentlemen, we had an agreement. No electronic devices except for the things I personally okayed. Not on this boat. Not on your person at any time during the trip."

Why was Wilson looking at me?

I said quickly, "I had a cell phone and a little GPS. Your guy, Vue, took both. I wasn't happy about it. And I expect to get them back—but those were the only electronics I had."

Wilson said, "Then this is just an oversight." He held out his hand to show me one of the two small flashlights I had left. "I didn't go through your gear. That's *your* job. I found this hanging on one of the lockers forward."

I was confused. "It's a flashlight, Mr. President. It's not a radio."

He looked at me until I realized I'd slipped again. "Sorry . . . *Sam*. But you've lost me. Are you saying we can't carry anything that uses batteries?"

He shook his head. "Not batteries. Computer components." He handed me the light. "Those little buttons— that thing's programmable, isn't it?"

The man was right. The new generation of LED lights used Intel chips; a few had memory cards. I hadn't even thought about it.

"I've got to be tough about this. You men are aware of my . . . timetable. There are things I want to accomplish. And I only have two or three weeks. I can't risk an interruption. That flashlight could have a tracking chip in it. Turn on the light, it sends a locator signal."

Tomlinson said, "Whoa, man. I've got a personal relationship with paranoia. We go *way* back. But the three of us are shipmates now, and you've got to trust Doc and me—"

I interrupted, "No, he doesn't. And he shouldn't. He's right." I had the cap off the flashlight, inspecting it. "There's no transmitter chip—not that I know of, anyway. But there doesn't have to be. Some computer components have their own electronic signature." I looked at Tomlinson. "If one of us wanted to signal our location, this is the sort of thing we'd use. There're GPS tracking sticks smaller than this. It's not my field, and I don't know how sophisticated the tracking equipment is—"

"It's the most sophisticated on earth. If people get serious about finding us, they'll pull out the stops." Wilson touched his thumb to an index finger, then his middle finger. "There are two ways to defeat superior technology. One, change the objectives of engagement. Two, change the arena of engagement. Do both and your chances improve.

"We're changing arenas. The technology they'll use is twenty-first century. But aboard this boat"—Wilson looked at the sail: a sanded wing transecting a tropic sky—"we've moved back in time a hundred years. Modern tracking systems are programmed to monitor *modern* threats. Not the stuff we're using."

Because Wilson had insisted, we'd stripped *No Más* of her VHF radios, EPRB emergency transmitters, GPS, and SONAR gear and left them with friends on Cayo Costa.

Tomlinson said, "I've done astral projection, soul travel—you'll learn that meditation is the *vehicle* of spiritual experience. But this is cool. We've shifted centuries."

"In terms of electronic signature. Yes. The National Security Agency has amazing monitoring technology. Details are classified, but I know their capabilities. Use a cell phone in the Afghan mountains and our people can triangulate the position within a minute. With prior authorization, we can have a laser-guided missile under way within ninety seconds. The technology is brilliant, but it's also very specialized. And that makes it vulnerable."

During our canoe trip from Ligarto Island to Cayo Costa, he'd asked if I'd brought a draft of the paper Tomlinson and I were writing. But this was the first time he'd mentioned the subject.

"An early indicator of overspecialization is when a technology no longer addresses the problem that made it necessary in the first place. Intercepting an adversary's communications dates back thousands of years. Our monitoring systems can track a cell phone on the other side of the earth. But they're not equipped to monitor the primitive transmitters you and your friends were using this morning." Wilson was looking at Tomlinson, expecting him to be confused, and maybe a little disappointed because he wasn't.

"The drums, man," Tomlinson said. "Yeah—transmitters. A communication system so old that our brains can't translate the language. But our hearts still understand."

Wilson said, "You could set up a network, send messages back and forth, and the finest surveillance systems in the world would never record a beat. Lots of noise but zero signature. Drums. When you're up against the National Security Agency, you're much safer living in the Stone Age."

DRUMS?

During the last year, I'd spent time in the Stony Desert, between Afghanistan and Pakistan, where domes of ancient mosques turn to pearl in moonlight. Was that how they avoided spy satellites—hammering out messages on rocks and goatskins?

Wilson caught my eye. "'Zero signature'—it's an interesting term. I came across it in my reading a year ago. When you think about it—*zero signature*—it has philosophical implications. People who accomplish nothing. People who stand for nothing. But it also describes someone who is very good at what they do. Brilliant reconstructive surgeons. Architects, petroleum engineers. And . . . other professions. Were you guys Boy Scouts?"

Tomlinson's expression read *Are you serious?* as I replied, "No. I've never been much of a joiner."

"Too bad. One of the founders was a great naturalist. He had a theory that every living thing leaves an uninterrupted track, from birth to death, that's readable to a skilled tracker. And he believed the converse was true: A skilled tracker knows how to cover his tracks. That's what we're going to find out."

"How, Sam?" Tomlinson was into the conversation, loved the idea that we'd switched centuries, I could see. I could also see that he was getting twitchy, tugging at his salt-bleached Willie Nelson braids. It was after six—*beer time*—but Wilson had ordered him to limit his alcohol intake and banned marijuana.

Wilson replied, "By the way we communicate. I'm going to use your drum technique tonight. Sort of." Meaning we'd find out. "But right now, we need to finish this electronics issue." He pointed at the flashlight. "Is that all you're carrying?"

"I've got another flashlight in my bag, but it's a simple penlight. I'll show you—"

Wilson put his hand on my shoulder when I tried to stand. "No need. Your word's good enough." His sincerity somehow added to my sense of indebtedness. "The question now is, what should we do with it—your light, and any other items aboard this boat that might compromise us?"

I was holding the little LED. A fine piece of equipment. Machined aluminum body and a dazzling beam. It wasn't as nice as the Blackhawk I'd left with Wilson's would-be assassins, but it was *nice*.

I said, "How about I take the light apart? You can stow it with your gear. These things are a lot more expensive than you might think—"

The former president was shaking his head even before I finished. "On a trip that's so personally important, is that our most secure option? I don't think Tomlinson's going to be shocked to hear that, in certain circles, you're considered a security expert of sorts. So I'll leave the decision up to you, Doc. Your call."

In only a couple of sentences, the man had voiced his unquestioned respect for my integrity and deferred to my superior knowledge and judgment.

Damn.

"Marion, your behavior is so predictable," Tomlinson said. "You're clinging, man. Material objects. Money. The sutras tell us that all suffering is rooted in selfish grasping. To experience reality, we must first divest ourselves of delusion." He was using his Buddha voice—the gentle, all-knowing tone he uses with his students, and, at times, to intentionally piss me off.

I held up a warning hand. "Okay. Enough. No more of your ping-pong Zen speeches. I'd rather throw the damn thing overboard than have to listen." And I did—flipped the flashlight over my shoulder. Didn't even turn to see it hit the water.

Tomlinson had both feet on the wheel, hands folded behind his head. He leaned and gave me a brotherly rap on the arm. "Sam? Doc's the sort of guy who, if I pointed at a meteorite, he'd study my finger. *Seriously.* Meditation frees us."

Wilson said, "Really? You're free of greed and delusion, huh? We'll see." He had returned to the companionway, talking to Tomlinson as he went down the steps.

WHEN THE PRESIDENT REAPPEARED, HE WAS carrying Tomlinson's leather briefcase, timing the sailboat's movement before he took his seat. The man was careful about getting banged around, I'd noticed.

"You stowed this in the bulkhead locker. The briefcase was open, so you're obviously not trying to conceal anything." Wilson removed a laptop computer, then a palm-sized wafer of white plastic—an iPod.

Tomlinson was suddenly sitting up straight, watching. "Careful there, man. If we take some spray, salt water could ruin the circuitry."

"I'm aware of that. Question is, why are these things aboard?"

"Because this is my home, man. Don't you have a computer at home? *Everybody* has a computer at home. Where else would I keep it?"

"I told you several times that I had to personally okay all electronics."

"Yeah. But you meant navigational gear. Radios, radar, my sonar—that kinda stuff. The bullshit twenty-first-century baggage no real sailor needs. I got rid of that crap. We're simpatico on the subject—"

Wilson was shaking his head. "Apparently not. I hate to force the issue, but this equipment has to go."

Tomlinson was twitching, tugging at his hair. "My *computer*? Sam . . . you can't be serious."

"I'll give you time to back up your files."

"You mean . . . throw it overboard?"

Wilson nodded.

"But it's a *MacBook,* Sam! It's not some IBM clone piece of garbage. We're discussing an engineering work of art."

Wilson remained stoic.

"*And* my iPod?" The president didn't resist when

Tomlinson reached, took the device, and held it lovingly. "This is my personal *music system*. I've got, like, my entire vinyl collection stored here. Jimi Hendrix outtakes from the Berkeley rally. Cream's last concert. The actual tape from the *Rolling Stone* interview with Timothy Leary!

"Sam, please"—I'd never heard Tomlinson beg before—"this is history, man. Think of what you're doing. You . . . you need to *shallow up,* Sam."

The president said, "Sorry," his voice flat.

Tomlinson leaned forward and touched my sleeve. "Doc—talk to him. Aren't there some basic safety issues involved here? He's asking me to sail to Key West without music *or* smoking a joint? Why, it's . . . *insane*. I've never tried anything so crazy. Say *something, compadre.*"

I was watching Wilson open the laptop—surprise, surprise. Tomlinson's screen saver was a photo of Marlissa Kay Engle, actress and musician. She was wearing a red bikini bottom, nothing else, smiling at the camera from a familiar setting. The woman I'd been dating was topless on the sun-drenched foredeck of my best friend's boat.

Wilson said, "I admire your taste, but your judgment is questionable."

"But it's only two months old. A MacBook with a SuperDrive, four gigs of memory, and the built-in video eye. You can't be serious!"

I studied the computer screen long enough to be sure of what I was seeing, then looked at Tomlinson, whose expression had changed. "Doc. I can explain."

I interrupted. "You're clinging, man. Don't grasp—it's

the root of all suffering. You're hung up on possessions . . . *man*." To Wilson I said, "Give me the goddamn computer. *I'll* throw it over."

Wilson closed the laptop, cutting us both off. "You take the helm, Dr. Ford. Mr. Tomlinson, go below and back up your data. Then deep-six this contraband."

As the president went down the companionway steps, Tomlinson sounded near tears. "But these are *Apple* products, Sam."

I nudged him away from the sailboat's wheel, saying, "You need to deepen up, pal."

12

Two hours before midnight, the president said, "I didn't anticipate our friend Tomlinson disappearing. So I've got to confide in you. We have to be in Central America in three days. By the afternoon of November fifth."

Tomlinson hadn't disappeared. As I had explained to Wilson, we were in *Key West*. The man was out having fun, not hiding.

Even so, we were walking the streets, searching.

I said, "By 'Central America,' you mean Panama? Or Nicaragua?" He didn't reply for several seconds, so I made another guess. "You're going there to kill the person who murdered your wife."

He walked half a block before saying, "No. *You're* going to kill him." His voice was low. "If you have moral reservations, tell me now."

I turned my attention to the tangled limbs of a ficus

tree, where bats dragged a fluttering light into shadows. "November's nice in Central America. Rainy season's ending, but tarpon are still in the rivers."

"Is that an answer?"

I looked at the man long enough for him to know it was.

"Then we don't have time to waste. Why the hell would he do something so crazy?"

"There's nothing crazy about Tomlinson disappearing in Key West," I said again. "The only reason he doesn't live here is because he knows it would kill him."

We'd anchored off Christmas Island, Key West Bight, at 5:30 p.m. An hour later, Tomlinson vanished into the sunset carnival of Mallory Square while I chatted with my friend Ray Jason, who juggles chain saws when he's not captaining boats.

It was Ray who reminded me that Fantasy Fest had just ended, a weeklong celebration of weirdness. A dangerous time to lose Tomlinson on the island because the party's wounded and demented were still roaming the streets.

Tomlinson was visible one moment, laughing with a couple of bikers and a woman dressed as a Conehead. Next moment, all four were gone. I didn't see him all evening, and he wasn't aboard *No Más* when I returned at 8:30 to ferry the president ashore.

Wilson thought it would be safe to spend an hour after dark reacquainting himself with Key West. He was peeved that he had to spend the time searching.

"Is he still mad about dumping his computer?"

"Giving him orders on his own boat? Sure, and I don't blame him. But he's too good-natured to be spiteful, and he's too much of a sailor to miss a tide."

Wilson had told us to be up and ready to leave at 6 a.m. Water turned early in the Northwest Channel.

We were walking Caroline Street, blue-water fishing boats to our right, lights reflecting off docks, showing masts of wooden ships. People roaming, tourists, bikers, Buckeyes, hip rockers and old hempsters, their faces cured like hams, browned by sun, salt, nicotine.

"He might be around here. These are his people."

Wilson stopped. "I hope you're right. We only have"—he squinted at his wrist—"a little more than seven hours."

"Unless there's something I don't know," I told him, "leaving an hour or two later won't make any difference. Channels here are a lot more forgiving than Sanibel."

"There's *a lot* you don't know," he answered.

We were back at Key West Bight after making the big loop around the island in cab and on foot. The president was wearing a Hemingway fishing cap, a goatee, and a camera hung around his neck. That was my idea—in a tourist town, a camera's the perfect mask. He could shield his face anytime he wanted.

Even so, he'd waited outside in the shadows while I hit Tomlinson's favorite bars: the Bottle Cap, the Green Parrot, La Concha, the VFW, Louie's. Tomlinson spent so much time in Key West, locals considered him family, so bartenders may have been protecting him when they said he hadn't been around.

The good news was, the bars had televisions, and networks weren't abuzz with news of a missing president.

At Margaret Street, we stopped in a circle of streetlight. The doors of Caroline Music were open: grand pianos glistening in sea air; guitars, horns, harps suspended from the ceiling as if buoyed by some composer's helium-laced fantasy. We crossed to the Turtle Kraals where dinghies were tied like ponies, ours among them. I said, "I'll run you out to *No Más,* then come back for Tomlinson. But let's talk first."

"You sound worried. Having a change of heart?"

"Maybe."

"Because what we're doing is dangerous?"

"Yes."

"Crazy?"

"*Yes.* 'Crazy' is what the press is going to call you if we get caught. Is it worth it? Think of what you're risking. Your legacy. The prestige of the office."

Wilson's eyes caught mine as we walked onto the dock. They were measuring. I'd hit his most vulnerable spot with accuracy—the man's reverence for the presidency.

"You're sharp. The office is bigger than all the men who've ever held it combined. But there's more at stake than you know."

"You told me getting even was for amateurs. You wanted revenge."

"Yes, but I'll say it one more time: There's more at stake than you know."

He was talking about the Panama Canal. I felt sure

now but didn't ask. With Wilson, every bit of data was a bargaining chip.

"If we sail in the morning, there are people I need to contact before we leave. Discreetly. People I trust."

"By telephone?"

"Yes," I said, lying because I was embarrassed. All my contact information had been stored in the cell phone I'd left behind. Worse, I'd even forgotten the numbers of people I call regularly because of one-touch speed dialing.

Operator assistance was no help—most people rely on cell phones and the numbers aren't listed. Not entirely a bad thing. I would've been tempted to call Marlissa Engle—if I could've found a pay phone that worked. Which I couldn't.

"I need to get to an Internet café," I told Wilson. "But first, you have to trust me with details."

"Impossible. I've already told you too much. The more you know, the more danger you're in. To paraphrase Andrew Jackson, 'If I'm shot at, I don't want another man in the way of the bullet.'"

I said, "Here's a quote that might change your mind: 'I not only use all the brains I have, but all the brains I can borrow.' Woodrow Wilson, twenty-eighth president. I'm offering you a loan."

He chuckled, then sobered. "There are historians who say if my brilliant relative had confronted Germany in 1914, instead of signing a Declaration of Neutrality, there would've been no war."

I said, "What do you think?"

"I'll answer that with another Wilson quote: 'Politicians use history to rationalize confrontation, religion to explain restraint, and academia to justify cowardice.'"

Because Woodrow Wilson was an academic, I asked, "Why would he say something like that?"

"He didn't. *I* did—after Wray was killed. I'm no academic." He looked at me. "Andrew Jackson did something no other American president had before or since. Any ideas?"

"No."

"He killed a man, face-to-face. Called the guy out, slapped him, and challenged him to a duel. The guy accepted, and Jackson shot him dead—a man who insulted his wife."

"Old West justice. Part of our history."

Wilson replied, "Being part of history is easy. Changing history—that's risky. Woodrow Wilson signed the Declaration of Neutrality *after* the assassination of Archduke Ferdinand. Ferdinand's murder—one bullet— started the war."

"Could he have stopped it?"

The president said, "Maybe. With a second bullet." Even through the tinted glasses, I could feel the intensity of his eyes.

"Ferdinand was an Austrian blueblood. The Serb who killed him was a bumbling kid. Nobodies. But, because of legally binding pacts, world powers were obligated to mobilize their armies. They depended on the legal machinery of the time as protection. Instead, it led them off a cliff, one country linked to another. Like blind horses."

"But the second bullet—used how?"

"Events don't change history, Dr. Ford. Only events that become *symbols* change history. After a first bullet is fired, how is the second bullet best spent? Appeasement— leave it in the chamber? Or retaliate blindly? Both guarantee war. Pick the right target, though . . . use the second bullet like a scalpel. Who knows?" His tone softened; he yawned. "I'm working on it. But I'm not going to come up with an answer tonight."

I stood. It was 10:35 and the bars across from the fuel docks were busy. "Then let me help. I'm going to grab a beer, Sam. Think it over."

IT WAS BEGINNING TO FEEL COMFORTABLE, CALLing him that. Sam.

Sailing from Sanibel to Key West, we'd spent the night trading watches, talking softly, as stars swayed overhead. Formality can't survive a small boat on a big sea. Wilson was a gifted storyteller and he had a profane sense of humor—especially when he got on the subject of journalists. Particularly a network anchor or two.

That was another reason I was sure Tomlinson hadn't disappeared because he was mad. We'd laughed too much and had had too much fun on the trip down—after declaring a temporary freeze on the subject of Marlissa.

Something else we'd learned during the sail was Wilson's method for contacting his unnamed ally— presumably, Vue. He'd alluded to it earlier. A form of drumming, he'd told us.

Accurate, in an ingenious way.

Exactly at midnight, I had gone belowdecks and found the president, wearing old-fashioned headphones, sitting at the galley table, among *No Más*'s familiar odors of teak oil, kerosene, electronic wiring, and a blend of patchouli and cannabis. Tomlinson, who was at the wheel, had just boiled a pot of French roast, so there was coffee, too. The president was hunched over a circuit board made of plywood, on which there were tubes, copper wire, and a brass-and-stainless armature—an antique telegraph key, I realized.

He'd waved me into the seat across from him and focused on the keypad. I watched him use it to tap out a series of dots and dashes. Then he pressed a headphone to his ear, took up a pencil, and made notes, left-handed, as his responder clicked away.

Years ago, I'd had to pass the FCC's Novice and Technician tests so I could legally use shortwave transmitters in countries that had reciprocal operating agreements with the United States. It meant learning to send and receive Morse code at five words per minute—not nearly as fast as the president was drumming out messages.

I'd lost the skill, but I still recognized some common shortwave abbreviations. *C*: − − . − − . (Yes, you are correct.) *R*: . − − . (Received as transmitted.) *TMW*: − − − − − − . − − − − . (Contact you tomorrow.)

Transmission concluded.

The president removed the headphones and slid the circuit board toward me. "Something else I learned in Boy Scouts. Made it myself." He sounded proud. "It's a simple continuous-wave transmitter with a crystal oscillator, runs on twelve volts. With this antenna"—he'd strung a copper wire to the forward bulkhead—"I can skip signals a thousand miles or more."

"You don't think the NSA can track that?"

"Sure they can. But they won't. I'm using a straight key on a thirty-meter band—primitive compared to the kind of communications they're set up to monitor. Even if someone stumbled onto it, they'd think I'm some kid. Drumbeats." He touched the telegraph key. "That's what this would sound like."

No Más lifted and rocked in the Gulf night as I took a closer look—an old telegraph key with copper contacts, springs, and a steel shorting bar.

I knew better than to ask who he'd contacted, so I asked, "Everything okay back home?"

"So far, so good. My Secret Service guys are getting antsy, but they still believe I'm locked away in my cabin, meditating." He sounded relieved.

WHEN I RETURNED TO THE FUEL DOCKS, I WAS carrying two Styrofoam cups filled with ice and Tuborg beer. I knew the president wanted to be back aboard by midnight so he could make his nightly shortwave contact.

We found a bench facing the harbor. *No Más*'s anchor light was a white star among many clustered off Christmas Island.

"That smell . . . heat and rain"—Wilson sniffed as if tasting—"it hasn't changed."

At night, a bubble of Caribbean darkness envelopes Key West, insulating the island from the mainland. Air molecules are dense, weighted with jasmine, asphalt, the musk of shaded houses. Rain on coral; heat, too.

"When I was in the Navy, we were stationed here for six weeks. The air base off Garrison Bight—I'd just completed amphibian training in San Diego, and we were still flying the Grummans. I didn't want to leave. When I finished my hitch, I wanted to come back and run a charter boat. Maybe buy a seaplane and fly tourists to the Tortugas and Bahamas."

"Why didn't you?"

"It was Wray. She had a higher calling. The woman was born with a need to serve. We couldn't have children, and I'm not the religious type. So we went into politics."

"Not religious?" His month in a monastery, the interest in Zen—then both were precedents for severing contact with security people.

"Unofficially? No. My wife, though, was religious in the best sense of the word."

He took a drink, shaking his head. "I hope I don't sound like some maudlin old geezer when I talk about her. One of the perks of being president is that when I bore people, they think it's their fault."

No, it wasn't tiresome. He'd mentioned his wife a few times while sailing. Stories that provided fresh insight. Wray Wilson's public persona was that of the solid, supportive First Lady who had overcome handicaps. According to Wilson, though, "She was the brains, I was the mouthpiece, and we shared the balls."

A tough, driven soul, was the impression. He loved her. He was also in awe. She compensated for her deafness, and slight speech impediment, by working harder, studying harder, than her contemporaries. The woman had a sophisticated understanding of the world, he said, that could only have been assembled in silence.

"I didn't go into politics because I wanted to be president," Wilson told us. "Hell, I didn't even want to be a congressman. Live in D.C. after some of the places I'd been stationed? I went into politics because I wanted to live up to Wray's expectations. At first, that was the *only* reason. Then it kinda swallowed me up."

He focus was inward. The Navy pilot chuckled. "I was more comfortable as a hero than a president. I'm right at home leading a charge. But I have no interest in assigning tents afterward. If it wasn't for Wray, I never could've pulled it off."

It was touching. I told him that as we sat looking at the harbor, sipping our beers, adding, "I prefer boredom to surprises. That's why I'm offering to help. I'm not an adrenaline junkie, Sam. Thrills are for amateurs."

The problem, I explained, was time. We didn't have enough.

"We have to be in Central America in three days? If the weather holds, it'll take us three days to sail to Mexico. After that, what? Nicaragua, where Mrs. Wilson was killed? That's two or three hundred miles overland. Panama is a couple hundred more."

I leaned forward for emphasis, because I was now whispering. "For me to eyeball an individual, to chart his habits, his schedule, it takes a week. And I have to know the area well enough to select a . . . a spot."

As I continued talking, listing the difficulties, Wilson sat looking at the harbor as if I wasn't there. When I'd finished, he nodded. "Useful information. But I told you from the beginning—don't worry about details."

"But we don't have time—"

He turned to face me. "When people say they don't have time, it really means they're not sufficiently motivated. That's why I'm going to give you another piece of information. I didn't plan on sharing it until later. You know more about aviation than most."

"Flying basics, sure."

"You can land and take off?"

"I can take off, sure. Landing? It depends."

"Then think about this: Wray's plane caught fire *after* it landed. A grass runway in the rain forests of Nicaragua. Do you perceive some significance?"

I said, "You've mentioned it twice, both times like it should mean something. It doesn't. Sorry. Something to do with the rainy season?"

"No."

"Was the plane low on fuel?" Fire was less likely if a plane was in a rain-sodden forest and low on fuel.

Wilson said, "You're getting closer, but that's not it." He thought for a moment, then stood and began walking.

I caught up with him at Flagler Station, where he turned left. The doors of Caroline Music were still open, ceiling fans fluttering. Music came from inside, the elegant refrain of one of the classics we all know but I couldn't immediately name.

I looked inside, still walking, then did a double take: A familiar scarecrow figure sat at the grand piano. The president was about to say something when I interrupted. "There he is. Tomlinson."

He followed my gaze. "Liberace lives."

"I should've stopped here first." The guy who owned the place was one of Tomlinson's buddies, but a music shop? An hour before midnight?

Wilson said, "That was one of our favorite pieces. He plays . . . *beautifully*. I didn't know he was a musician."

My brain had matched melody with a name— "Moonlight Sonata"—as I told him, "I didn't, either."

13

When Tomlinson disappeared, he was wearing British walking shorts, tank top, hair braided. Now, though, he was dressed formally: black slacks, white dinner jacket, hair brushed smooth to his shoulders, sun-bleached, with streaks of gray. He was hunched over the piano, fingers spread, face close to the keys, like a nearsighted novelist at a typewriter.

Wilson and I entered the shop unnoticed to listen. It was like stepping into a musician's attic: a cramped space, no air-conditioning but cool, instruments overhead, violins, guitars, swaying with ceiling fans like the pendulum of an antique clock. There were reading chairs, a chess set, a workbench of disassembled artistry. Red-shaded lamps melded shadows with the reticent lighting of a Chinatown whorehouse. If Sherlock Holmes lived in Key West, it would've been here.

When Tomlinson finished, Wilson and I waited for the last note to end before I said, "Ten years I've known you and I've never heard you play."

Tomlinson looked, threw his hair back, and focused. Said, "Marion?" as if coming out of a trance while his brain relocated. "You've never heard me because I don't play anymore. Pianos disowned me when I moved to a sailboat. Can you blame them?"

"Because . . . ?"

"No room, man. It was a form of infidelity. Pianos demand space and I chose not to provide it. Occasionally, I'll find a very forgiving instrument"—he touched the ebony wood with affection—"that'll play *me*. This is one of the few who accepts my fingers. This piano is saturated with sea air, I think. We're both sailors." Tomlinson's eyes drifted until they found the president, then brightened. "Sam! I've been trying to contact you! That's why the piano." His fingers moved over the keys. "Like the Pied Piper. I knew you'd show up if I played."

"I don't get it."

"For the music, of course." Once again, Tomlinson began "Moonlight Sonata"—left hand rolling the repetitive bass notes, right hand coaxing a reluctant melody.

Instead of being confused, Wilson grew serious. "Why that passage?"

"Because I watched you on the beach yesterday and the sonata's first movement was *all over* you. Like an aura." Tomlinson continued playing; notes reluctant, understated.

"Knock off the baloney."

"For real, man. It's what I *heard*. I was getting *No Más* ready. You walked to the point."

"That's true. But why 'Moonlight Sonata'? Out of all the songs in the world?"

"'Cause I felt it, man. This sort of thing happens to me all the time, Sam. I'm like a wind tunnel. Energy blows right through me."

Tomlinson's eyes were cheerfully numb. From Wilson, I expected cheerful forbearance. Instead, he became more serious. "*Prove* it's true."

By the way he tugged at his hair, I could tell Tomlinson wanted to be done with the subject. "I can't prove it, but I'm right. I knew if I played the sonata, you'd show up. Same with 'Clair de Lune.' It was there, too, with you and your wife on the beach. Debussy."

Chords changed; Tomlinson's fingers slowed. Another familiar classic—fragile, inquisitive.

I was reminding myself that Wray Wilson had been deaf from birth as the president said, "Cayo Costa. That's where I proposed to Wray, forty-one years ago. Both songs had special meaning. But no one is aware of the significance. *How do you know?*"

Tomlinson was into the music. Maybe he didn't hear. Wilson looked at me as if to ask something. I shrugged, palms up. Started to say, *Tomlinson does what he does, no one understands.* But then stopped as another man entered the room. A huge man, leprechaun-shaped, with a red beard, glasses, and an Irish cap. Shy expression; a gentle-giant smile as he greeted Tomlinson, "Ready to go, Siggy?"

Siggy, as in Sighurdhr M. Tomlinson.

It was Tim something, who owned the music shop. He was wearing a white dinner jacket, too.

Tomlinson stood, wobbly but grinning. He located the president, who was still in the shadows. "Sam? It's okay. The Gnome's cool—I told him I have two amigos who are on the run from the feds. As if dealing with outlaws is something new, huh, Gnome?"

Gnome and Siggy. In pirate towns, nicknames are preferred.

TOMLINSON AND TIM HAD BORROWED JACKETS from some waiter pals so they could crash a party.

Not just any party.

"There's a convention in town," Tomlinson said. "Broadcast journalists from all over the country!"

Wilson appeared interested but uneasy.

"And guess who the keynote speaker is?" Tomlinson used his index finger. *Shushhhh*. "It's the guy you talked about on the boat. Like God dropped everything else just to bring you two together. *Walt Danson*. He's in Key West!"

"You're kidding."

"No, man. I never joke about karma."

Danson was a network anchor. Years ago, Wilson had told us, at a Georgetown party, that the anchorman had made a crack about Wray Wilson's speech impediment. The president had never responded publicly, but he still seethed privately.

"Where?"

"At the Flagler Hotel. He was in the private bar when I left." Tomlinson's eyes floated a question to the Gnome.

"They moved the party down the street to Louie's. Danson and a couple of network big shots."

"Can you get us in?"

"If your buddies don't mind serving drinks. I've got extra jackets in the car."

Wilson was saying "Don't be absurd . . ." but the big man interrupted, concerned. "I can't loan tuxes to just anyone, Siggy. Are your friends dependable?"

Tomlinson made a blowing noise as he searched his pockets. "Are you kidding? Compared to these two golden boys, gravity's a party drug. Speaking of which"—he'd found something and held it for inspection, a joint—"I think it would do us all some good to, you know, shallow up a little. What'a you say, Sammy?"

Wilson ignored him. His tinted glasses sparked like a welder's mask as he turned to me. "Walt Danson. I can't believe that vindictive old lush is in town. It's so damn tempting, but I can't take the chance. He's seen me too many times."

I told him, "Out of the question."

But Tomlinson was shaking his head, waving us to follow. "Guys! Unbuckle your belts a notch, let your snorkels breathe. The way Danson's pouring down scotch, he wouldn't recognize his own mother if she was wearing a photo ID. Isn't that right, Gnome?"

"He's stinko, Siggy. Starting to turn mean when I left."

"Sam—*seriously*." Tomlinson was following the Gnome out the door. "*Think* about it. When'll you get another chance like this? Next lifetime, maybe?"

THE FLAGLER HOTEL WAS ON REYNOLDS, BLOCKS from Dog Beach and Louie's Backyard, the place where the broadcasters were now partying. It's the only reason Wilson allowed Tomlinson to stop.

The hotel was a 1920s mastodon, refurbished, but it still had the look of Prohibition cash and Havana politics.

The Gnome's car blended: a 1972 Eldorado convertible. Maybe green, maybe gray. Hard to tell under the streetlights, despite a Caribbean moon. The president and I sat in back but refused to try on waiters' jackets. It was pleasant riding in a convertible, but he wasn't going anywhere near a room full of reporters.

Tomlinson kept trying. "You got to let go of the whole negative vibe thing, man." He sounded very sure of himself, the top down, his hair like a flag, gifting cops and street people with a regal wave of the hand as he and Tim, the Gnome, passed the joint back and forth.

Each time, I responded, "We are *not* going to Louie's."

Finally, Tomlinson gave up. I told him we should call it a night and go back to the boat. He agreed—but didn't sound happy.

"Then we might as well drop off the jackets while we're here."

Wilson told him fine, make it quick.

Gnome used staff parking at the Flagler's side entrance,

pulling up outside the service elevator. Beyond a set of Dumpsters, I could see palms, then a vast darkness where the lights of freighters were held motionless by the Gulf Stream. They were as solitary as campfires.

Tomlinson said, "This won't take long. Go for a stroll on the beach, if you want."

Wilson said, "No, thanks. I'm afraid you'll pull your vanishing act again."

The Gnome was walking around the front of the car, but we could hear him say, "Are you afraid the feds might recognize you, Sammy? Screw 'em. This is hotel property. Fuckers can't *touch* you in the Conch Republic, man."

Wilson shook his head irritably. I empathized. It was tempting—crash a party and serve drinks to a bunch of broadcasters, including Walt Danson. Wilson had *enjoyed* telling the story about Andrew Jackson killing the man who had insulted his wife.

The circumstances were so unlikely, it was unlikely anyone would have recognized him. The former president looked so *different* now. With his head shaved, the burn scar, and beatnik beard, Wilson looked like just another casualty of the service industry.

It would've been interesting to find out.

The night became interesting.

Still wearing their white jackets, and each with a jacket draped over an arm, Tomlinson and the Gnome were waiting for the elevator doors to open when the Gnome turned toward the car. "Hey, guys? I forgot about the pants. They're in a box in the trunk. You mind?"

I leaned over the seat to pop the trunk as Wilson got out. The trunk was a Curiosity Shoppe of broken violins and guitars, but he found the box of pants, which he gave to me, plus two jackets. We were handing the uniforms to Tomlinson when the doors of the service elevator flashed open.

The interior was illuminated with a bright, industrial light. Inside were two men and a woman, well-dressed, obviously not hotel employees, judging from their confused expressions.

"Sorry," the woman said. "I'm very sorry. I must've hit the wrong button." She hesitated. "Do you men work here?"

Trying to sounded sober, the Gnome said, "Oh, yes. This is our workplace."

"*Good*. We could use some help."

That was obvious.

All three looked like they'd had a lot to drink, but one of the men was drunk. He sat on the elevator floor, legs crossed, his expression blurred and surly. The woman and her companion had been struggling to lift him to his feet when the doors opened.

I recognized the woman as a broadcaster with a cable news network. Suzie . . . Cindi . . . Shana. A name that was similar. She had a cheerleader face, the body of a trophy bride, and the arrogance of a man who would marry one.

I recognized the drunk, too.

It was television icon Walt Danson.

* * *

"MR. DANSON IS ILL," THE SECOND MAN TOLD US. He was tall, with bland features and feral eyes. "Food poisoning, we think—the kind of publicity your hotel doesn't need. Can you help us get him to his room?"

Danson opened his eyes for a moment, took a moment to find the man; glared. "Fuck you, Harry. You *wish* I was poisoned. That'd make dumping me a lot easier, wouldn't it?"

"Now, Walt," the tall man said for our benefit, "is it smart to use that kind of language, old friend?"

Danson waved his hand, dismissing him. "You don't have any *old* friends—*Mister* Program Director." The anchorman leaned his head against the wall and closed his eyes.

Harry turned to us with a stage gesture. "See what I mean? He's feverish. We're counting on your professionalism."

The Gnome straightened vaguely, as if at attention, as Tomlinson said, "We are professionals, sir."

The program director exchanged looks with the woman, his expression saying *Simpletons*. Then his eyes moved from me to Wilson, who'd turned his back to the elevator and was returning to the car. "Excuse me—sir? Don't leave. I'm talking to *you*. Hey—*old man*!"

Wilson froze. Thought about it for a moment before turning to face the elevator. He wore the expression of a convict who expected to be identified.

I watched the TV people closely. No flinch of interest or recognition. Just impatience. They'd been drinking, they were tired, and they were now dealing with inter-changeable objects—hotel staff.

They didn't notice Wilson stiffen when the program director asked, "Are you deaf? Or don't you understand English?"

"I understand English just fine, sir," Wilson answered, sounding passive with his Southern accent, under control.

"Then listen to me. We need all four of you men. We'll pay you—but only if you can keep your mouths shut. Agreed?"

Without waiting for an answer, the man stabbed a finger at me. "Same goes for you." He paused. "You wait tables here?" His tone saying I didn't look like a waiter.

"Mostly maintenance." I had a white jacket over my arm. "I only wear the monkey suit when there's a convention. Either way, we don't need you to lecture us about hotel etiquette."

Piss him off, maybe he'd tell us to go away.

Instead he said, "Smart-ass, huh? Okay. You're in charge. Make sure the two stoners and the old man don't do anything stupid."

Tomlinson and Tim were already on the elevator, bracing Danson so he wouldn't fall over. Wilson came up behind me, touched his hand to my back, and gave me a little push. He *wanted* to do it. When I didn't move, he pushed again.

I said, "After you . . . Sam," and followed the president to the corner of the elevator, then stood in front of him.

Harry's cell phone began to ring as he said, "Shana, why don't you go back to the bar? I can handle it from here."

The program director was checking caller ID as the woman stepped into the elevator. "Get real, Harry. Leave Walt when he needs me? The man's been like a father."

Danson opened his eyes long enough to roll them. "A father, huh? I'm the only network suit you haven't fucked, so that *explains* it." *Funny.* He was still laughing as his head clunked against the wall.

"Dear old Walt Danson," the woman said fondly, touching the back of her fingers to man's head. "Why don't you tell me what you *really* think," showing she could take it—there was something odd, though, about the way her hand lingered by Danson's face.

She was palming a digital camera, I realized . . . no, a tape recorder.

Danson mumbled, "Women correspondents? *Chorus girls,* is more like it. Kick your legs high enough and the network hacks think you got something between your ears . . ."

Ugly. Impossible to ignore, but not for Harry, who was on the cell phone as he pushed the button for the top floor, talking loudly.

His words blurred as the old anchorman rambled . . . until I heard Harry say, "Repeat that. *Who* disappeared? WHO disappeared?" There was a long pause. "You're *shitting* me!"

I stiffened. Tomlinson started to turn toward the

president but caught himself. The doors had closed. It felt as if the oxygen had been sucked from the elevator.

The program director's voice became strident. "Are you *sure*? Did he disappear or was he kidnapped? Yes . . . I know . . . I know. Jesus Christ, *find out!*"

A cable clanked. The elevator began its ascent. We listened to Harry say, "Are you still there? Hello . . . Can you hear me?"

Kept repeating it until he gave up. He'd lost reception.

THE FLAGLER'S PENTHOUSE FLOOR WAS RE-stricted access so there was no one in the hall as Tomlinson, the Gnome, the president, and I guided Danson to his door, then waited while the woman tried to get the plastic key to work.

On the elevator, she'd asked Harry, "Who disappeared?"

Harry tried redialing a couple of times before he answered, saying, "Nothing's confirmed yet," looking from me to Tomlinson, meaning he couldn't talk.

Or maybe he didn't want her to know . . .

The program director was first off the elevator, walking fast toward the stairs, phone to his ear, saying, "Workman? Jesus Christ, I was just talking to Bentley. Go get him!"

The woman called, "Harry! What the hell's going on?"

The program director turned long enough to make a calming motion—*No big deal*—then pointed down the hall, mouthing the words *Be right there*.

So far, though, it was just the five of us, plus the drunken anchorman. Danson had been babbling most of the way as Shana patted his head, and fed leading questions.

"Who's the stupidest network anchor, Walt? Any of them ever accept sex for favors, Walt?"

Danson was drunk, but he was also cagey. I noticed he began softening his replies, throwing some compliments in—his reporter's bullshit alarm going off, maybe, sobering the receptors. Did he know what she was doing?

"My darling girl, don't you wish you had that beautiful little tape recorder I gave you for Christmas? Why . . . you could try to blackmail me with some of those questions."

Yes, he knew.

Then, as we dumped him on the bed, Danson turned it around on the woman, saying, "Shana, you fool—you really think Harry's coming back? We work for *different networks,* sweetie. New York calls a program director this late? There's something big going on. He *wants* you to play nursemaid. But the son of a bitch doesn't fool me." Suddenly, the old anchorman was sitting, not sounding so drunk now, as he picked up the phone.

I said, "If that's all you need, we'd better get going," nudging Tomlinson, then Wilson, toward the door. But Tim, the Gnome, didn't move.

"Hey," he said, "what about a little something for the cause?" He put his huge hand out, palm up.

The woman was concentrating on the anchorman, who was saying into the phone, "Yes, *the* Walt Danson, young lady. And if you care about your career, you'd better get Bentley on the line *immediately*." Weaving, eyes glassy, he used his TV voice to mitigate the slurring—an old pro used to rallying from a whiskey haze.

The Gnome cleared his throat. "Has the service been satisfactory, ma'am?"

The woman ignored him until he cleared his throat again. "Stop that disgusting noise! What do you want?"

Gnome said, "The mean guy promised us money," as the anchorman snapped, "Hello . . . Baker? Yes, I know Harry's on the other line. But I'm still managing editor, so he *will* take my call. Jesus . . . I'll wait . . . but not very goddamn long!"

The woman started to say to the Gnome, "Yeah? Well, *I* didn't promise to pay you—" but then gave up, whispering *That jerk* as she pointed at her purse, which was on the bed near Wilson. "Hand that to me."

Wilson leaned to get the purse but fumbled it and the purse fell. He knelt to retrieve what spilled onto the floor.

The woman was coming around the bed, saying "Clumsy old fool," as I moved between her and the president, telling everyone, "Forget about the tip. We're leaving now."

In the abrupt silence that followed, I realized I'd just said something that no waiter would ever say.

The woman was oblivious. But Danson noticed. As he waited for Bentley, he put his hand over the phone and stared at me. After a moment, he said, "You work hotel maintenance?"

Even drunk, he'd caught that.

Before I could answer, the president replied, "Yes, sir, he does," sounding smooth and Southern. "Personally, I'd be very happy to accept any gratuity you kind people might offer."

Head down, Wilson handed the purse to the woman with a slight bow—the compliant servant.

Danson was still staring, thinking about it. Interested but drunk, having trouble focusing as he turned his attention from me to Wilson. "How long have you been in Key West?"

"Longer than I planned to be, sir."

"You're from Georgia. No . . . the Carolinas." The anchorman stumbled over *Carolinas,* but he got it out.

"You have an educated ear, sir."

"Your face—is that a birthmark?"

The woman snapped, "Walt! Why the hell do you care?" as Wilson touched his cheek. "No, a fire. Not so long ago."

"You look familiar."

"Maybe so. We often remember people by their scars."

"It's not that. You remind me of someone." Danson turned to the woman, who was handing a wad of bills to the Gnome. "Who's that actor? On the HBO series? He looks a little like him," but then Danson's attention suddenly returned to the phone. New York was on the line.

"It's about time, Bentley! Tell me everything you told that asshole Harry. Who's missing?"

I took the Gnome by the wrist and pulled him along, trailing Wilson and Tomlinson across the room.

The president had his hand on the doorknob as the old anchorman said "My God" in a whisper before gathering himself. "Yes. I would say it's one hell of a story."

The Gnome said, "Call if we can be of assistance," to the woman, who paid no attention because she was sitting on the bed now, eyes eager, listening to Danson say, "Yes, well . . . that's the question. Kidnapped or did he just take off? Where was he last seen?"

I held the door, waiting to file out, staying calm, hearing Danson say, "Florida? We're *in* Florida. Check his bio—wasn't he stationed in Key West for a while? Christ, for all we know, he's someplace around here."

I was imagining the anchorman's eyes boring into my back as I stepped into the hall.

As the door swung closed, Danson was saying, "That's what I'm saying. For a wimp like Kal Wilson to do something so crazy? It means he's gone insane."

14

Twenty minutes after midnight, under sail aboard *No Más,* President Wilson dropped his headphones on the galley table and pushed the telegraph key away. "Damn. He's either not receiving or he's afraid to send."

"Your contact on the mainland?"

"It's Vue. I can tell you that now. He has a similar setup on Ligarto Island." Meaning, the shortwave transmitter.

The reason the president could tell us was that we'd pulled anchor and were under way. Five hours ahead of schedule. Presumably, we'd be together for the next three days, on our way to Mexico. No risk of security breaches.

Tomlinson was at the wheel. As we talked, the sailboat's engine cavitated, the hull shuddered. *No Más* rolled, cookware rattling, then resumed her beam–sea rhythm. He was steering south toward the sea channel, the darkness of the Atlantic Ocean beyond.

"I knew the Secret Service would figure out I was gone. But I was hoping to have at least a couple of days' head start." Wilson had said variations of the same over the last hour.

I was wondering about the man's timing. Would being discovered endanger whatever it was he had planned? I decided the subject was taboo for now. Instead, I asked, "What will the Secret Service do to Vue?"

"Hopefully, he saw it coming and got off the island. He works for me, not the Secret Service. But he's good at anticipating what the agents are thinking.

"I left a letter in my cabin, handwritten, exonerating him. I said I was leaving because I wanted time alone. That Vue didn't know I'd left until it was too late to stop me."

"If he didn't see it coming?"

"Taken by surprise? They'd put Vue in a room and question him for a long, long time—pointless, because he won't tell them anything."

Even so, Wilson was troubled by the prospect of his friend being detained. His hands disseminated, boxing the transmitter, coiling the antenna. My guess: He had been counting on Vue's help throughout the trip.

Wilson straightened for a moment, alert to a change in the sea. He'd taken off the goatee but not the synthetic scar. I watched him cross the cabin and press his face to the porthole. "We're passing Fort Taylor, the old Key West sub base. Wray and I spent a few nights at the Truman Summer White House; his personal quarters—another perk of being president. You'd be amazed at how simple the furnishings are. Politicians weren't treated like royalty in those days."

He returned to the table, something on his mind. I waited, not surprised when he said, "I'm more worried about Tomlinson's friend, sitting in a room right now being questioned. Tim. He's a nice man, different . . . but he has no reason to protect me. The FBI's good at asking the right questions."

"Tim has no idea who you are."

"But what if Danson or Shana Waters recognized me?"

"They didn't."

I wasn't as confident as I tried to sound.

Wilson said, "I wish I'd have gotten a better read. Any new impressions come to mind?"

He'd asked variations of that question as well. I said, "Like Tomlinson said, the timing was more like fate. I'm still puzzled by Danson. One minute, he's nearly unconscious; next, he's a functioning drunk. Was it because he figured out the woman was trying to entrap him? Or because his radar sensed a big story?"

Wilson said, "You obviously haven't spent much time with the White House press corps. The answer's both. Wait . . . that's unfair. Not to the press corps but to people like Danson who make it to the top.

"The ones who excel tend to be either decent professionals or they're ruthless thugs. Both types appear non-threatening; both are shrewd, but they are types. Tonight, you met one of the worst."

"Danson," I said.

"No. The woman, Shana Waters. She was an intern at

CBS our last year in office. My wife was at the first press conference Shana attended. The two never exchanged words, but Wray took me aside afterward and told me to never let her get me alone.

"Danson is a borderline thug. He's heavy-handed, biased as hell. But the man can cry on cue, and he looks like everyone's favorite uncle. Shana, though, is a jackal. She's after the anchor job and he knows it. So maybe he was trying to trap her by pretending to be drunker than he really was. The man's not stupid. None of the top dogs are."

"Your wife had good instincts."

"Yes, but she had more than just instincts. She knew things about people. Wray sometimes saw events before they happened. In that way, Tomlinson's like her." Wilson smiled as he removed the telegraph key from the box. "Extrasensory perception. You don't believe in that sort of thing, do you, Dr. Ford?"

"Mystic visions, no."

"You seem uneasy."

"I am. I'm surprised you *do* believe. It worries me—there's a lot on the line."

"More than you know—as I've said." He was reattaching wires to the telegraph key for some reason. He began to tap the key, not sending, playing. "What if I called it 'telepathy' instead? The physics are similar to the telegraph. Our brains are chemical-electric transmitters. So is this key when it's connected to a battery." He drummed out a series of letters. No . . . it was the same letter over and over, I realized.

Dot-dash-dash. Dot-dash-dash.

W . . . W . . . W.

"Wray spent her life in the kind of silence you and I will never know. But she could hear music through the bones of her face. If she laid her head on a piano or touched her teeth to the wood. That's how she learned to play. It's also how she learned Morse code.

"When we were in the White House. I'm sure you heard all the cynical jokes. Always holding hands, like we were pretending. We weren't.

"In all the years we were in politics, no one ever figured out the truth. When we held hands, Wray could tap out signals to me with her finger. Morse code. Warning me. Coaching me. Reminding me of a name; sometimes telling me to shut the hell up when I was midway through some idiotic remark."

The president laughed as he continued to send and resend the same letter. *Dot-dash-dash.* I sat, fascinated, sensing the weight of the sea through the sailboat's skin, and also the weight of Kal Wilson's despair. He had lost his partner.

"You tell me," he said. "How did Tomlinson know the importance of the two songs? 'Moonlight Sonata' and 'Clair de Lune.'"

"Maybe he heard you mention them in an interview."

The man was shaking his head. "No one knew. Morse code had been our secret language since we were children. Let me show you something." He slid the telegraph key to the middle of the galley table. "In the first movement of 'Moonlight Sonata,' the left hand plays three notes over and over. The notes are C-sharp, E, and G-sharp. Do you perceive the significance?"

He'd asked the same question about Wray Wilson's plane catching fire in a rain forest.

"I'm not a musician, sir."

"You don't need to be. You know the piece. Try humming those three notes."

I felt ridiculous but I made an attempt. *"Bumm bum-bum. Bumm bum-bum. Bumm bum-bum."*

He was nodding, conducting with his right hand while his left hand moved to the telegraph key. He resumed drumming out *Dot dash-dash* . . . *Dot dash-dash* . . . *Dot dash-dash* as I hummed.

I finally figured it out.

"In Morse code," I said, "the sonata plays the letter *W* over and over."

"That's right. *W*, as in Wilson. When we were children, the sonata was our distress signal. The way the little deaf girl summoned the kid who'd become her protector. Me, the jock hero and Boy Scout.

"As we got older, it meant more. Beethoven was deaf when he wrote the piece. He was also in love with a woman he knew he could never have. Because of her handicaps, Wray had felt the same was true of a guy like me. Unattainable. *WW* stood for Wray Wilson—her name once we were married."

I nodded, not sure how to respond, so I asked, "And 'Clair de Lune'?"

Wilson chuckled. "I'll do us both a favor by not asking you to hum it, but listen." The telegraph key clattered with a series of dots and dashes too fast for me to read, but the rhythm was similar to the beginning of the Debussy classic.

"In Morse code, the first few bars of 'Clair de Lune' spell out *I-L-U*. Several times. Think about the melody." He began tapping the key. "Hear it?"

I said, "Yes. But you lost me. What does *I-L-U* stand for?"

The president shook his head, a wry expression. "No one will ever accuse you of being a romantic, Dr. Ford. I'll let you figure it out. But how did Mr. Tomlinson know? That's what I'm asking you."

I thought about it for a moment. "He has uncanny intuition, I'll admit. He observes details, I think, that most of us miss, and his subconscious processes the data in a way that may seem mystical. But it's not."

"I think you're wrong. He had nothing to observe regarding those two pieces of music. Yet he knew. My wife was the same way. You didn't want him to come on this trip, did you?"

"No. I'm afraid he'll get in the way—for what you have in mind."

"Once again, I think you're wrong. He knows things. That's why I chose him."

"But you never met Tomlinson before. And the only time we met—"

"Cartagena, Colombia," the president interrupted. "My motorcade was coming from the airport, on the road by the sea. Secret Service had done its usual superb job. We had Blackhawk helicopters, more than a hundred agents working the streets. But the only one who noticed something odd about that little gray fishing boat was you, a vacationing tourist—or so I believed at the time."

The gray boat was made for pulling crab traps yet the men aboard were fishing. They were also holding their rods upside down. I'd been in a fourteen-foot Boston Whaler watching the motorcade. I'd rammed the boat just as they fired the rocket. A SAM.

The president continued, "You both know things. But in different ways. That's why I chose *you*. One of the reasons, anyway."

"There are other reasons?"

"Yes. That's something else I'm going to let you figure out for yourself. It'll come to you. The significance."

That word again.

I STARTED TO GET UP FROM THE GALLEY TABLE, but the president held up an index finger: *Wait a minute*.

He was removing wires from the telegraph key, boxing it again. "Before you go topside, there's one more thing I want to show you. I said the top TV people were either decent professionals or thugs? The same's true of politicians."

When I started to speak, he held up the finger again. "I'm making a point."

He reached into his pocket and placed a palm-sized digital recorder on the table. It was silver.

"Look familiar?"

"It's Shana Waters's. Danson said he gave it to her as a present."

"That's right. I dumped her purse intentionally. She stuck the recorder in there when she helped us get Danson on the bed." The president removed his glasses and looked at me with his farmer's eyes, telling me something. "My wife was the good and decent half of our presidency. I was the *other* half. I have a lot more in common with that shark that was cruising the drop-off. I want you to know that."

He seemed to think that would reassure me.

I touched the recorder. Digital. Expensive. "What's she going to think when she finds it missing?"

"That Danson took it, of course. Those two are in a kind of occupational death dance. You didn't pick up on that? They despise each other, but they also get some kind of perverse satisfaction out of their secret battle. Who can outdo the other. He gives her a fancy recorder, she uses it to blackmail him, he steals it back. Like chess."

"You could ruin Danson with what's on here."

The president nodded. "But I won't. I may use it, but not to ruin him." In reply to my expression, he explained, "My life's evolved to a point where I trust old enemies more than new friends. At least I know what they want. You'd have to spend four years in the White House to understand what I mean." He paused, suddenly alert. "Do you feel that?"

He meant the way *No Más* was taking the sea. The wind was off our port side now.

I said, "We've tacked. Tomlinson's turned west toward Mexico."

Wilson stood, lost his balance, then steadied himself. His face was pale in the cabin's light, his skin looked as fragile as paper. He found the chart, saying, "That man needs to establish a priority list. I told him to steer south until he heard from me. Here's where I want to go." He rapped his finger on an island that was only a few miles up the road from Key West. Big Torch Key.

It made no sense. Why would he want to remain in Florida when the feds were looking for him? I said, "Are you sure?"

"Very sure." With a pencil, he circled a smaller island off Kemp Channel. "This is our destination. There's a private estate, with a good anchorage."

"Is someone expecting us?"

Wilson said, "Let's hope not," handing me the chart.

ABOVE DECK, I SLID IN NEXT TO TOMLINSON, put the chart in his lap, and said, "He believes you're psychic. Even though you're a hundred eighty degrees off course. He says you need a priority list."

Tomlinson flicked on a little red lamp as I pointed to the island Wilson had circled. "I tried making a priority list once but it came out more like triage."

He checked the compass, then the horizon: fragmented moon in the west, navigational markers flashing in the early morning darkness. "I'm not off course. My route's just twenty-five thousand miles longer." He touched the chart. "You're serious?"

"That's what he wants. Turn us around."

"*Why?*"

"Go below and ask him."

Tomlinson shook his head. "No, thanks. Let the man have his space."

It had been the same way on the sail from Cayo Costa to Key West. Kal Wilson was not an individual who invited familiarity, so Tomlinson and I spent most of the time topside while he slept or read below. If the president wanted conversation, we waited until he engaged us. But even idle talk with the man consumed an inordinate amount of energy. I wasn't sure why, nor was Tomlinson. Wilson had a presence that was tangible, like heat or cold, and required total attention. So we kept our distance—not easily done on a thirty-five-foot sailboat.

Another factor: The man was ill. It was apparent only when he didn't know we were watching.

Tomlinson asked, "You ready to come about?"

"Let 'er go." I slid beneath the boom as *No Más* pointed into the wind, stalled, then fell toward the lights of Key West. When Tomlinson gave me the word, I cranked the mainsheet trim, feeling the starboard side lift beneath me. The sailboat began to accelerate southeast as canvas leveraged wind.

"You still pissed off at me?"

"That's a hard one to answer. I've got so many reasons."

He reached into the cooler he keeps on deck and opened a Corona for me, saying, "I'm talking about Marlissa."

As if surprised, I said, "Oh . . . *her*. I'm not mad."

"Which means, you're majorly pissed-off."

"Damn right. We've always had a gentlemen's agreement that we don't date the same women at the same time and we don't discuss details if it happens later."

"I didn't break the agreement, man. It was her. Marlissa's no gentleman. Like that TV woman, Shana what's-her-name. *Very* hot. But poison."

"You're serious?"

"Two of a kind. But I'm like a kid at Christmas when it comes to women. I can't wait to unwrap them, even if I don't like what's inside. At the marina, Joann, Rhonda, and the other woman said I should warn you. In a way, I guess, maybe I did."

"Don't expect me to thank you."

Tomlinson said, "I won't. But you're welcome," as he hunched over the chart. I watched him put a thumb between our position and the nearest obstruction. Then I watched him hold his arm out, sighting over three fingers held parallel. They were old sailors' tricks for measuring distance.

After a while, he asked, "When we were in Key West, did you call Marlissa?"

"Never crossed my mind," I lied. "Why would I bother?"

"To find out the truth. She would've denied it."

"Think so?"

"Yep. Hell, Doc, I *wanted* to call her—I don't have your willpower. Know why I didn't? Because I couldn't remember her damn number. I had it on speed dial so I never memorized it. Pathetic, huh?"

I smiled. "Yeah. Pathetic." Then we both sat back, drinking beer and laughing . . . after I'd told him the truth.

15

The significance of a plane catching fire *after* it had landed in a Nicaraguan rain forest? The answer came to me in a dream. I was not the same man when I awoke.

We found the island. We found the estate, with its sheltered harbor. When *No Más* was anchored and secure, I made a bed on the bow. Last time I checked my watch, it was 3:30 a.m.

It returns sometimes. My dream. It is a nightmare played in the flames of a long-gone blaze, my index finger twitching on a trigger as young men nearby, alive but terrified, lay frozen in their innocence, eyes fresh with homecoming, haylofts, ghettos. They are not yet scarred by the darkness that frees them to admonish their killers by killing in return.

Shooting a human being in a fit of temper is one

thing. To do it professionally, when you are exhausted, filthy, and afraid, half a planet from home, is another.

The brain, undirected as we sleep, organizes random thoughts into patterns. Synapses are gaps between cells. Like sparks, neurotransmitters arc between. Dreams are the chemical-electric by-product, and they are meaningless—with rare exceptions.

For the last few days, my subconscious had been struggling to connect random phrases and events. They became fragmented as I ascended into sleep:

"Wray's plane caught fire after it landed. No survivors. Suggestive?"

"You know more than you realize . . ."

Significance . . . ?

". . . one of them a brilliant plastic surgeon, near a volcano in Nicaragua . . ."

"You've been following events in Panama . . ."

"Thomas Farrish is the most dangerous man on earth . . ."

"Not the only reason I chose you. You'll figure it out . . ."

Nicaragua . . . fire . . . Managua . . . fire.

Nicaragua . . . burn scars . . .

"You are the perfect man for the job, Dr. Ford. When I visit you at the lab, I'll sign a photograph for your son . . ."

Fire. My son.

How does the president know I have a son?

As I slept, random data sparked until it catalyzed the old, familiar dream. Once again, I was returned to that place, suffocating with dread, and the stink of flames fueled by innocence.

FIRE.

I sat up, sweating in the chill, gray light of a November morning, seeing water, the sailboat's mast, relieved to know it was only that damn dream. Again. But the relief was soon replaced by a sickening awareness.

After landing safely, a chartered plane caught fire in the jungles of Nicaragua.

I now understood the significance.

Seven people had been burned alive, one of them a plastic surgeon. I knew their murderer.

Praxcedes Lourdes.

It was the sociopath who had kidnapped my son, who maintained contact with Laken even after being extradited to Nicaragua. Writing letters or e-mails, describing his "symptoms," and discussing behavioral anomalies caused by injury and birth defects. A predator's ruse to keep the prey within grasp.

Prax was out. The Man Burner was free. He was killing again.

TOMLINSON WAS IN THE AFT BUNK, ASLEEP, BUT the president was gone.

I felt a moment of panic but then took stock. It was an hour before sunrise. The world was shades of charcoal and pearl, a few stars showing. But there were dock lights and sodium security lights on the island. I could see that our dinghy was tied next to a boathouse a hundred yards away. I stuffed my shoes in the back of my fishing shorts, jumped from the stern, and swam.

The main house and outbuildings were Mediterranean-style salmon stucco with roofs of red tiles. The lawn hadn't been tended in weeks and the pool was clogged with palm fronds. I assumed the place was empty but banged on the back door, anyway. No response. The door was locked.

I pressed my face to the window and saw furniture covered with white sheets and a television that had to be twenty years old. The island was a multimillion-dollar property, but seldom used.

"Ford. I'm in here." Wilson was outside the boathouse, wiping his hands on a mechanic's rag. Behind him, the horizon was banded silver, silhouetting the tops of trees. He turned and disappeared, closing the door behind.

Unlike the other buildings, the boathouse was a remnant of Old Florida: cypress-shingled, built on low stilts, barn-sized, large enough to house one of the elaborate wooden yachts from that period.

But there was no yacht. Instead, when I stepped through the door I found the president standing on the pontoon of a single-engine airplane. Amphibious—it could land on water or a runway. He had the engine cowling open.

Hoping I was wrong, I said, "Praxcedes Lourdes—was it him? Is he the one who . . . attacked Mrs. Wilson's plane?"

The president turned in my direction, holding an oil dipstick, then returned his attention to the engine. "I knew you'd figure it out."

"Are you sure?"

"I'm sure of my sources."

"Then that explains why you came to me. You know what Lourdes did to my son."

"Motivation is important." Wilson turned again, briefly. His expression had changed, as if a mask had slipped. "I *want* that son of a bitch. And you're going to help me get him."

"Then you were right. I'm the perfect man for the job."

"I told you you'd get used to it."

"But my son—"

"He's in no danger. He's still in California with his mother—I confirmed that before I met you at the party on Useppa Island. And Lourdes, hopefully, is still in Central America."

"Where?"

"On the run. That's all I know. He escaped—or so they say."

"Bullshit." I was shaking, I realized. My clothes were soaked on this cool morning, but it wasn't just that.

"I agree. Someone bought his freedom. There are powerful people who don't want him caught. Elections are coming up in Nicaragua and Panama. You know what that means."

Yes, I knew. Lourdes had been raised by Miskito Indians in Nicaragua. In his early teens, he'd murdered his adopted family by torching their hut.

It was the beginning of a lifelong fetish even though he, too, was badly burned.

An element of Lourdes's fetish was his fantasy of harvesting an attractive face from a victim. That's why he'd kidnapped my son. Lourdes's face was a horror of scars and plastic surgery gone wrong.

Threaten a village with a visit from the "Man Burner" and the vote was guaranteed. Among the superstitious, he was believed to be a monster with inhuman powers. They were right.

"Who has the most to benefit from using someone like him?"

"The determined or the depraved. Or both."

An evasion.

"No matter who's paying him, sir, it's possible he wasn't after you. There was a plastic surgeon aboard."

"Yes. Dr. David Miller. A good friend. Brilliant."

I said, "Lourdes could have been after him," and explained why.

"I don't see how he could have known David was on the trip."

"The Wilson Center has a Web page. Could it have been mentioned there?"

The president hadn't considered it. I could tell. "Possibly."

"Are you certain all seven people aboard that plane died?"

The subject was painful and it made him impatient. "*Yes.* You're getting off track—my contacts are convinced Lourdes was hired to assassinate me."

"Because of the elections? But you no longer have any influence—" I stopped myself.

I watched him check and recheck the dipstick, then close the engine cowling, before responding. "You're right. I no longer have the political influence I once had. But I told you before that events don't change world history. Events as symbols change history. I'm a symbol. A far more powerful symbol than an Austrian archduke. There are religious zealots, as I've said, who are determined to start a world war. Armageddon. They long for it."

I replied, "In that case, if someone hired Lourdes, he's not the only one you're after."

The president had been standing on the floating dock next to the plane. Now he stepped onto the main dock and walked toward me, using the mechanic's rag to clean his glasses. His eyes were luminous—the light of obsession.

"I'm after anyone who had something to do with murdering my wife and six other good people. Most of them friends."

His voice became incrementally louder as he got closer—a man no longer struggling to keep his anger in check. "But first, I want *him*. I want the sick son of a bitch who poured gasoline in a plane, struck a match, then blocked the door. Can you imagine anything closer to hell? That image is in my head, asleep or awake. What it must have been like to be trapped inside.

"*It was me they wanted!* But Wray suffered, my poor, dear girl. Now do you see why I'm willing to risk so much?"

He stopped; stood looking into my eyes, his own eyes

coal black through his tinted glasses, nostrils flared, and I took a step backward, intimidated by his rage. It seemed to be directed at me. In a way, it was.

"There's another reason you're the perfect choice, Dr. Ford. It's because I know you had the chance to kill that animal nearly a year ago. He kidnapped your son. Lourdes came close to cutting the boy's throat—I read the Coast Guard report! You had him alone on that ship for how long?"

I knew better than to try and explain the complicated circumstances. "Long enough, sir."

"You *knew* he was a murderer. Burned people alive because he likes it. You had a perfect opportunity." Wilson was shouting now. "Killing him would have been easy for you. I'm *aware* of your skills. A zero signature professional. Yet you did nothing! Why?"

I hadn't had time to process the implications of Lourdes's involvement. Suddenly, I understood: If I had killed Lourdes when I had the chance, Wray Wilson would not have died in a burning plane. A different assassin might have been hired, but Wray would not have endured that horror.

"I have no excuse, sir. I've regretted it for many months. Never more than now."

"What Praxcedes Lourdes did was the first bullet. You are the second bullet, Dr. Ford. This time, you will not leave that round in the chamber. There will be no more appeasement. Is that clear, *mister*?"

I found myself standing straighter. "Very clear, sir."

The president had his index finger in my face, leaning

close enough so that I could feel the heat of his breath. "I want the heads of the people who did this. The ones who started it by putting a bounty on my head. And I want that *twisted motherfucker*."

I demonstrated my allegiance by remaining calm. "Get me close, sir. Turn me loose. You will have him."

"Good." Wilson looked at the plane for several seconds as if letting the precision of its lines calm him. The plane was white aluminum with green trim. A four- or five-seat Maule, mounted like a trophy on ski-shaped pontoons. The plane looked new, but black grease was smeared over the ID numbers on its side.

"We leave at exactly zero-seven-thirty hours. Roust Mr. Tomlinson, and collect the gear you need. Weight is a problem on a small plane. We're traveling light. Stress that. You have a little more than an hour."

"The gear I need isn't on the boat," I said. "It's hidden in my lab. That's why I want to contact friends in the region. Trust me, Mr. President, I'll do it in a way that's discreet. I won't implicate you. I'm . . . *good* at this."

He wrestled with the idea before saying, "There's a phone in the house, but don't use it. This island's owned by one of my oldest, most trusted supporters. He's an invalid. Vue uses the place sometimes, and it's possible Secret Service will make the connection. But there's a computer. Vue's. I think it's hooked up for the Internet, but I'm not certain."

"What's our destination? I can give rendezvous points without spelling it out."

"Are you certain?"

I said it again. "Trust me."

He used the rag to polish a smudge off the plane's silver propeller before he said, "I want to visit the place where my wife died. It was on an island in Lake Nicaragua. Their government put a memorial there. I've never seen it."

"The central part of the lake?"

"No. Far south, near the Costa Rican border."

The Solentiname Islands. I'd been there during the Sandinista-Contra wars.

"After that, we go to Panama?"

Wilson nodded. "Officially, Panama's Independence Day is the first of November, but they celebrate the end of Independence Week on November fifth. That's when it was officially recognized as a sovereign nation.

"There's a ceremony scheduled at the Canal Administration Building at noon. All the principals are expected— including the U.S. ambassador."

Ambassador Donna Riggs Johnson was a brilliant woman, but unpopular for the stand she'd taken against leasing the canal to an Indonesian company.

Wilson was a historian. I suspected he mentioned Archduke Ferdinand for a reason.

I said, "Someone plans to assassinate her." A statement.

"I believe so. I couldn't warn her through regular channels—my source would've been put in danger. But I've made sure she knows. Ambassador Johnson's not going to announce it publicly, but she won't attend the ceremony."

"Someone hired Lourdes to kill you. Will they be attending?" I was thinking of Thomas Farrish and the Islamic clerics he was associated with.

"We'll discuss that at another time." The president looked at the plane again. "The keys to the back door are under the mat. I still have my preflight to finish."

As I was walking toward the house, Wilson stopped me, calling, "Doc? I *do* trust you."

I SENT THREE E-MAILS, TWO OF THEM TO MEN who spend extended periods in the jungle, so there was no guarantee they would get them in time. I knew several people in Panama City because of my recent consulting job, but they were scientists. These were the only two contacts who could provide the sort of assistance I needed.

One was to an American mercenary I'd met a couple of years ago, Curtis Tyner. *Sergeant* Curtis Tyner. Tyner is a little over five feet tall, has bristling orange muttonchops, carries a swagger stick, and collects shrunken heads as a hobby. He became wealthy as a jungle bounty hunter, and as a facilitator of small wars.

We were going after people inviting the Apocalypse? Curtis Tyner could provide them a personal introduction.

I wrote:

Sergeant Tyner, I'm on a collecting trip, after a rare species of shark. Spoils may be significant. Can we discuss over a Chagares water & rum in a day or two?

> Sunset at the yacht club by the American Bridge, or I
> will be staying at a favorite hotel. Cdr. mWf.

The Chagares River flows into the Panama Canal. A popular place to watch sunset is the Balboa Yacht Club, near the Bridge of the Americas, and the El Panama Hotel is a favorite of the CIA and Mossad.

Tyner would understand—but I gave the message some thought before sending it. Did I really want to return to Balboa? I'd witnessed a different sort of nightmare there.

It was an emotional reaction, I told myself. Avoiding the place was irrational.

I sent the message.

In Spanish, I wrote a second e-mail to Juan Rivera, the Castro-style revolutionary who was Kal Wilson's old adversary but also my old friend.

> Gen. Lanzador, I would be honored to join you for
> batting practice. I will soon be at the lake where we
> once fished for sharks. Unfortunately, it will be neces-
> sary for you to provide all equipment. Moe Berg

Lanzador is Spanish for "pitcher." As in baseball. At one time, Rivera had been a good one, and he was still miffed that the major leagues had never drafted him. Moe Berg had been a professional baseball player in the 1930s and '40s—and a spy for the OSS. I knew Rivera would get it.

I wrestled over how Wilson might react to involving

Rivera, a man he had every reason to despise. But it was true: I had no equipment.

I sent that e-mail as well.

Finally, I e-mailed my son, telling him Lourdes was on the loose, he was killing again, then added, "Please believe this: He is not your friend. He will murder you if he gets the chance."

When I returned to *No Más* to collect our gear, I asked Tomlinson, "Do you have your ball glove aboard?"

Tomlinson had been sleeping, but he was instantly interested. "Of course. Glove, spikes, and the bat Spaceman gave me."

Wilson was concerned about weight on the amphib, so I said, "Leave the bat but bring the rest."

I told him we were leaving for Yucatán, 7:30 sharp, by plane.

16

The reason we had to leave at exactly 7:30, Wilson told us, was because that's when the downward-looking radar on nearby Cudjoe Key was scheduled to be lowered for maintenance.

"Fat Boy?" Tomlinson said. "The balloon, you mean."

Yes, the balloon. It was a "Tethered Aerostat Radar Detection System," a white, bovine-shaped inflatable attached to several thousand feet of cable. Day and night, it hovered above the Keys, tracking ships at sea and low-flying planes. Some, especially Tomlinson's hemp-loving kindred, considered the balloon a malevolent icon, the all-seeing eye of Big Brother. They called it "Fat Boy" because of its shape, and as a sinister reference to another top secret government program.

We were in the plane, taxiing in shallow water, Wilson in the left seat, me in the right. Tomlinson, with his long legs, was in the back, stretched out among our gear. We wore headphones, using the plane's voice-activated intercom system to converse.

The president said, "They do a major systems maintenance once a month and today's the day. We'll have a window of between forty minutes and an hour. By the time they're up and running, we should be about a third of the way to Mexico.

"But if we're early, or late, radar will red-light us, and DEA or Homeland Security will scramble planes to intercept us. We can't miss the window."

Tomlinson was impressed. "Sam, I'm not even gonna ask how you got Fat Boy's maintenance schedule. It's got to be, like, top secret, right?"

His tone wry, Wilson said, "Yes. Entrusting smugglers with the schedule might be considered counterproductive. But no one expects a former president of the United States to try *anything* illegal. It's another one of the perks. I never have to go through metal detectors or airline security."

Tomlinson said, "You're shitting me. No one ever checks?"

"Never. It would be a breach of international protocol. And old acquaintances in the military trust me with all kinds of useful information."

All the potential scenarios—Tomlinson was having fun with them in his mind. "Look, if you ever get tired of traveling around, making speeches? And you're willing to share—down the road, I'm talking about. We could make a lot of money with that kind of access. Not that I'm into the whole materialism thing. I see it more as spreading the gift of mellowism."

Wilson was in a brighter mood, now that we were under way, and he smiled. "'Mellowism,' huh? My friend, with your gift for language you would be a superb diplomat. It's not as easy as it sounds. To say nothing, especially while speaking—that's diplomacy. Teddy Roosevelt's line. Or was it President Carter?"

Tomlinson sat back, enjoying it. "I wouldn't mind being an ambassador. Colombia, maybe—that would be cool. Jamaica would be okay if it wasn't for all the assholes at the airport. Speaking of which, where're we gonna land?"

I watched Wilson reach to switch off the plane's transponder, the VHF radio, then the GPS. Our electronic signature was now zero. He checked his watch, then turned to look out the port window. Fat Boy should have been visible. It wasn't. Wilson said, "We're not landing at an airport. But we *will* land. That's about all I can promise you."

His hand on the throttle, we began accelerating— seventy . . . eighty . . . eighty-five knots—the water's surface tension drumming the pontoons, the plane lifting, fishtailing as it broke free. Then we were banking low over Content Keys, the plane's shadow preceding us, skating across shallow water veined with gutters of jade.

I was surprised when the president immediately leveled off. He noticed as I checked the altimeter: a hundred fifty feet.

"For the next hundred miles, we're going to maintain

this altitude. Our cruising speed will be a hundred fifteen knots—about a hundred thirty miles an hour. A little faster over ground with the wind shift. If we'd shed a hundred pounds of gear, we could probably do one forty."

It looked as if we would barely clear the treetops of the mangrove keys ahead. Tomlinson whistled softly, getting into it. "This is more like surfing than flying. Man"— he whistled again—"give me a rope, I could ski behind this thing. Hope we don't run into any tall ships."

Wilson said, "Let's talk about that. We've got a range of almost six hundred nautical miles, so fuel's not a problem. But eye fatigue could be. There's no autopilot—too much weight. So, Ford? I'm going to need your help. We've got clouds to the west, which is good. Less chance of losing the horizon. Even so, flying this low will be a hell of a strain on the eyes. So we'll do it in shifts. Half an hour on, half an hour off. You okay with that?"

"Fine," I said.

"You want to see how she handles?"

"Okay." My feet found the rudder pedals as I put my hands on the control yoke. It was embossed with a white MAULE M7 insignia.

"You know the gauges—fuel, air speed, altitude." Wilson was pointing. "Here're your trim controls. Keep your eye on the horizon indicator. We want the wings level."

I tried easy turns to port, then starboard. I climbed briefly without adding throttle, then pushed the yoke forward, my stomach alert to a slight increase in g-force. At only a hundred fifty feet off the deck, I didn't have room to try anything else.

"You seem comfortable."

"I've steered a lot of planes in a lot of places. Pilots need breaks. But I wouldn't want to try a water landing unless I have to."

"Don't worry about that. The important thing is, keep us level, use your compass. We're traveling the old-fashioned way: dead reckoning. Just a chart and a pencil. Pretend you're Lindbergh crossing the Atlantic. Just lower."

I felt the yoke move as the president resumed control. I slipped my feet off the pedals.

As he said, "At this altitude, we'll be invisible. Like ghosts," I was looking out the window, seeing water change from green to silver, then blue, as the bottom fell away.

There was a pod of dolphins hobbyhorsing as we banked again, westward, toward the Gulf of Mexico.

DURING THE FLIGHT, WITH ME AT THE CON-trols, Wilson used a mini earphone to listen to Shana Waters's digital recorder. After five minutes, he said, "I don't know what's stronger, Shana's ambition or her sex drive."

He passed the recorder to me and I fitted the earplug beneath my headphones.

Danson wasn't the only man Waters had taped. She had recorded lovemaking sessions with at least two men whose names I recognized—a U.S. senator, and an anchorman from an opposing network.

I raised my eyebrows as I handed the recorder back to him.

"She has the makings of a great politican," the president said. "Too bad she went into broadcasting."

He was serious.

By 11:10 a.m., Florida time (10:10 Yucatán time), we were forty miles off the Mexican coast. Wilson activated the GPS long enough to confirm our position, then turned south, keeping distance between us and the tourist destinations of Cancun and Cozumel.

An hour later, we landed south of Cayo Culebra on an isolated bay. The water was Bombay gin blue. Coconut palms shaded a shack built on stilts at the mouth of a river. There was a rim of white beach where pigs rooted.

As Wilson idled the plane toward shore, he asked, "What's *Cayo Culebra* means in Spanish?"

Tomlinson said, "'Island of Cobras'?"

I said, "Close. 'Island of Snakes.'"

Wilson appeared pleased. "Perfect."

He was in a good mood. We'd crossed the Gulf without close contact with ships or planes, and he was comfortable enough with me at the controls to get more than an hour of sleep. First part of the mission accomplished.

But then he said, "Uh-oh. Something's wrong," not happy anymore.

He was still wearing the tinted glasses, but he had removed the fake burn scar—he expected someone he knew to come out of the shack and greet us. Vue. My guess. Wilson didn't say.

But someone *had* anticipated our arrival, because there were ten six-gallon gas cans on the dock, all full.

We got out, secured the plane, and went to work.

"I don't like this."

Tomlinson was holding the huge funnel, while I poured gas through a leather chamois into the wing tanks. The president was standing behind us on the dock, his head moving as if he suspected that eyes watched from the shoreline. "There should've been at least a note."

There wasn't. I had checked the shack.

"From who?" I asked for the second time.

Wilson didn't reply—for the second time.

He was studying the pigs, now coming along the beach toward us—the farmer in him paying attention.

"Those aren't domestic hogs. See the tusks on the boars?"

The animals were black, hump-necked, with elongated snouts.

"What were they rooting for?"

"Crabs," I said. "Sea worms."

The president frowned. "That's why they're moving the way they are—more like a pack. They're hungry. Trip and fall, those hogs would gut you, then eat you. Mr. Tomlinson? You are supposed to have a gift for knowing things. What's your read on this place?"

Tomlinson appeared nervous—unusual. "Well . . . it seemed kinda fun until you started talking about a bunch of damn pigs eating us. I mean . . . the water's nice and clear. Lots of coconuts that would go real good with rum. But you're right. Sam? Those bastards are coming after us."

Tomlinson looked from the pigs to me, his expression a mixture of awareness, dread, and disgust. "Doc? Is he right? I've never even thought about it before. Getting eaten by a fucking pig?"

I asked, "Don't you usually smoke a joint about this time of morning?"

"I get a late start every now and again. But what do you expect me to do when I'm in a airplane?" He couldn't take his eyes off of the pigs.

I smiled. "Relax. I wouldn't take any naps on the beach. Otherwise, we're okay."

"Geezus . . . I'd like to believe that. They've got cloven hoofs, man. Like the devil. Who knows what happens after that. Eat you, then they could shit out your soul. That really could be the *end*." In a louder voice, he said, "And I'm a *vegetarian*," as if he wanted the pigs to hear.

Wilson said, "Sharks don't care about your ideology and neither do those hogs. Vegetarians are edible and no amount of broccoli's going to change that." He was looking at his watch, his mind on other matters. Was he considering waiting for someone . . . or something?

After a few seconds, he muttered, " 'Island of Snakes.' *Perfect*," but not pleased, the way he'd said it before.

I had emptied the ninth gas container into the wing. Tanks were full. Because I said I wanted to go for a swim after we'd refueled, Wilson caught my eye. "I'd planned on overnighting. But I think we need to get our butts out of here."

Meaning we'd have to improvise.

I said, "Let's go."

* * *

AT 1:20 LOCAL TIME, WE LANDED IN A BAY OF Honduras backwater, where we saw men fishing from handmade boats with outboards. We pulled up on a beach near a couple of pickup trucks—one of them a new Dodge. We bought fuel, then ate achiote chicken with tomatillos and chilies made by a woman cooking outside her hut.

Wilson remained alone, directing the operation from a distance. He'd brought a can of aviation fuel to augment the local gas and he had us add it.

"Mountains ahead," he explained. He didn't have to remind us to filter the gas through a chamois.

Because Tomlinson and I carried food to him, one of the locals said to me, "He must be a very important man in your country. A *jefe*."

A chief.

Five minutes later, we were under way, pointed south.

The largest country in Central America is half the size of Florida. Borders moved below us as topography, rain forests, low volcanic craters striated with green, and rivers that appeared as switchbacks, water black as blood. With window vents open, we flew low enough to smell earth, leaf, water. Once, as we approached a village, Tomlinson said he got a whiff of simmering beans.

We went cross-country, avoiding cities and the few major highways. Wilson had a bush pilot's instincts and we used valleys as cover. It wasn't until somewhere near the border of Honduras and Nicaragua, while following the contour of low mountains, that we ascended to forty-five hundred feet. Even then, we stayed low enough to enrage howler monkeys, who shook their fists at us from the tops of trees.

I was familiar with this country. Took pleasure in the remembrances of my years here. As Tomlinson used ruler and dividers to track our position on the chart, each landmark he mentioned brought back people, events, missions—not all pleasant. But unpleasant memories are useful gauges and mine verified all the fun I'd had. For me, returning in this unorthodox way was a little like coming home.

As a military pilot, the president had flown in and out of the Panama Canal Zone many times, he said, but never over this area. Not at deck level, anyway. It was the end of the rainy season, but we'd drawn a rare cloudless day. He enjoyed himself. It keyed memories of what he said was the best thing about getting elected president: Air Force One.

"No other perk comes close," he told us. "The White House and staff were great, don't get me wrong. You have a basketball court, putting greens, tennis, a private movie theater, even a bowling alley—which I never used. It always struck me as a little sad, frankly, because it was about the only thing Richard Nixon enjoyed during his last days. Bowling alone."

In the West Wing, he said, Friday was Oreo yogurt day, and the kitchen turned out the earth's best french fries, 5 p.m. sharp.

"But there was something special about that plane," he

told us. "The backup, too—neither is officially Air Force One until the president steps aboard. Wray loved the whole ceremony because it meant freedom. Walking across the South Lawn to the helicopter, she'd be smiling. Her *real* smile. And it got bigger when she stepped off and saw Air Force One waiting, the honor guard at attention.

"We could relax there. Her office was forward, next to mine. She'd work while I'd do an hour on the elliptical. Or she might go aft and make sure there were plenty of souvenirs for the press corps to take home. Matches, china, blankets. Those people take anything not nailed down. But even they loosened up a little once we got airborne.

"President Clinton used to go back and play cards all night with reporters. Shoot the bull like a regular guy until reporters hammered him over that intern business. Harry Truman—he called his plane *The Independence*—he'd loosen up with a couple of drinks, and he always had the pilot notify him when they were over Ohio. Senator Taft was from Ohio and Harry hated the man. He'd get up and take a piss over Ohio every time.

Wilson laughed, hands on the yoke, looking military with his buzz cut and earphones, straightening the microphone when he spoke. He had a lot of stories about Air Force One, most assembled from his talks with the crew: Gerald Ford was their all-time favorite president because he was such a decent man. President Reagan was the most charismatic, Carter was the most family oriented, George H. W. was the funniest, Clinton was the smartest, and Lyndon Johnson was the crudest and rudest.

"If he got a steak he didn't like, he'd dump it on the

floor. He made military aides wash his feet and cut his toenails."

Tomlinson said he'd read somewhere that Johnson had huge testicles and, after a few highballs, he wasn't shy about showing them.

"Didn't he walk around naked on Air Force One?"

Wilson ignored the question. He wasn't going to confirm something negative about a member of the club.

"The best thing about that aircraft," he said, "was to land in Peking, or Baghdad, or Cartagena"—he gave me a slight nod—"and to look back at that great big gorgeous 747 from the tarmac. UNITED STATES OF AMERICA, in that don't-screw-with-us lettering, and the presidential seal. Like it had been chiseled from the Rockies; a force that had come a long distance to protect, to do good things, to stand for something . . . better."

For a moment, I thought Wilson had gotten choked up. But then I realized he was concentrating on the instruments. We'd have to switch fuel tanks soon.

"What does the crew say about you, sir?"

"Well . . . I hope they say they enjoyed working for me. Leadership is the art of getting someone to do something you want done because they want to do it. Eisenhower said that. They loved Wray. Like the rest of the staff, they knew the kindness in my speeches came from her—she was more than my occasional ventriloquist. But they respected my record as a pilot, if nothing else. So they worked hard to please us. No boss can ask more than that.

"Before we decided not to run for a second term, our

strategy guys said I should do my last few press conferences standing in front of Air Force One. It communicates such power. Wray was heartbroken when we decided not to do four more years. A big part of the disappointment, I think, was how much she enjoyed her time on that aircraft."

"Sam?" Tomlinson had gotten so used to calling the president that it seemed natural. "If the late Mrs. Wilson wanted to run again, why didn't you?"

Wilson's expression changed. "Check the history books. That's a question I've answered too many times to repeat."

He pushed his microphone armature up.

End of conversation.

17

Tomlinson said, "It's the Days of the Dead. *That's* why I've felt this weird vibe. All afternoon—since those damn pigs attacked us."

We were standing outside a hut roofed with palm thatching. The thatching was a foot thick, intricately woven. A Halloween-style tableau had been constructed outside the door: candles carved as skeletons, a table with offerings of liquor and twists of tobacco.

It had taken me a moment to remember that in Mexico and parts of Central America, the first two days of November are celebrated as Dias de Muertos. *Days of the Dead.*

Deceased children are honored on November 1st, adults on November 2nd. Today was the third, but the shrines would be around for weeks.

I said, "The pigs didn't attack us. You were paranoid.

Probably some type of withdrawal." I was trying to humor him because his expression was so serious. Dread and disgust, like before.

"No," he said. "They wanted me, man. I could see it in their piggy little eyes." He cringed. "I was never afraid to die until I thought about getting eaten by a pig. A fucking *pig*, man. Anything but that."

We were on the remnant of a volcano that protruded from Lake Nicaragua. It was one of the largest of the Solentiname Islands, an archipelago of more than thirty islands clustered at the lake's southern end.

We'd landed at 5 p.m., near a settlement of three huts, all furnished but empty. A man had been waiting for us on the dock. Vue. He had a backpack and a couple of boxes with him, plus a row of gas cans. It was as if he'd just arrived himself.

The little giant had appeared upset. Maybe because he didn't expect us until the next day. Which didn't compute—he also seemed in a hurry.

He'd nodded at Tomlinson and me as he helped Wilson out of the plane, then immediately steered the man toward a private spot ashore to talk. As they started down the dock, I heard Vue say, "Mr. President, I'm very sorry I fail you. Secret Service discovered you missing yesterday morning. And there is more bad news . . ." Vue's voice became a whisper, and I didn't hear anything else.

Since then, Tomlinson and I had been left on our own. A relief for all three of us, probably. I got the plane secured while Tomlinson carried our gear to the door of the shack. Part of my duty was to tie the aircraft fast near overhanging trees, then cover it with camouflage netting Wilson had packed.

The man was good at details.

When I was finished, I returned to the hut. Presumably, we would sleep here. Wilson had an ally in the region who had a lot of power—that was apparent. The Solentiname Islands are isolated, but not all of the islands are uninhabited. About a hundred people, mostly fishermen and artists, live in the area. Yet someone had arranged for these huts to be vacated for our use.

It was now only 6 p.m. but volcanoes to the west were already silhouetted, mushroom clouds tethered to their rims. The Pacific Ocean would be visible from those craters.

"Do you think we should interrupt them to ask which hut we should use?" Tomlinson meant Wilson and Vue, who were standing near the lake's edge, focused on their discussion.

I said, "The man doesn't have any problem giving orders. He'll tell us if we take the one he wants."

Spooked by the tableau, Tomlinson had stacked our gear outside the hut. I took a backpack, opened the door, peeked in, and saw beams of raw timber with hammocks strung between supports. Oil lanterns on a table.

"Nice," I said. "Smells like wood smoke."

I went inside, claimed a hammock, then searched until I found cans of Vienna sausages and an unopened bottle of Aguadiente hidden in a sack of rice. I opened the bottle, poured half a tumbler for myself, a tumbler three-quarters full for Tomlinson, then went outside to find him. He was leaning against a tree smoking a joint.

"I guess you won't be needing this," I said.

"What?"

"It's cheap cane rum."

He thrust his hand out and took the glass. "The hell I won't."

We drank the warm liquor and talked about the things travelers talk about—home, mostly. Friends; what they were probably doing right now.

"Vienna sausages." Tomlinson smiled. "One of nature's perfect foods. Drink the juice, then eat the little bastards. One of the few staples I miss since becoming a vegetarian."

Later, I went for a swim, then dozed off reading by lantern light. Moths found their way into the hut. Their wings threw gigantic shadows.

Around nine, Wilson tapped on the door and poked his head in. "We can hike to the site from here. We'll leave before first light. Six-thirty sharp."

I was half asleep and confused. After the door closed, I said, "Hiking where? What's he talking about?"

Tomlinson was in a hammock across the room. He had the Aguadiente bottle cradled beside him. Half empty.

"The site where the plane burned," he said, his voice monotone. "The man wants me to visit where his wife died."

I AWOKE TO THE RUMBLE OF THUNDER AND A rain-fresh wind filtering through the thatched roof. It was 6 a.m. and Tomlinson was already up. He had a fire going outside, coffee steaming. I took a leak off the dock, went for a swim, and returned as storm clouds assembled in pale light to the east.

"I dread this," Tomlinson said, handing me a mug of coffee.

I took a sip, then another, saying, "It's bad. But it's not that bad," trying to get him to laugh.

He did. But then said, "I mean visiting the crash site."

"I know."

"I'm pulling out today around noon. Sam gave me the news a little bit ago. Vue and I are driving to some hacienda near the Panamanian border, taking excess gear to lighten the load. It's only a hundred twenty miles and he's got a rented Land Rover. I'll fly home from San José or Panama City tomorrow night."

I was surprised.

"Visiting the wreck is the only reason he wanted me to come on the trip. He wants to know what his wife experienced when the plane caught fire. And any other details. He's aware I have psychic powers."

I said, "So he's told me. But I'm curious—what convinced him? He's not what you would call a frivolous man."

"You can say that twice. He's about as warm as a brass hemorrhoid tester. But . . . likeable, too, in a weird way."

"You never met before the party on Useppa?"

"No."

"Do you agree his interest in Buddhism was just an act?"

"I've known that since we left for Key West."

"So you weren't invited because of your book?"

"I doubt if he read it."

I asked again. "Then what convinced him you have psychic powers? I assume he hasn't told you the reason."

Tomlinson's reaction was unexpected. I've known him so long, I can read his mannerisms nearly as well as he can read mine. There was guilt in his expression—confusion, too.

"As a matter of fact, he *did* tell me. Not everything. But enough to jog the old memory banks. And to know what he said is true." His laughter was forced. "Kind of a shocker. I'm a little embarrassed I didn't tell you."

"You've known for a while?"

"Since a few days after the party. We met privately for drinks on Cabbage Key. He rented the Cabbage Patch so we could talk confidentially."

I was looking beyond a hedge of banana plants, where stalks grew heavy-fingered like yellow fists. President Wilson and Vue were walking toward us as I said, "There's no reason to be embarrassed. For the last couple of years, your memory's been returning a little piece at a time, I know that. Electroshock therapy erases memory. It's documented."

The gentle smile on his face told me he was aware I was being kind. "Well . . . truth is, I've remembered bits and pieces of what he told me for quite a while. I guess I was ashamed. You see"—he broke off several bananas and tossed one to me—"back when I was at Harvard I got involved in a research project. I needed money.

Didn't know what I was getting into—a secret sort of deal at the time. But it all came out later. A program called 'Stargate.'"

I did a bad job of hiding my surprise because then Tomlinson said, "So now you understand why I'm ashamed. I worked for those right-wing weirdoes more than a year."

I was familiar with the project. There was no right-wing association and only critics called it "Stargate." The Pentagon referred to the project as "Asymmetrical Intelligence-Gathering Research." It began in the 1970s when U.S. intelligence agencies learned that the Soviets were recruiting clairvoyants and telepathic savants to work as "psychic spies."

The CIA and U.S. Defense Intelligence Agency took it seriously enough to establish a similar program. The project was funded until the mid-'90s, and employed many dozens of "psychics" over a period of twenty years. Some in the intelligence community say it produced usable product, others say it was a waste of millions.

I was smiling despite the implications. "You worked for the CIA?"

"Isn't that a kick in the pants?" Tomlinson said. "Somewhere, right now, Tim Leary is rolling over in his grave. But it's not like the agency gave me a decoder ring and showed me the secret handshake. I sat in a room at a military base in Maryland while a guy in a lab coat asked me questions. I remember looking at a lot of maps and pointing at places. That particular extrasensory gift is called 'Remote Viewing.'"

"You convinced researchers you had the gift?"

"They told me I had the highest score ever recorded on their test. A lot of what happened, though, is still foggy. Big chunks missing."

I said, "The highest score?"

"Well, they said one of the highest scores. But I knew what they meant."

It was the way the agency would have couched it. He was telling the truth.

Tomlinson, eating a banana, waved at Wilson and Vue, who were close now. "Sam found the classified records. That's how he knew. He told me what he wanted before you showed up on Cayo Costa—quite a shock to see you, Doc.

"No offense," he added, "but I told Sam you were very negative about the whole psychic thing. You might get in the way. I love you like a brother, man. But I still can't figure out why he asked you to come along."

THE WRECKAGE OF THE CESSNA HAD NOT BEEN removed, as I expected. In isolated places worldwide, carcasses of planes are routinely abandoned where they fall. Their fragility makes a mockery of wealth and complexity. I've seen locals smile a little as they pass by.

I wasn't prepared, however, when Tomlinson told us, "They didn't find all the bodies."

I translated for the guide as the president and Vue stared at my friend as if he were making a bad joke.

"Bodies from the plane, you mean? There were only

seven people aboard." His face pale, Wilson was looking at the stone marker beyond the runway where trees thinned, and the lake, six hundred feet below, was a motionless blue. Next to the stone were five white crosses and two Stars of David.

The Nicaraguan government's way of honoring the First Lady and her group.

Tomlinson, with eyes closed, facing the jungle opposite the marker, repeated, "They didn't find all the bodies."

The wreckage was a quarter mile from the huts, all uphill until we got near the top, where there was a natural terrace—ideal for the small runway. After lighting incense and candles, Tomlinson had walked around the perimeter, saying:

> *Whatever beings are gathered here . . . of the land below or skies above. Listen respectfully to what is being uttered now . . .*
>
> *May all those beings develop loving-kindness toward human progeny. They that brought them offerings by day and by night, let extraterrestrial beings diligently keep watch over them . . .*

They were words from one of his favorite Buddhist sutras. He repeated them over and over, as a chant.

But after half an hour, uncomfortable with religious ceremony, I slipped off alone. The rain forest on the north side of the volcano was dense. Beneath canopy shadows, the chirring of tree frogs was an oscillating chorus. I found several tiny frogs, three inches long, that were iridescent scarlet with black flecks at the dorsum. They were from the genus *Dendrobate,* which the indigenous people call "poison dart frogs." Roasted, their skin secretes alkaloid poison that's deadly—effective when arrows are dipped in it.

Flora and fauna I saw were common to the region. It was the end of Central America's rainy season. In this cloud forest, water had been converted into rivulets of vines, rivers of fern, and pools of green forest canopy, water's flow slowed by absorption, then delayed by photosynthesis.

I jotted details in my notebook.

When I returned, Tomlinson and the president were alone near the stone monument talking. Tomlinson had his hand on the man's shoulder, comforting him.

When they rejoined our group, Wilson's face had paled, but he was stone-jawed, in control. It was then that Tomlinson stopped abruptly, closed his eyes for a moment, and said it: *They didn't find all the bodies.*

When the president snapped, "Damn it, that's impossible!" Tomlinson touched a finger to his lips and waved for us to follow.

He walked like a man using a stick to dowse for water, feeling his way. He led us through jungle, down the volcano, to a wall of vines that, when parted, revealed a stone cistern. It was ancient; the hieroglyphics on the outside were Maya-like.

Tomlinson leaned over the cistern for a few seconds, then spun away, hands on hips. His chest was heaving as he asked, "You said the plane was supposed to pick up a sick woman and her child?"

The president was moving toward the cistern. "That's right. A pregnant woman. But she and her son left earlier in a boat. That's what locals told our investigators."

"They never got to the boat."

"Oh no. Don't tell me—"

Tomlinson moved to slow Wilson as I stepped to the opening. I looked, turned away, cleaned my glasses, then looked again. There was an adipose stink about the place.

"You don't need to see this, sir."

The cistern was ten feet deep. At the bottom, among forest detritus, were two bodies, an adult and a child, judging from their sizes. The corpses were contorted by what may have been abrupt muscle contractions prior to death. Animals had been working on them for months. Two charred mummies. Their skulls were discernible, shrink-wrapped in skin.

Both had been set ablaze, possibly after death, but, more likely, while they were alive.

Their contracted poses were significant. But it wasn't only that. The screams of seven people in a burning plane wouldn't have been enough for Praxcedes Lourdes.

He liked to watch his victims run.

18

Tomlinson and Vue left by boat before noon with some of our gear to lighten the plane. It would give us additional range and speed. But Vue had brought a couple of boxes for us—food, I was told—so the difference would not be striking.

Once ashore, they would drive a rented Land Rover south to a safe place to overnight.

As they said good-bye, I heard the president tell Tomlinson, "When you get back to Sanibel, you will receive an envelope containing the information I promised you."

I wondered if a similar envelope would be awaiting me.

An hour later, a single-engine aircraft—another Cessna, Wilson said—circled the island once, showing an interest that made us both uneasy. The Maule was covered with camouflage netting, but that was no guarantee.

It was rare to see a plane in this part of the world. The airstrip hadn't been used in months. Locals still traveled by dugout canoe and fished with nets woven by hand.

The plane banked as if to make another pass but turned south instead. Had the pilot lost interest? Or had thunderheads, stalled to the east, forced him onward?

I'd been trying to buy time, hoping General Juan Rivera would show, but also thinking *I don't need a weapon. A bullet is not how Praxcedes Lourdes should die.*

No, I didn't need a weapon. I knew what it was like to have the man by the throat; to feel reflex contractions caused by fear, not flames. Bullies are driven by cowardice. It was the only normal human characteristic I could assign to Lourdes.

But Kal Wilson was an impatient man. This island was now poison to him.

"We need to get under way." Wilson had been worried about the weather, now there was a plane to think about.

I said, "I really think you should cut me loose. He was here, I can pick up his trail. When the local police arrive, I can talk to them. Maybe they'll know something."

Wilson's expression said *Why are we having this discussion again?* "That was six months ago."

"But Lourdes grew up here. There's a settlement of Miskito Indians not far, on the coast. They have a communications network better than any telegraph. They'll know he's out. They might know where he is. They're terrified of him, so they keep track."

Wilson wouldn't budge. "We have to be in Panama by

tomorrow. Why are you stalling? You're expecting someone, aren't you?"

I told him yes, that I'd e-mailed a man who might have
the equipment I need.

"Who?"

Wilson had every reason to despise Juan Rivera, even
though both men had been out of the political spotlight
for years. But that's not the reason I replied, "I'd rather
not say, sir. He would expect me to keep his name confi-
dential."

"Did he tell you that?"

"No. But I would expect the same of him."

"Sorry. You said you need at least a day to get set up?
This will give you extra time."

No, I had said I needed a week but didn't correct him.
The president was still shaken by what we'd found on the
rim of the volcano and by what Tomlinson had told him.

What that was, exactly, I didn't know. I'd gotten Tomlinson off alone, but he was emotionally drained. I didn't
chide him when he opened the silver cigarette case he carries while traveling and lit another joint.

"Bad?"

He inhaled, waited for a moment, attuned to his internal chemistry, before he exhaled. "Horrible." Meaning,
how Wray Wilson had died. "Praxcedes Lourdes was
here. The evil one. He had three or four men with him."

Although the case was plea-bargained, Tomlinson had
been deposed as a witness against Lourdes because he is
friends with my son. Tomlinson had actually faced Lourdes once, in a courthouse hallway.

Since that day, he has always referred to Lourdes as "The Evil One," as if the term should be capitalized.

There are times when I wrestle with the possibility that Tomlinson really does have extrasensory powers. But then I remind myself it is a mistake to confuse empathy with telepathy. For Tomlinson, the pain of others is as palpable as vapor, as contagious as a virus. It seeps into his brain, then his soul. He doesn't just empathize, he absorbs. Tomlinson says he loves people for their flaws because flaws are the conduits of humanity.

Like many who spend their lives outdoors, he also has a heightened awareness of sensory anomalies. The stink of charred adipose is uncommon at sea.

I asked, "What did you tell the president?"

"The truth. You can't lie to a man like that. But I softened it as much as I could. There were details . . . details about those poor, poor people . . . what they went through before . . . before . . ."

Tomlinson stopped as if waiting for pain to fade. He looked at me with his wise, sad Buddha eyes. "For Wray Wilson, the worst part was the silence of the flames. Water, wind, earth, and fire—all elemental. But combustion isn't a substance, it's a chain reaction. To a woman unable to hear? Fire is deafening."

I packed the camouflage netting as the president went through his preflight. We left the volcanoes of Lake Nicaragua behind, flying south.

Less than two hours later, we landed at a place I hadn't seen for many years—the Azuero Peninsula, on the Pacific coast of Panama. Rock, opal sea, jungle. There was a tuna research facility nearby operated by my friend Vern Scholey.

As Wilson idled the plane toward what looked like a seaside cattle ranch, he told me, "A man's supposed to meet us here at three. But we're early and he's one of those pompous asses who's always late."

I knew he wasn't talking about Vern.

Four hours later, at sunset, the man arrived. Turned out the pompous ass was Kal Wilson's adversary, General Juan Rivera.

Rivera hadn't gotten my e-mail. And he wasn't in Panama to see me.

19

General Rivera told President Wilson, "The American newsman Walt Danson is in Panama searching for you, old friend. I am saddened I must damage our reunion with this bad news. If he was not such a famous *journalista*" — the general's eyes sought mine in a knowing way — "I would have him kidnapped. But kidnapping famous people is time-consuming. They are demanding, and so nervous about how their food is cooked. As you comprehend, we have very little time."

Wilson was looking at me. "How could Danson possibly know I'm in Panama?"

"It is not a thing I understand," Rivera replied, moving imperceptibly to distance himself from me. "I can only tell you it is true. Something else that is more bad news: Only two hours ago, I was sitting at an outdoor cantina in the jungle watching the news on CNN, and the sexy *gringa*—Shana Waters?—she was interviewing fishermen who said you purchased gas from them for your craft. This was on a beach, and she was wearing a blouse that my new wife said was quite expensive. One of the *campesinos,* he titled you 'The Chief.'"

Rivera was a showman, performing for an audience even when there was none. He was enjoying this chance to impress the president with his English. I interrupted. "Did she describe the plane?"

"Yes. Very accurately."

"What about the location?" If Waters was on our trail, she might be selfish enough to keep the story exclusive.

"She said . . . Honduras. 'Somewhere in Honduras,' is the way she said it. Such a sexy *gringa*—in my humble opinion. The entire world is searching for you, Mr. President. The news is on every screen. But if Shana Waters succeeds, do you think it is possible that you could arrange an introduction?"

As an aside to me, Rivera added, "It is a thing I miss. Being interviewed by the *journalistas* of New York and California, particularly women. They are so . . . *receptivo*. It is one of the reasons I have decided to"—he stumbled for a moment—"decided to abandon my retirement from the revolution." He smiled. "Do you not agree, Mr. President? It is the time for revolution once again."

Wilson, who was not smiling, said, "Yes, General, I agree. It *is* time for a change. First, though, we have to deal with this security problem. How do Waters and Danson know I'm in Central America? And for Waters to broadcast from the exact spot where we refueled—that was an unscheduled stop, remember?" He was speaking to me, as my brain reviewed the linkage: *Key West . . . Danson, Waters . . . Tim the Gnome . . . Tomlinson . . . Me . . . Wilson . . . Vue . . . Rivera.*

I said, "Only you, me, and Tomlinson knew about that stop."

"Is it possible one of the fishermen recognized me?"

"No, they didn't get close enough. If someone had binoculars, maybe, but unlikely. No one was expecting us."

Both men were now staring as I considered alternative explanations, both probably wondering who had tipped off the TV people, me or Tomlinson.

We were in the foreman's cabin of a working cattle ranch owned by a friend of Rivera. The room smelled of leather and horses. Rivera had ordered privacy. Except for men cutting wood in the distance, the president and I had seen no one until Rivera landed on the beach in an old Huey helicopter, blasting sand and spooking horses. With him were four men in military khaki, plus the pilot. All wore sidearms.

As I approached Rivera, we both spoke at the same time, surprised, the general saying "What are *you* doing here?" as I asked "How did you *find* me?"

It wasn't until Rivera greeted Wilson with a bear hug that I understood that the powerful, unseen force providing assistance to the president was the same man I wanted to assist me.

What had Wilson said in Key West?

I trust old enemies more than I do new friends. At least I know what they want.

Something like that.

I was sure the maxim now applied to me.

RIVERA WAS TELLING US HOW HE KNEW WALT Danson was in Panama to search for the president.

"He arrived in the capital this afternoon, trying to charter a helicopter. He came in a craft from Managua too small, he said, for his crew and equipment."

I was picturing the single-engine plane that had circled us, as Rivera continued, "Walt Danson went to the only *avión* company in Central America that I do not trust. Those *malvados*. But even there I have extra eyes. Loyal comrades in the flying business eager to help. As you know, I own a beautiful helicopter."

Through the office window, I could see the Huey's tail section. Someone had used green spray paint in an attempt to cover MASAGUAN PEOPLE'S ARMY, stenciled in white. The aircraft had to be twenty years old. Like its owner, the Huey had seen better days.

As a young revolutionary, Rivera had been among the most charismatic figures in Central America. Like Fidel Castro, he was driven and ruthless. Unlike Castro, he actually was a good baseball player. Three years pitching in the Nicaraguan League elevated Rivera to icon status. I am a mediocre catcher; still play amateur baseball. The sport is what brought us together, even though we were on opposing sides in two revolutions.

But great revolutionaries are seldom great administrators and Rivera was no exception. He was an inspiring leader but an uninspired bureaucrat. Dressed in fatigues, with his beard and field cap, Rivera photographed like a film star. In a suit and tie, though, he looked like an out-of-shape vacuum cleaner salesman who smelled of cigars.

The apex of his career in mainstream politics, ironically, was when he outmaneuvered Wilson in a show-down over illegal Latin immigration and then publicly snubbed the U.S. president at the Conference of American States.

It was incredible that the two men had forged a secret friendship. Or maybe inevitable . . .

In Key West, Kal Wilson had admitted he was more comfortable as a hero than as president. He loved leading the charge but hated arranging tents afterward.

That was true of Rivera, I felt sure. I once saw him on horseback, leading his troops toward a Contra stronghold—not exactly a cavalry charge, but Rivera didn't turn and run when he started taking fire, nor did his troop.

In some ways, the two men shared threads of a similar destiny. Their political stars had blazed, then dimmed, at about the same time. Both were horseback anachronisms in a young, impatient world that was guided by committees and administered by computers.

The public will tolerate an incompetent politician. But not a failed hero. The people have so few.

ON THIS NOVEMBER EVENING, RIVERA WAS dressed as he had as a younger man. His camo fatigues were tight around the belly, his beard was gray, but his eyes were as brown and bright as his polished boots.

He was still a showman. Probably still ruthless. You didn't have a conversation with Rivera, you listened to a speech. I noted key points as he continued to talk, explaining at length how he knew Danson was in Panama.

Danson was accompanied by a two-man crew, he told us. They had a lot of equipment, but the Cessna from Managua had been the only plane available. They needed a larger aircraft, plus they'd somehow offended the pilot.

"Television stars are vulgar," Rivera counseled. "I have met many and can assure you of this truth. You may be aware, Mr. President, that *I* was invited to be a television star, even though I am not a vulgar man. But I refused out of loyalty to my people."

Wilson was diplomatic. "It was the viewing public's loss, General."

Because of his destination, Danson had been told he needed a helicopter, Rivera said—significant. He also wanted to charter a ten-passenger plane and keep it standing by because he expected "friends" to arrive soon. Cost was of no importance.

My guess: If Danson found the president, he planned to import a bigger crew. He was in contact with New York, so he was also aware that Shana Waters was only a half a day behind him . . . and behind us.

An example of the occupational death dance Wilson had mentioned.

Rivera said, "There is no doubt why they are here. One of my comrades overheard the cameraman mention your name. Not once but twice. They also overheard the place where the famous Danson wanted to go." Rivera was growing more serious. "My friends are very good at overhearing. There is no mistake."

The place, he said, was near the village of Muelle de San Carlos.

The general focused on me a moment. "Is that name not familiar, my old catcher friend?"

It was, but I'd been a lot of places and heard a lot of names. Then I remembered.

"John Hull owned a farm near there," I said.

Hull, with the help of the CIA, had built a dirt airstrip sizeable enough to land cargo planes. Colonel Oliver North and associates had used the strip to transport food and arms to the Contras during the war in Nicaragua.

"It is true I had a base near John Hull's, but this camp is far to the south. You should remember this property. A secret camp that is also a farm. You do not remember the excellent baseball stadium my men constructed?"

It was a rocky infield with a couple of benches, not a stadium.

"Of course," I said, smiling—until I saw that Rivera was not smiling. Danson was on his way to Rivera's secret camp, I realized. That's why he'd chartered a helicopter.

The president had figured it out. "Son of a bitch— your farm—that's where I sent Vue and Tomlinson. They're there right now, spending the night. What time did Danson's helicopter leave?"

"Only a few minutes before my comrade contacted me

with the information. That was a little more than an hour ago, after I saw the sexy *gringa* in her pretty blouse."

"How far is your camp from Panama City?"

"About an hour's flying time."

Wilson began to pace. "If Danson isn't there yet, he soon will be. *Damn it.* How could he know?"

Rivera said, "It pains me that I also must ask this question. How did the famous man learn of my secret base?"

Walt Danson had the GPS coordinates, Rivera informed us. He gave the coordinates to the pilot of the helicopter he chartered.

"The exact coordinates?" I asked.

"Yes. Written on a paper."

I turned to the president. "We're being tracked. There's a telemetry transmitter somewhere on the plane. It's the only way to explain how Waters knew where we refueled in Honduras, and why Danson—" I stopped, aware that I'd overlooked the obvious. If the plane was bugged, why wasn't Danson flying here, to the cattle ranch? Instead, he was bound for a place near the Caribbean coast.

If there was a bug, it was no longer on the plane.

Wilson was right with me. "Either Tomlinson is feeding them information, which I doubt, or there is a transmitter in the gear Vue took from the aircraft. If Vue or Tomlinson had planted the bug, they would've made sure it stayed on the aircraft. If either one of us had planted a bug, we wouldn't have allowed them to take it from the aircraft."

Reasonable. And comforting. The president's logic, by including us all, cleared us all.

The "Angel Tracker" chip in the president's shoulder had been the size of a rice grain. It would have been easy to hide a transmitter anywhere in the plane. Perhaps in one of the containers that we'd transferred to Vue's SUV.

But *who*?

I WAS REPLAYING THE LINKAGE, STILL PUZZLED, as Rivera said, "Thank God, no matter how it happened. My great worry was that you were at my camp, Mr. President. I have not explained why. The *avión* company is owned by *extranjeros*. It is a word we use."

The general looked at me for help.

I said, "The charter company is owned by *foreigners*? I don't understand. Almost everything in Panama is owned by foreigners."

"They are Muslims. But not Latin Muslims. You see? They are foreigners. Brought here by Dr. Thomas Bashir Farrish, that *cabrone*. If the famous Danson knew your location, then the foreigners would also know because it is their helicopter. They might sell the information to other journalists. Or even give it to someone who wants to kill you."

Wilson stopped pacing as the implications crystallized. "Islamicists own that charter company?"

"The same people, Mr. President, who offered money for your head. That is why I am overjoyed you are safe. With such men, the way their brains work; killing civilians, children—they are foreign in that way, also. They are *malvados*. Capable of anything."

Malvados. Evildoers.

I said, "Farrish is behind all this?"

"He's a main player," Wilson replied.

"Because of politics? Or religion?" Change the political makeup of Central America and Panama could cancel the Indonesian company's lease.

His expression severe, Wilson said, "Both. Islamicists consider me a prize. I'm a *symbol.* The cleric who offered the reward is Altif Halibi, an Indonesian. Halibi is a disciple of the cleric who converted the billionaire playboy into a billionaire Islamicist."

Meaning Thomas Farrish.

"Halibi visits Farrish in Panama often. Either one of them—or their lieutenants—could've hired Praxcedes Lourdes, along with a dozen other psychopaths, to kill me. Halibi doesn't have a million dollars to pay as a reward. Farrish does."

Four days with Kal Wilson and I finally understood why he wanted to be at Panama's Independence Day ceremony. All the "principals" would be there, he had said.

I was picturing it, imagining what my role would be, as Wilson told Rivera, "If Farrish's people believe I'm at your camp, they could send someone after me. We've got to warn Vue. Is there a way to contact them, General?"

Rivera appeared embarrassed. "All winter, at that place, we had a generator and a telephone line. Even the Internet and a hot tub. But then the rainy season arrived, and after so many storms—" He shrugged. They were all out of service.

I suggested, "Morse code?"

Wilson said, "I can try. Vue and I are supposed to make contact at nine and again at eleven. But maybe he's already hooked up." As the president jogged toward the bedroom, where he'd placed his bag, he called, "Does your camp have an airstrip? Or a lake?"

"No, I am sorry. Besides, it will soon be too dark for your plane to land."

Through the office window, beyond the helicopter, the orange rim of the Pacific was fading. It was twenty to seven, and I was thinking of Tomlinson. He'd had a rough day, finding the bodies, and then driving hours to a remote farm. He would be in a marijuana-and-rum stupor by now—maybe for the best.

"General Rivera," I said as I opened my duffel, "I need to borrow your helicopter. And a weapon."

"Of course. I will come with you. But"—Rivera looked toward the bedroom where Wilson had disappeared—"but it is very important that the president and I are in Panama tomorrow morning—"

I interrupted. "That's why you're staying here. The president's security—and your security, General—that's primary. All I need is your pilot."

Wilson reappeared at the door. "I am not going off and abandoning Vue, goddamn it! You can shit-can that nonsense right now, mister."

I said patiently, "You're not abandoning him, sir. You're sending me. Our bargain was that I get you here and then back home safely. Let me do my job . . . Sam."

Rivera said, "Sam? Who is this Sam?"

I had my shirt off, pulling on a black wool watch sweater. I would need it in the helicopter. My jungle boots were in the duffel, too, worn soft but glassy with wax. "Mr. President, if you have plans for Panama now's the time to share the details. I'll get to the Canal Zone tomorrow, but I may be late."

"But what if Danson's still at the general's camp? He'll recognize you from Key West."

"I'll offer him a drink and wait for Shana Waters to show up, then—" I paused. My sarcasm had produced an accidental clarity.

I was kneeling, tying my boots. I looked up. "Shana Waters's tape recorder—the one Danson gave her. Where is it?"

Wilson stepped from the bedroom toward me, then began to nod. "That damn *digital recorder*."

I said, "I listened to it on the flight from Key West, then gave it back to you."

Wilson was still nodding. "And I put it in the box with the things we didn't need. Vue took it. The bug's in her damn digital recorder!"

It made sense. Danson had tracked the signal to Lake Nicaragua, then either followed the Land Rover until he realized he needed a helicopter or maybe until his pilot decided he'd had enough and dumped the crew in Panama City.

Wilson said, "Danson, that shrewd old bastard. He gave Shana a recorder bugged with a telemetry chip. Maybe to blackmail her or just to keep track of where she was. That clever bastard."

An expensive recorder. Something she wouldn't throw in a drawer.

But Waters was now tracking Danson. How?

The president said, "Maybe they had exchanged gifts at Christmas."

I thought about it and nearly smiled. "Yeah." Two of a kind.

I was no longer concerned about TV reporters.

I was picturing my friend alone on a farm—a place with pigs, most likely—and Praxcedes Lourdes outside, watching from the darkness, assessing Tomlinson's facial qualities.

The two had met, once, in a Florida courthouse.

Lourdes would remember.

20

Five miles out, the helicopter pilot said "Fire" as if he wanted me to pick up a weapon and open fire. A moment later, though, he said, "Something's on fire," and I knew he was talking about Rivera's camp.

I was in the cargo hold and couldn't see what the pilot was seeing. He said it in such a flat, indifferent tone, I doubted the seriousness.

The man was hard to read. When we lifted off from the cattle ranch, I had asked if he was going to use conventional lights or night-vision gear to land. It was dark by that time. He had replied, "Neither. I've landed in that field at least five times. Why would I want to see it again?"

Pilots.

Rivera's camp was farther than I remembered. We were in the air more than an hour. I sat alone near the open door as we flew over jungle, the forest canopy awash in mist. Occasionally, I saw pockets of light: isolated villages, fires burning, the night strongholds of rural people linked by darkness, strung like pearls, bright and incremental, from a thousand feet.

Ahead, a half-moon was rising, white as hoarfrost in the tropic night. Its surface was pocked by geologic cataclysm and a wisp of earth shadow.

At a hundred twenty knots, there was the illusion that the moon was pulling us as if we were waterborne, suctioned by tide ever deeper into darkness. The thrumming of helicopter blades echoed in the lunar silence. The silence allowed me to think, to visualize.

I'd been to this camp before, but Rivera had drawn a rough map anyway, and I memorized it.

It also gave me time to assemble, then dry-fire the weapons the president had unexpectedly provided—they were in the boxes Vue had loaded onto the plane. There were five to choose from: a rifle, two handguns, a shotgun, and a submachine gun.

I selected two: a Russian-made sniper rifle with sound arrester and a pistol. Both had been fitted with infrared sights. Put the red dot on your target, squeeze the trigger.

I was tempted to select a second pistol that was also Russian made—a rare PSS silent pistol, used by KGB assassins. It was palm-sized and used special ammunition that, when fired, was no louder then the click of its own trigger.

Where had Wilson found a KGB silent pistol?

But it was a specialty piece and held only three rounds, so I left it with Rivera and Wilson. I was comfortable with the weapons I selected.

With chambers empty, I fired them over and over as we flew southeast. I worked the slide and bolts until my fingers were intimate. I loaded the magazines, learning the subtleties of their feeder springs.

The rifle had a Startron scope, which I had used before. The occasion was made necessary by two former KGB agents who aspired to be salesmen.

When I touched the scope's power switch, the jungle below was transformed into green daylight, minutely detailed. Except for the iridescent glow and the slight whirring sound, we might have been flying at midday.

I adjusted the focus and experimented with the scope's windage and elevation knobs. With the scope off, I activated the laser sight and aimed at the jungle. A red dot kept pace beneath us, sliding over treetops.

For each weapon, there was high-tech ammunition. Prefragmented bullets: maximum stopping power; no ricochet.

I also had a knife, the *hadek* I'd taken from the bearded killer. And I had written instructions from the president, sealed in an envelope.

He had told me what was expected of me tomorrow in Panama. Wilson had been stationed there as a Navy pilot, he knew the area well and made suggestions about what to look for and where to position myself. He jotted a few key words, he said, so I wouldn't forget.

The man really was *good* at details.

* * *

ONE OF RIVERA'S MEN WAS SITTING FORWARD, next to the pilot. The general had insisted. His name was Lucius. He was twentysomething and humorless. Lucius had a fuck-you-kill-them-all attitude. It matched my mood perfectly.

Rivera's men were notoriously loyal. I was delighted with the general's choice.

The helicopter's pilot didn't introduce himself—not unusual in Central America when circumstances are questionable. He spoke Spanish with an Israeli accent and English with a Mississippi accent. So when he said "Fire!" it came out "Fah-er!" sounding like a Jackson door gunner I'd once flown with.

That's why I had my hand on the pistol when he elaborated: "Up ahead. There's something on fire."

The chopper's cargo area was lighted with overhead red bulbs. I secured my weapons and ducked forward. I put a hand on the right seat, steadying myself, as we tilted in descent. Ahead, I saw a petroleum blaze, black smoke boiling starward.

We angled lower, accelerating. I felt the temperature drop as we traced the course of a river, the quarry scent of water fresh in the cabin. But then there was heat and the smell of combusting rubber.

"Helicopter crash?" I was thinking of Danson.

"No, diesel doesn't burn like that. That's gas." As we got closer, the pilot said, "Yeah. It's a car."

I whispered, *"Christ."*

Rivera had told me the only vehicle that should be at the farm was the Land Rover that Tomlinson and Vue had driven from Nicaragua.

"If you spot any vehicle larger than a mule," he had said, "expect trouble."

There was a hacienda now visible and we buzzed it doing a hundred knots at treetop level. As we passed, the cockpit jolted unexpectedly and the pilot shouted "Shit" in Spanish, a word that has an ironic, musical sound.

"What's wrong?" I thought maybe the vehicle had exploded beneath us.

"Some *pendejo* is down there shooting!"

There was a sound of a hammer hitting aluminum, three times fast, and the helicopter jolted again.

"Hold on!"

We banked into a climb so steep that I nearly went skidding out the open doors.

Clinging to the pilot's chair, I could look straight down and see an SUV burning. It was the Land Rover.

A safe distance away, there was also the shape of a pickup truck. Rivera's camp had visitors.

Yes, expect trouble.

WHEN I TOLD THE PILOT TO LAND, HE DIDN'T even turn to look. "When I'm being shot at? Fuck you, I'm not getting paid enough." He began to bank west, saying, "We'll be back in Panama City in time for drinks at the Elks Club."

In Spanish, I said to the twenty-year-old curmudgeon

Lucius, "Order him to land. General Rivera will hear of this."

Lucius was wearing a special forces boonie hat and tiger-striped camo. He had unbuckled the seat belt, grabbed his assault rifle, and was facing the open cargo door ready to return fire—reassuring.

But he surprised me, saying, "I don't care what you tell Rivera. I would like to put a bullet in those *culos,* take their money and necklaces. But if the pilot chooses not to land, that is his decision. The old fool doesn't frighten me."

He was speaking of the general.

I was no longer reassured.

"I am asking for your help. There are friends of mine down there."

"Why should I care about your friends? What are they to me?"

Lucius's tough-guy act, I realized, *was* an act. He sounded relieved.

I returned my attention to the pilot. "Cut me loose. After that, I don't care what you do. Put us on the ground long enough for me to bail and you've done your job."

We were now climbing as we turned. "No way. We've taken, what, at least ten rounds? My advice to you is, get your ass back to the cargo hold where you belong and shut the fuck up."

These were Rivera's men? In Nicaragua, I had watched his men walk into fire following the general on horseback. Rivera had fallen further than I realized.

The .45 caliber pistol was in a holster on my belt. I put

my hand on it as I asked Lucius, "Is the pilot in command or are you in command?"

Lucius gave me a look of disgust. "There is no one in command. We are here because we get paid."

I was losing patience. "My friends are in trouble. Please tell the pilot to land."

Lucius tilted the barrel of his M16 toward me—a threat. "The important thing, *yanqui,* is that you are not in command. If the pilot has decided we are returning to Panama City for drinks at the Elks Club, then that is what we will do. The pilot gave you an order. Move your *culo*—"

I was watching the helicopter's altimeter. We were at three hundred feet. I didn't let Lucius finish. With my left hand, I reached as if to touch the pilot's shoulder. But then I turned my palm outward and grabbed the barrel of the assault rifle and yanked it from his hands.

I had the pistol drawn. I jammed the barrel into the back of the pilot's neck as I said to Lucius, "Don't point."

I tossed the assault rifle out the open door.

"You idiot *cabrone*!"

"You want to go after it?" I shoved the pistol barrel hard into the soft spot beneath the pilot's skull. "Drop us down to a hundred feet."

"*Why?*"

"Because it'll kill him if I throw him out from here."

"You're bluffing."

Yes, I was bluffing, but also watching as Lucius unsnapped his holster. I swung the pistol toward his face, hoping the little red laser dot would blind him and also scare him. Lucius shaded his eyes with his left hand as he pulled the gun with his right.

"Don't do it!"

He wouldn't stop. As Lucius lifted the gun toward me, I put the pulsing red dot on his boot and fired.

"Mother of God!" The gun spun from his hand as he fell against the chopper's controls, clutching his foot. The helicopter rocked, began to climb, and nearly stalled.

The gunshot was so loud that, for a moment, I thought the slug had caromed off the deck and hit me in the temple. My ears were ringing.

As the pilot struggled to regain control, I reached and dragged Lucius into the aisle.

"You're insane, man. You're gonna kill us!"

I stuck the pistol against his neck again. "Insanity's for amateurs. Do exactly what I tell you to do. Understand?"

Lucius was still screaming, trying to get his boot off.

"Okay! But keep that kid away from the controls. Christ, he's getting blood all over everything."

I told the pilot to do three touch-and-goes—brief landings, each with only a few seconds on the ground.

"Circle the hacienda, but stay a couple hundred meters away."

There were men with weapons near the burning Land Rover. I hoped to confuse them. At which spot had the helicopter off-loaded attackers?

The third time we touched down, I slipped off the landing skids onto the ground. I kept the pistol pointed at the pilot. He gave me the finger as the helicopter lifted away.

21

Fifty yards from the burning Land Rover, I saw why I hadn't been confronted as I approached the adobe ranch house, with its garden corrals, and horses grazing in the outfield of Rivera's homemade baseball diamond.

Shana Waters had the full attention of the men sent to assassinate Kal Wilson. Three of the men, anyway.

Maybe there were others out there in the darkness, decoyed to the helicopter's first or second landing spots. Or inside the house, where another fire was burning, judging from the strobing windows.

But I doubted it.

The men recognized Shana. It was in the familiar, leering way they said her name: *Shaaa-nah!*

It was not unexpected. People in remote villages worldwide who five years ago didn't have telephones now

watch satellite television by the light of cooking fires, indifferent to the diesel hammering of a generator.

An American TV star alone in the jungle? A fantasy
opportunity they were not going to miss.

Or maybe the men had already gotten to her and were
back again. The expensive blouse that Rivera had found
fascinating was torn at the shoulder and her hair was a
mess. She'd been carrying a backpack and its contents
were scattered on the ground.

But the woman was not yielding without a fight.

Waters had her back to the burning car, holding a
pitchfork. It was three-tonged, the kind used for lobbing
hay to cattle. As the men circled, she jabbed the pitchfork
at them. Each time she lunged, the men dodged out of
danger, laughing and chanting her name. *Shaaa-nah!*

When they laughed, she swore. The woman had a
New Yorker's command of profanity.

It only made them laugh harder, and they conversed
among themselves in languages I'd heard recently—
Halloween night; the men who paddled to Ligarto Island
to kill Kal Wilson.

Indonesian and Arabic.

These weren't the same men, but, like the others, all
three had automatic rifles slung over their shoulders.
They'd come to kill.

Had they?

I'd hoped to hear Tomlinson's voice call from the house.
Or Vue's. Instead, there was only the snap of flames as the
SUV's interior and tires burned. And the leering laughter
of the men as they taunted the famous broadcaster.

But the woman was tiring. Pack behavior is choreographed to exhaust prey, not overpower it. It is the saddest dance in nature. Shana's eyes were glassy; her slacks mud-stained . . . or bloodstained.

She was nearly done. The men knew it. They had not shot her for a reason.

The wind stirred . . . then shifted.

I was crouched, watching from the shadows, but then stood taller, testing with my nose. The garbage-dump smell of burning rubber was replaced, for a moment, by the scent of burning meat.

The stink of scorched adipose tissue is distinctive. The stink was coming from the open windows of the house.

I looked from the house to the men.

I, too, was carrying weapons. I holstered my pistol, slipped the rifle off my shoulder, and slammed the bolt back, shucking a round into the chamber.

Certain sounds are also distinctive.

The laughter stopped. The men turned to look. So did Shana Waters.

I drew the pistol and walked toward the fire.

I was holding the rifle at waist level in my left hand, the pistol in my right.

IN ENGLISH, I SAID, "WHAT HAPPENED HERE?"

The woman's expression was a mix of shock and rage. "They burned Walt Danson *alive*! For no reason! They killed everyone!"

"The president's bodyguard?" I had trouble assembling the next sentence. "And a friend of mine—Tomlinson?"

"*Everyone!*"

I felt a slow, chemical chill in the back of my head. It radiated through the brain stem, to my chest.

Tomlinson dead, Vue dead, and three more, including Danson. Shana Waters had her story. If she lived to report it.

As I stepped closer, the men began to drift apart, widening the circle—a typical pack response. Their hands also moved to the slings that held their assault rifles.

"Where're the bodies?"

"In the house. It's horrible."

I indicated the three men. "Are there more?"

"There were five, but two must have left with the pilot in the helicopter. I didn't see. That's the reason I'm still alive—"

I interrupted. "I'll get details later."

My eyes moved from man to man. "Do you speak English?"

They stared at me blankly, one of them shaking his head, as Waters said, "Yes, they speak English. They're a bunch of fucking liars." She was pointing the pitchfork at them as she backed free of the circle.

In Spanish, I said to the men, "There was a man here. A *yanqui* with long hair. His name is Tomlinson. Where is he?"

I could see that they understood. They didn't answer.

"She says you killed him. Why?"

One of the men spoke. Maybe he interpreted the

expression on my face accurately. "The woman lies. We have only just arrived. We have no knowledge of what has happened here."

"That's difficult to believe. Why are you carrying weapons?"

"It is a dangerous world."

I replied, "I've heard the rumor. I will give you one more chance. Did you kill him? Or was it Praxcedes Lourdes?"

They knew Lourdes. I could tell by their reaction. The man said, "We know nothing."

"You know how to lie, that's clear."

"Believe what you want. We saw the fire and came to help this silly *puta*. Call the police, if you like. We will only speak to the police or our attorney. And stop pointing those ridiculous guns at us or we will have *you* arrested."

Attack your accuser—an old gambit.

One of the men managed to laugh. The third man appeared terrified. Of the three, he was the only one with good instincts.

I thumbed the pistol's hammer as I said to Waters, "Do you understand Spanish?"

"A little."

She hadn't understood.

"They want us to call the police. They want their attorney."

"They're a bunch of murderers, for God's sake—"

"Do you have a cell phone?"

"Of course, but there's no signal. I tried while they were—"

"Walk toward the house. Maybe you'll get a signal there. These men know their rights."

"But I tried to call a dozen times!"

"Try again. I'll stay here."

"But why?"

"*Do it.*"

When Waters was a dozen yards away, I shot the first man in the chest, the second man in the side of the head, and the third man in the back. Two shots each. Stop-action. Like film frames of a man attempting to turn and run.

It's not like in the old westerns. No matter where you shoot a man, he continues to function until the hydraulics or the electrical systems fail.

The man who told me he would only speak to the police or his lawyer was still moving. I stepped close enough so that the pistol was directly over his head. His eyes were open, looking up at me, and he lifted his chin, exposing his neck—a reflexive gesture of submission I have witnessed before in men about to die. It is a primitive request: Be quick, be painless.

Waters, I realized, was watching.

"Keep walking!"

The woman turned. I fired.

22

Walt Danson, the television star, had not died a Hollywood death.

Nor had his two crewmen.

Praxcedes Lourdes had enjoyed himself here. Shana Waters had watched through the window, she said, until she couldn't stomach it anymore, then run away.

"What could I have done to help? Me against five men? Six, really, because our own fucking pilot set us up—the coward never got out of the helicopter. And my damn cell phone was useless!"

Shock, as it fades, is commonly replaced by guilt.

Waters had caught up with Danson as he was boarding the helicopter in Panama. They had compromised, using the same helicopter and sharing Danson's crew.

They were disappointed not to find the former president at the camp, but they both recognized Vue; Tomlinson, too. Still a damn good story, she said, even though Vue refused to talk.

Danson and his crew were setting up outside the hacienda getting ready to shoot, so Waters decided to take a look around. Maybe Wilson was at the camp but *hiding*.

When the five men arrived in a Toyota pickup truck, she was near the baseball diamond on the far edge of the property. Waters heard the first scream as she was returning to the house.

"It's the only thing that saved me. My God, to think how close I came . . ." The woman put a hand to her stomach, eyes dazed, as if she might vomit. "By that time, they'd herded everyone into the house. They knew who Walt was. Those bastards had watched him on satellite. An American *anchorman*. So they went after poor Walt right away."

At first, she thought the men were robbers. Waters watched through a side window as they collected billfolds and jewelry. Tomlinson got some abuse because he had neither, she said.

"But then *he* came in. A guy the size of a football player, smoking a cigar."

It was Praxcedes Lourdes, though the woman didn't know his name.

They were all wearing ski masks, she said, or had their faces wrapped—turbans were easily adapted.

"But the big man wore this bizarre silk mask, the kind they use in operas. It was white, with huge Oriental eyebrows and a fucking smile. Like a clown, but with an opening so he could smoke."

Yes, it was Lourdes.

Lourdes always kept his face covered because of his scars—the failed plastic surgeries, too. He'd been burned to the bone on the cheeks, much of his chin, and the top of his head. His mouth was an exposed wedge of teeth, like a dental schematic—skeletal, like a cadaver used in medical school.

He might seem a sympathetic figure, unless you knew the truth. He'd been scarred by a fire he set himself while murdering his family.

Lourdes sometimes wore surgical gauze, or bandage wrap, plus sunglasses—practical, when traveling by day. Most often, though, he preferred a monk's habit, because of the hood, and he liked masks, which are common in Central America. During the war in Nicaragua, rebel Contras often wore light mesh masks that allowed them to eat and drink without revealing their identities.

It sounded like the mask Waters was describing.

"He had one of those propane torches, the kind with the screw-on cylinder. He used his cigar to light it. I could hear the hissing noise even through the window while he adjusted the flame."

By that time, she said, the men had taped Danson's hands and tied him to a pole in the center of the main room. The rope allowed the anchorman to walk around it in a tight circle.

I pictured a pony on a leash, although Waters did not describe it that way.

Then, with everyone watching, Lourdes began to

goad Danson around the pole. Burning him with quick blasts of flame on the butt and back. Both Vue and Tomlinson attempted to intercede, but were knocked to the floor with rifle butts. Vue, she said, had to be taped like a mummy because he was so strong.

Lourdes continued his torture of the anchorman.

"One thing I found out—Walt was one tough son of a bitch. I always thought it was an act, but it wasn't. He was so damn . . . *brave*. I could have never endured what he did."

Lourdes was a performer. He often filmed victims, as I knew. He loved an audience. Torturing a TV star with men watching was the sort of thing he would enjoy.

Her breath catching, Waters said, "I thought it would go on forever, the cruelty. But then . . . then . . . then Walt's hair caught on fire. I've never seen anything so hideous in my life. But they were *laughing*. Those men thought it was hilarious—like some sick, slapstick comedy bit. See the anchorman's hair burn!"

That's when she ran away.

SHANA WATERS HID IN THE TREES UNTIL THE HElicopter they had chartered flew away, soon followed by the truck. After waiting ten minutes, she went inside the house but got only a quick look before the truck returned and the three men surprised her.

I said, "Maybe the pilot told them he'd brought a woman. A trap."

"Maybe," she said bitterly, "but it's more likely he

thought I was dead. The coward had to realize what was going on, but he made sure he didn't see it.

"It was existential. I covered the Middle East for two years and it's the only thing that comes close. Tie men and burn them alive? I thought Kal Wilson was a spineless figurehead, but I respected Vue. And the old hippie Tomlinson? If he was a friend of yours, I'm so sorry."

We were standing near the Toyota pickup truck. I had confirmed that the keys were in it, it was fueled and ready to go. I didn't want to stay at Rivera's camp for a minute longer than was necessary.

I was nearly done. Waters had locked herself inside the truck, waiting while I searched the hacienda.

I found Danson. His hands were still taped, but he was no longer tied to the pole. In an adrenaline-charged frenzy, he had popped the rope, only to crash into a wall so hard his head had shattered plaster. A blind sprint.

His two crewmen were in a bedroom tied facedown on a mattress that was still smoldering.

Existential. Yes.

It was not a place to linger.

But where were Vue and Tomlinson?

Because I had to hold my breath, I made several trips in and out of the house. Checked every room and closet. Then I took the night-vision scope outside and searched the property.

There were hogs in a pen.

If Tomlinson was clairvoyant, his sudden loathing for the animal suggested that's where I might find him. It was a sickening possibility, but I opened the gate and looked as the hogs scrambled free.

He wasn't there.

I returned to the house and searched some more until I was convinced there were only three bodies, not five. After that, I focused on details.

I confirmed that the TV crew's wallets and valuables were missing. I confirmed that their wallets were not in the truck or on the three men I had killed.

I went through *their* wallets. They had twenty-seven hundred dollars among them in euros, pesos, and dollars. I took the cash, and a piece of ID from each.

The only other thing valuable I found was the digital recorder that Danson had given Waters as a present.

The recorder wasn't left accidentally. It had been placed on Danson's chest as a rose might be placed on a corpse.

When I exited the hacienda for the last time, I showed the recorder to Shana. She was shocked to see it. I told her it contained a telemetry chip and watched her reaction.

"Walt was spying on me? Jesus Christ, he gave me this recorder for my birthday!"

Sincere.

"You didn't have any trouble following him across Honduras. Or finding him at the airport where he was chartering a helicopter. Why?"

"I'm a journalist. It's called having good instincts."

A lie, which I didn't challenge.

That's when I told her that Tomlinson and Vue were missing.

"How can that be?"

"Did you actually see their bodies?"

"No. I could barely make myself look at Walt, then I went to the bedroom and . . . It was so awful being inside, I just assumed . . ."

I said, "Either they hauled their bodies away in the truck and dumped them, or Tomlinson and Vue left on the helicopter with the man who was wearing the mask."

"You think they might be alive?"

I handed the recorder to her. "If they are, there's a reason. And there's a reason he left this."

There was a little red light flashing on the recorder. The recorder had a message function, Shana explained. Someone had used it.

I started the truck as she got in. In the cabin light, she read the digital time signature.

"This message is only an hour old."

"Play it."

PRAXCEDES LOURDES'S VOICE IS UNFORGET-table. He has a smoky, mixed-breed accent that grates like a wire brush on metal. When he speaks English, there is a grandiose quality, like a theatrical child desperate for attention.

Dr. Ford, you self-important twit. If you want to see your playmates alive, bring me the president today by sunset. Just the two of you, at his favorite landing strip. You know the island. I'll tell that pompous fool what his wife was screaming as she died. No tricks.

I am God to the Indios and they will be watching.

Lourdes had a drunken, raspy laugh.

I put the truck in gear and started down the dirt drive as Waters played the message again.

I said, "He didn't expect the recorder to be found until tomorrow. That's why he says 'today at sunset.'"

"The one with the mask?"

"Yes."

"What island is he talking about?"

"It doesn't matter. He's not getting the president, and Vue and Tomlinson won't live through the night."

In fact, they were probably already dead. But if Lourdes had postponed killing them, they might still have a chance—if I could find them.

"Shana? You knew exactly where we'd refueled in Honduras and you found Danson? How?"

"I told you. I'm a professional journalist. I have good instincts."

We'd come to a dirt road. I had to decide whether to turn north or south. "Can you live with it?"

"I don't know what you're talking about."

"You said you respected Vue. Can you live with the way he's going to die? Lourdes enjoys what he does. Tonight, he found five new toys. He didn't want to use them all at once. So he saved a couple for later. Like dessert. With Vue and Tomlinson, he'll make it last a long time. Can you live with that?"

She'd been using her tough broadcaster's voice. The

voice she used now, though, revealed uncertainties. "I don't see how I can help."

"If I knew where they are, maybe I could do something. I searched Danson's body. They took all his valuables—including something *you* gave him. A present, maybe. That's how you knew we'd landed in Honduras, isn't it? You were tracking Danson, stopping where he stopped. Where was the microchip? In his watch? It had to be something expensive or he wouldn't have carried it."

After a long silence, she said softly, "His wallet."

I waited.

"I had it custom-made in Singapore, so the chip was sewn in. I was there doing a story on telemetry implants. They've been putting them in pets, their children, old people with Alzheimer's. The medical advances they're making in Asia are incredible.

"Walt was so damn competitive. The idea he'd never beat me again with another exclusive seemed . . . well, fun at the time. We were always playing dirty tricks on each other."

"They have his wallet, Shana. Unless they threw it out of the helicopter, we can find them."

She opened her backpack, then a purse. "I'm sorry I didn't admit it right away. The idea of following them . . . my God"—she shuddered—"it makes my stomach roll to even think of seeing that hideous mask again."

The face was worse, though I didn't say it.

The receiver was about four inches long, with a screen the size of a matchbook. It took a minute to acquire satellites. Then she pressed the zoom toggle until an outline map of Central America appeared.

There was a flashing dot. She moved the cursor to the dot, then zoomed closer. The flashing dot remained stationary.

"They're here," she said.

Lourdes was on the Caribbean border of Costa Rica and Panama, about sixty miles away.

I expected him to be in Nicaragua.

Waters said, "We're going straight to the police and tell them, right? Or we're driving until I get a signal and then I'll call the police. *Right?*"

I had turned south, truck tires kicking gravel.

"Right," I said. "First chance we get."

23

At the side of the road, there was a sign visible in the truck's lights, the writing in Arabic and Spanish. Shana Waters asked, "What does *Granja de Panal* mean?"

"'Honey Farm.'"

The telemetry chip inside Danson's wallet was sending a steady, pulsing signal from somewhere inside the fenced confines, about a quarter mile ahead. Tomlinson and Vue might be near.

"Lourdes is staying on a honey farm? It would be funny if it wasn't so disgusting."

But it made sense. Osama bin Laden had been in the honey business before he went underground, and the honey trade is still a primary source of funds for terrorist groups. Honey is shipped in industrial drums—ideal for smuggling weapons, conventional, chemical, or nuclear. When the U.S. Treasury froze the assets of the three major honey producers in Yemen, Islamicists moved some operations to Colombia.

It was 11:15 p.m. I put the truck in gear and continued down the road, accelerating as I passed the gate with its chain and NO TRESPASSING sign. There was a light, the shape of men guarding the shadows.

I drove another quarter mile before I got out, collected my rifle, and told Shana Waters to keep driving.

"Fine! And I hope to hell I never see you again!" She floored the accelerator, showering me with dust.

We had not become friends during the trip. The woman had endured two hours of bad roads and rain, plus she was pissed off about her cell phone. I had asked to borrow it, when she finally got a signal, and called the El Panama Hotel on the chance that Curtis Tyner had checked in.

When I was done, I threw her phone out the window.

Waters was momentarily shocked, then furious.

I had to do it. She would have called the police. The woman had been only a dozen yards away when I murdered three men—something she had conspicuously not mentioned as we drove.

When I refused to go back for the phone, she had screamed, "Who *are* you!" It was an accusation, not a question.

I replied, "I'm the guy who saved your life and I'm asking for a little time in return."

She gave it to me, in a chilly, relentless silence.

As the woman sped away, I felt relieved to be alone—until I heard a distant turbine whine coming from inside the compound. It was a helicopter. I watched as the helicopter levitated above the forest canopy, its landing spotlight maintaining contact with the ground until the craft tilted southwest. The light went out and the helicopter flew away toward Panama's Pacific coast.

Damn.

Was it possible that, after hours of hard driving, I'd missed them by only a few minutes?

The telemetry receiver was in my pocket. I hurried to check the illuminated screen.

Yes, it was the same helicopter. Danson's wallet was aboard. Maybe Tomlinson and Vue were aboard, too. Or . . . could the pilot be returning to Panama City alone . . . ?

No. If he'd wanted to do that, he could have left hours ago.

I whispered profanities and checked the sky, hoping *another* helicopter would materialize. I was thinking of my call to Curtis Tyner.

It did not.

So I was alone, on a dirt road in the jungle. No transportation, no way to communicate with the outside world. Because it was possible that Tomlinson and Vue had been left behind, I decided to stick with my original plan and search the honey farm. If nothing else, I might find a vehicle to steal.

As I turned toward the fence, though, I heard the truck skid to a stop. Waters had seen the helicopter lift off. She was coming back for me.

"The only reason I'm doing this is because"—she

made a growling sound of frustration—"because you're the only person I know in this whole goddamn country who's still alive and even I'm not bitch enough to go off and leave you alone."

For the first time that night, she began to cry.

VUE WAS INSIDE.

Alive? I couldn't tell because the woman was accurate when she said they'd taped him like a mummy.

But no sign of Tomlinson. No sign of Lourdes.

I was standing on a stump at the rear of a corrugated-metal building, looking through an open window. It was a processing and packing plant, set back several hundred yards from the road. There were stacks of boxes, unused commercial hives, a conveyor belt for bottling, and a wagon-sized centrifuge.

Commercial beehives contain removable frames. When the combs are full, the frames are slotted into a centrifuge that spins the honey free. My crazed uncle, Tucker Gatrell, had kept a few hives on his ranch because he liked orange blossom honey in his coffee.

This was a prospering business, not a front for Prax-cedes Lourdes. But it *was* a front for weapons smuggling, judging from the metal crates stacked near the window and screened from the main entrance by machinery. The crates were labeled NIRINCO/PRC.

NIRINCO is China's primary weapons manufacturer. The company produces many thousands of AK-47-type assault rifles a year.

Lourdes had been hired by a wealthy and highly motivated group. It was not a commercial enterprise, it was a terrorist organization.

Vue was lying immobile next to the centrifuge, near a table where two men with beards and skullcaps sat smoking Kreteks and talking as they concentrated on assembling something—kites, I realized. Vue's guards were enjoying hobby time while he lay bound with duct tape, legs, arms, and mouth.

The temptation was to use the rifle. One round each. But I didn't know for certain these men had been involved in the earlier atrocities. Unless pathology is involved, murder always claims at least two victims. By sparing them, I would spare myself.

I checked the sky once again, hoping to see a helicopter. Nothing.

Using the gun was *tempting*.

Instead, I went to a row of active beehives not far from the processing plant. I had weaved my way through many dozens of boxlike hives on the hike from the road. Unlike the others, these hives were smaller and set apart in a screened area as if to protect them from other insects. Odd. Maybe they were prized bees.

It didn't matter to me as long as they had stingers.

I walked to the hives and stepped beneath the netting. It had been raining for most of our drive, but now it had stopped.

Typical.

Because I wanted the bees to believe it was still raining, I carried a bucket I'd found and filled from a puddle.

I chose the closest hive and began dripping water on the top. Inside, the buzzing of ten thousand bees noted the activity with a slow oscillating roar that calmed gradually as I poured more water.

Rain.

Bees are precision-coded. Unlike people, they do not venture out into the rain.

When the bucket was empty, I gently, *gently,* picked up the hive and went toward the building, walking with the smooth gait of a waiter carrying a tray. Without slowing, I stepped up onto the stump and tilted the hive through the open window . . . then I jumped back, slapping at my neck, then my arm, then my neck again.

Shit.

These bees were armed. Each sting was like an electric shock, and I was very glad seven feet of metal now shielded me from the hive—or I would have been pursued.

I stepped back and listened. Metal buildings cause an acoustic echo. The choral buzzing of bees became an ascending roar. The roar soon mixed with the voices of two startled men. Their kite making had been interrupted.

I shouldered the rifle, drew my handgun, and moved to a side window to watch. I expected the men to walk quickly but calmly for the front door. They were used to working with bees, presumably. I figured they would let the bees settle for a few hours, or maybe the whole night, then return with a smoker to calm the hive and to figure out what happened.

It would give me time to slip in, brave a few more stings, and grab Vue.

But the men did not react as expected. Nor did the bees. The bees amassed from the hive and moved like an iridescent waterspout toward the men. The men were already slapping at the colony's attacker scouts when they began to run. They threw open the double doors and came stumbling outside.

To my amazement, the bees followed. When a bee stings, an alarm pheromone is deposited. These men were marked and the entire colony went after them, drawn by the scent, and also by the mammalian body heat and movement.

The men were screaming now as they ran. There were security lights out front and I watched as the bees swarmed outside, gaining on the men, then covering them like ants. One man fell, then the other. When the last of the hive arrived, both men were thrashing beneath layers of bees.

The hives behind the building were isolated from the other hives for a reason, I realized. Along with importing illegal weapons, these people were raising Africanized honey bees—"killer bees," as they are known. Introducing noxious exotics into the United States was a favorite form of unconventional warfare among terrorist types.

If I hadn't used the water, the colony would have swarmed me instead. They could've swarmed me *anyway*.

My mouth was sticky dry. The swarming sound of bees is an atavistic sound that signals the legs to run. Far worse, though, were the sounds made by the dying men. Inhuman moans, childlike pleas for help. They would've been better off if I had shot them from the window. It would have been a kindness for me to shoot them *now*.

But moral assessments are as tricky as the vagaries of our uncertain lives. I did not fire.

I had to get Vue. The bees would soon return to the building searching for their smashed hive.

I bolted inside and knelt over him.

"Vue? Vue?" I shook him.

He opened his eyes.

I USED THE BADEK I'D TAKEN FROM THE BEARDED killer to cut the duct tape and I pulled Vue to his feet. But he couldn't walk. His legs were numb, he said.

"Give me a few minutes." His voice was amazingly calm for what he had endured.

"We don't have a few minutes." Bees were buzzing by my ears. I grabbed the big man's wrist, pulled him over my shoulder in a fireman's carry, and waddled outside far enough from the lights and the swarming bees to be safe.

As feeling returned to his legs, Vue stood and began taking experimental steps. Soon he was swinging his arms and rolling his neck muscles.

"I pissed in my pants. I bet I smell very awful."

I told him not to worry about smelling very awful. I had extra clothes in the truck.

"Where's Lourdes?"

"He knows where President Wilson is staying tonight! We must warn him."

"What?"

"Lourdes found my shortwave transmitter and he hooked it up inside." Vue indicated the processing plant, which was full of bees by now. "The president made contact at eleven. When that helicopter lands, the president will expect us to get out, not Lourdes. Lourdes knows Morse code!"

Vue sounded shocked. I was only mildly surprised. Lourdes was expert at using computers and electronics to trick victims.

The gate where I had seen guards was several hundred yards away, but I was worried they might come back to check on the plant so I was steering Vue away from the building. "What about Tomlinson?"

Vue stopped to look at me. "You not find him?"

"No."

"They had him tied just like me, only not so much. But then Lourdes take him away, so maybe they both on the helicopter."

I checked my watch. It was ten minutes before midnight. The flight to the cattle ranch where Wilson and Rivera were staying would take at least an hour. The helicopter had lifted off at 11:15.

"Can you run?"

"I try!"

"I have a truck and someone waiting. There's still a chance we can intercept Lourdes."

"A truck is no good. Too far, too far! The president will be dead by time we get there."

That's not what I meant. I had checked the sky once
again. This time there *was* a helicopter, approaching low
from the southwest and closing fast.

I fished a flashlight from my pocket so I could signal
the helicopter when it was closer.

Lourdes had a deal with his employer, Vue told me as
we jogged. He had overheard enough to piece it together. If Lourdes delivered the head of President Wilson, they would provide him with a new face and a new
identity in Indonesia. They had the surgeons and the
technology to do it.

He'd kept Vue and Tomlinson as bait.

"You ever see that bastard without his mask?" Vue
asked as we neared the truck. "He hates you. But he
wants the president *more*."

Maybe that's why he'd taken Tomlinson, I suggested.
Lure me in.

But Vue said, "No, I think the reason is different. He
said Tomlinson has a nice face."

24

Sergeant Curtis Tyner told Shana Waters, "You should live with me in the jungle for a few months. Get to know the oil prospectors and headhunters—birds of a feather, really. Then you'd realize I'm considered a damn fine-looking man in this part of the world."

Tyner had landed in his futuristic-looking, five-passenger Bell helicopter and immediately offended the woman by telling her that if she was as smart as she was good-looking she would have had an anchor job *before* she turned forty—a suave endearment, in Tyner's strange mind.

"You have to live outside America to be an expert on the American media, and I *am* an expert," he explained, attempting damage control. "I have seven satellite dishes in my compound and more TVs than a sports bar. What else am I going to do in my spare time, socialize with monkeys? New York should hire me as a consultant."

Now, as we flew toward the Pacific coast of Panama at a hundred forty knots, Tyner had offended her once again by suggesting she return with him to the Amazon Valley of Colombia.

"You're not for real," Waters said, dismissing him.

Tyner turned and looked at her bosom. "Neither are those. But that doesn't mean it wouldn't be fun getting to know you better."

Curtis Tyner *was* unreal; among the most bizarre characters I've encountered. He's about five feet tall, with amber-red hair and bristling orange muttonchops of a type that I associate with Scottish bagpipers from a previous century. Tyner would resemble an orangutan if it weren't for his handlebar mustache.

He had stepped out of the helicopter, extending his hand, saying "Damn glad to see you again, Commander Ford! Game's afoot, huh?" then ordered us aboard. His tiger-striped pants were bloused into jungle boots, a black beret angled low over his right eye, and he slapped a leather swagger stick into the palm of his left hand as he approached.

Pinned onto Tyner's beret was a golden death's-head and also the winged intelligence owl of the IDF. Most impressive was a green pyramid pierced by a stiletto—Delta Force. SEAL teams, Green Berets, and Rangers are in awe of Delta Force. For good reason. They are *operators,* the selected amalgam of the country's special forces.

Delta personnel are the secret soldiers that Hollywood, and the American public, does not know about.

As a bounty hunter and special warfare consultant, Tyner had seen places and done things that even an experienced journalist like Waters could hardly guess at.

I found him interesting as a character, but also scary and offensive in a way that tickled the gag reflex. The man *did* collect shrunken heads for a hobby. Becoming expert in military tactics and killing had made him rich—a *big* man—and he had an unsettling mannerism that psychologists would find interesting: He unconsciously rubbed his hands together as he talked, as if washing them.

I did not doubt Tyner's expertise, nor his connections. Chiseled in stone over the entrance to his mansion was the watch phrase BY WAY OF DECEPTION THOU SHALT DO WAR.

When it came to hunting down Praxcedes Lourdes, Tyner was my first choice. He would not have paused to consider beehives if he had a gun.

TYNER WAS NOT A PURIST. THE HELICOPTER'S control panel was aglow with GPS, radar, infrared imaging screens. Ten miles out from the cattle ranch, he asked, "Should we go in soft or go in hard, Commander?"

Meaning, should he make a combat ascent onto the property or should he do a few touch-and-goes a mile out to insert me and Vue? We could then approach the ranch in stealth.

It was 12:30 a.m. We had made up time in the fast Bell aircraft, but Lourdes had probably already been on the ground for twenty minutes or more. The image of Kal Wilson and Juan Rivera walking out to meet that helicopter only to be surprised by Lourdes and his men was sickening.

I said, "We don't have time for soft."

Tyner hummed his approval. "Lock and load, gentlemen. Safeties on until I give the word."

In my headphones, I heard Shana demand, "Why the hell don't you just radio the police?!"

Tyner said, "Because it kills the profit margin," as he tilted us downward, a dive that left my stomach behind and the woman silent.

The Pacific Ocean was ahead, the waning moon a smear of orange behind rain clouds. I could see the lights of the cattle ranch.

Was that a fire burning?

Yes. But small, like a campfire.

"I don't see a helicopter. Do you?" We'd leveled off, and shot past the ranch house and corrals at a hundred knots. Tyner banked around for another look.

No . . . no helicopter. Something else: Wilson's plane was no longer moored in the lagoon.

"Are you sure we have the right spot?"

I was sure. I recognized the bay and the layout of the ranch. Even so, I checked the telemetry receiver. The flashing dot was steady: Danson's wallet was somewhere on the ground below.

"Then there's something wrong. I don't like it."

Nor did I.

Near the campfire, a couple of men were staring up at us. The men I'd seen cutting wood, possibly.

"Put me on the beach. I'll check it out."

Tyner said, "Okay, but I'm going airborne the moment your feet touch sand," meaning he suspected a trap.

THE MEN WERE *VAQUEROS*. THEY WORKED ON the ranch with cattle and horses. But they were nervous as I approached—shifting their weight from foot to foot, machetes within easy reach.

They were relieved when I told them I was a friend of Juan Rivera.

"You are the *yanqui* named Ford?" one asked.

"That's right."

"He told us you might return. The general was once a great *caballero*." The *vaquero* smiled. "It is a shame we no longer have men like him."

Men who work with horses and cattle are also sometimes called *caballeros,* the Spanish word for "knight." The man was talking as if Rivera were dead.

"No," the man explained, "the general is not dead. It is a way of speaking of people who lose their heart at a certain age."

This was not a trap. These men knew Rivera.

The plane that floated on water, the *vaquero* said, had flown away more than an hour ago with Rivera and his *yanqui* friend aboard. Afterward, a helicopter landed. Men searched the house, and one of them tried to set the barn on fire. The man was very angry, the *vaquero* said, screaming profane words in a strange accent.

Lourdes.

"But we extinguished the fire. That is all we know." Once again, the *vaquero* was shifting from foot to foot.

"Did the angry man ask you questions?"

"No. He did not see us. We . . . know who this man is. The stupid peasants in the mountains call him '*Incendiario.*' A monster. We do not believe in monsters, but neither are we stupid."

The two *vaqueros,* I realized, had watched from hiding until Lourdes was gone.

"How did you know it was *Incendiario*?"

"Because of the helicopter he uses. A yellow helicopter. The *Indios* speak of it. And also because"—the two men exchanged looks—"because one of his men fled and we could hear *Incendiario*'s voice as he searched. He swore to burn the man alive if he found him. Even as his yellow helicopter left the ground, *Incendiario* was screaming."

I said, "A man escaped? Where is he?"

The *vaqueros* exchanged looks once again. The man who had not spoken said, "Do you have a paper that proves you are this man Ford?"

I showed them my passport.

The men studied it so intently that I realized they could not read.

"The man who escaped rolled from the helicopter while the others were searching the house. His hands were tied behind his back, and we are the only ones who saw him. He ran along the beach to the corrals, then past the barn. But he stumbled as he climbed a fence. He fell into the pen where we keep the *puercos*.

"Those animals are wild. We trap them in the forest, and they sometimes kill our dogs."

It was a place, the *vaquero* said, where even *Incendiario* would not search.

Puercos.

Pigs.

It was Tomlinson.

TOMLINSON CALLED TO ME, "IF PIGS COULD FLY, man, I'd be pasted on some statue right about now!" Trying to be funny, but, instead, he sounded robotic, possibly in shock.

I was searching the pen with my flashlight, seeing black-haired hogs with tusks, belly-deep in slop after the rains, a Stygian nightscape too dark for the light I was using to probe.

But when I called Tomlinson's name, he answered, "Over here!" then moaned something indecipherable before attempting a brave front. *If pigs could fly . . .*

I used the flashlight to signal the helicopter—*Land immediately*—then ran around the outside of the pen, sweeping the beam back and forth until I saw a section of Tomlinson's arm and hand, skin white as rice paper, protruding above the pack. He was waving to be seen, either sitting in mud or on his back—I couldn't tell—surrounded, or pinned, by the hogs.

I vaulted the fence and landed in muck up to my calves. I was trying to get one of my boots free when Tomlinson yelled, "Don't show fear! They won't hurt you!"

I got the flashlight up in time to see two pony-sized boars charging me. The clicking of their tusks was the sound of bone on bone.

I wasn't going to risk it. I slogged back to the fence, got a leg over the top rail as one of the hogs grabbed me from below, locking onto a length of shoestring like an attack dog. The shoestring gave way and I fell backward off the fence, landing so hard it knocked the breath out of me. I came up fast, drawing my pistol, holding the flashlight along its barrel in a two-handed grip.

"Don't shoot them. They're my friends!"

Friends?

I *wanted* to shoot. It was one of the scariest things I'd ever experienced. But I touched the hammer release and used the flashlight instead.

The hogs scattered when they charged me and I could see Tomlinson plainly for the first time. He was sitting in mud, back erect, legs folded into full lotus position, arms thrust outward, fingers and thumbs making circles. Around each wrist were cuffs of frayed rope, his hands no longer tied. He squinted with the pain of the light in his eyes.

"I was afraid you were Praxcedes and came back for me. He was going to burn me tonight." Tomlinson's voice was still monotone. Absurdly, he continued to meditate. Yes, in shock.

I was moving to the other side of the pen, hoping the pigs would follow. I said, "Tomlinson, get out of there. Lourdes is gone. You're safe now."

A lie because he wasn't safe. The pigs were losing interest in me, snorting and gnashing their tusks as they refocused on Tomlinson. I had the gun out again, flashlight laid along the barrel. I touched a red laser dot to the head of the boar that was now chewing my shoestring.

"Praxcedes wanted my face for a surgical transplant. But he found out I'm the wrong blood type. He needs O-positive. Vue's O-negative, but the surgeon told him that could work. Praxcedes wanted you and the president to watch me burn."

"Tell me later. Get out of that pen."

"But there's no danger. You shouldn't have run."

The boar would have been eating my leg right now instead of my shoestring if I hadn't run.

I listened to Tomlinson tell me, "When I first fell in, I thought I was a goner, man. Pigs *all over* me. Know what they went for first? My *hams*. Funny or what? Instead of eating my butt off, though, they chewed my ropes. I communicated with them, man. They *freed me*."

I said, "Uh-huh. Regular heroes." I was moving the laser dot between the two boars. "I'm asking you as a favor, climb out of there."

"Okay. But they're gonna miss their new buddy."

I pulled the hammer back as Tomlinson got to his feet, slinging mud from his fingers. His pants had been ripped to tatters. I couldn't tell if he was injured. The pigs, I noticed, continued to root where he'd been sitting, playing tug-of-war with bits of plastic bag.

When he got to the fence, I hurried and helped him onto the ground. Fear is exhausting; shock is debilitating. Tomlinson was so weak, his legs were straw until he got an arm over my shoulder.

The stink was incredible.

"Sam and Rivera knew Lourdes was coming. How, I don't know, unless Sam locked onto my telepathic warning. Which is *possible*. It made Praxcedes crazy. Crazier. I had time to get my legs free. Man, I bounced out of that helicopter like a bunny."

I said, "You need a bath in disinfectant. Pigs may like you, but bacteria don't play favorites."

"Nope, salt water is best. Salt water cures anything. Whoops!" I was helping him toward the beach, but he stopped to pat the back of his pants. "I'm missing something, man. Hey!" He searched his front pockets, then tried his back pockets again—they had been ripped away.

"Damn. The pigs got Danson's wallet." He was looking back at the sty. "I was going to return it to his family. It was inhuman what Lourdes did to that man. They tied him to a pole and used a blowtorch—"

I gave him a shake. "I know, I know. Don't talk about it."

Tomlinson took a deep breath, shuddering as he inhaled, then let the breath go slowly. He was teetering near the abyss but fighting it.

"Okay . . . but I have to go back for his wallet—"

"*No*. I'll get it."

He was still feeling for his pockets. "You're patronizing me, man. I can tell."

"Exactly."

I was watching the helicopter descend toward an open area between the ranch house and the beach. It looked like a spacecraft, with its blinking lights and powerful landing beam. I told Tomlinson that Vue was aboard and in good shape. The news buoyed him. Tomlinson is a resilient man. A lightning rod for positive energy, he describes himself, and maybe that's true. He seemed to rally.

"Doc, if you do go back"—it took me a moment to realize he was talking about Danson's wallet again—"it would be *nice* to find it for his family. But while you're there? I had some Ziploc baggies rolled up in my back pockets. About two ounces of prime weed."

I shined the light toward the pen where the animals were still rooting among the remains of plastic bags.

"I thought pigs are evil but they're not. They're actually very mellow once you get to know them."

I said, "It's probably because you're a vegetarian."

SHANA WATERS TOLD ME, "I CALLED NEW YORK and told them about Walt. Until it's confirmed, though, and his relatives are notified, they'll hold the story. *Try,* anyway. A lot of TV people aren't going to get any sleep tonight."

Tyner had given her a satellite phone, saying, "Keep it. Bring it along when you visit me in the jungle."

Waters had replied, "Sure—when the Amazon freezes. I can tour your art collection." Sarcastic but taking the phone, anyway.

She thought Tyner was kidding when he replied, "I'd *like* that. Most people don't consider shrunken heads art."

Waters had spent the next hour on the phone, pacing between the porch and kitchen, where I had sliced a haunch of smoked beef, provided by the *vaqueros,* and opened canned beans and canned spaghetti I'd found in the cupboards.

Shana had also told New York that she knew where to find Kal Wilson—Panama City.

The amphib needed a lighted municipal airport to land at night. Panama City was the closest, but it wasn't a guess. We found a note inside the ranch house that was crumpled and partially burned. Presumably, it had been tacked to the door when Lourdes arrived.

If you came for my head, you will find it at the Panama Canal Administration Building, noon, tomorrow. Kal Wilson

Wilson knew a killer was coming. How?

Vue had the best explanation. The president wasn't forewarned telepathically, he was tipped-off tele*graphically*. Telegraph operators develop a unique style on the key. "Fist" is the term, Vue said. He and the president had been practicing Morse code together for months.

Wilson may not have known Lourdes was coming, but he knew it wasn't Vue who sent the message.

What Waters didn't share with New York were the specifics. Tomorrow's Independence Week celebration was a huge story and she wanted to be the only network reporter broadcasting live.

"It's what Walt would have done," she told me. We were walking toward the Pacific, where rollers conveyed starlight before collapsing onto sand. "The network's going to send a crew from Miami first thing. Just in case, we're also arranging for a local crew to be standing by."

It was 2:30 a.m., and I'd left the hammock I had commandeered as a bed, too restless to sleep. What I really wanted to do was go for a swim. But I had surprised Waters, who was standing on the porch smoking a joint. She wanted to walk with me.

When she offered the joint, I shook my head and asked, "Did Tomlinson give you that?" I'd thrown his clothes away while he was swimming and couldn't imagine where he'd hidden it.

"No. I gave *him* one. Two joints, actually. His day was even worse than mine, and I figured he could use it. I'll buy more when we get to the city."

I was tempted to tell her to keep away from the pigs but said, "Very kind of you."

"I *like* him. And he was such a mess."

True, but cleaner now. I had searched the barn until I found veterinary-grade disinfectant soap and a bottle of Betadine. I poured half of each into a bath and told him to go soak. He walked into the bathroom carrying a bucket of ice, a bottle of tequila, and three limes.

"I'm going to attack the bastards from the inside,

too," he said. Meaning bacteria. He was weak but getting better.

As we walked, Waters talked about Key West and Danson. Neither of them recognized the president, she told me.

"I've been in so many hotels, staff people become shapes without faces," she said. "Have you ever run into a friend at some place totally unexpected? They look so *different* until we make the association. He reminded Walt of an actor—see what I mean?"

It wasn't until an hour later when she discovered her recorder missing and confronted Danson that they made the connection. After that, they had stood toe-to-toe, arguing, blaming each other for blowing the biggest story of the year.

"It was so damn funny the way we battled back and forth," Waters said, "trying to beat each other. It's true that I've wanted his job for years. But I'm still going to miss him."

I wondered.

Waters spoke with warmth and regret. But I couldn't be sure if she was sincere or trying to manipulate my opinion of her. She wanted to interview me about Wilson—she'd mentioned it in an offhand way, as if I'd already agreed.

Maybe I had, in her mind. This was a woman expert at leverage and she'd been within viewing distance when I shot three men.

But the closest she came to hinting at it—if she *was* hinting—was when she stopped, looked at me, and said,

"In Key West, I knew you were no maintenance man. Even drunk as he was, Walt knew it, too. Who're you with, the CIA? I'd say the Secret Service, but they're not allowed to . . . *do* the sorts of things you seem good at."

I said, "I'm a biologist. I was hired as a consultant on the new canal. I was with the president because I'm familiar with the area."

She chuckled, shaking her head. "That's insulting. Do you really expect me to believe that?"

I said, "It happens to be true, but you're right—it's not the whole truth." She was not expecting me to add, "I should know better. Some of the things I heard on your recorder are memorable. I apologize for underestimating you. It won't happen again."

The woman cleared her throat. "You listened?"

"Only portions. It was a long flight."

"Where is *my* recorder?"

"I have it. I'll return it—tomorrow. When President Wilson says it's okay."

Waters nodded, letting it sink in. "Did Tomlinson steal it? Or did you?"

I nearly smiled. Wilson had said that no one expects a former U.S. president to break the law. "What does it matter?"

"I thought you might admit it. Tomlinson's too religious and Kal Wilson wouldn't have the nerve. You're *different,* Ford. Nerdy and industrious—like setting out food for everyone. But underneath, you are one very damn cold customer."

The woman stopped, relit the joint. Inhaled a couple

of times, holding it like a cigarette, then offered it to me once again. When I refused, she said, "Boy Scout, huh? I don't *think* so. You and I have a hell of a lot more in common than either one of us is likely to admit. Scary, huh?"

She turned her back to me and began doing something—unbuttoning her blouse, I realized. I replied, "When you put it that way, yes."

"I can't imagine what you think of me after hearing what's on that recorder."

"Don't worry. I averted my ears when it got personal."

She laughed. "Like a boy who covers his eyes when a western gets too romantic."

"I didn't hear any romantic parts."

"That's because I'm a realist, not a romantic." Waters slid her blouse off, unsnapped her bra. With the practiced immodesty of an actress, she tossed them above the tide line. Then, using fingers to brush her hair back, she turned to face me. Curtis Tyner and Juan Rivera shared the same fixation, and their interest was not unwarranted.

"Ford? You should let your hair down. Because I'm getting my hair *wet*. After the day we've had, we both deserve it."

The woman shimmied out of her slacks and panties and I watched her walk into the sea.

25

Use a predator to lure a predator . . .

Kal Wilson had said it about a hammerhead shark that was shadowing a barracuda. Cayo Costa, five days ago.

It seemed like five weeks ago. I should've felt tired after so little sleep and so much travel. Instead, I felt energized.

I am not fanciful when it comes to speculating about emotion attributed to creatures not of my species. When people say their cat, or dog, "believes he's human," I attempt to smile as I edge away. But I have speculated— fancifully, I admit—that the single-minded focus of a shark might be the purest sensation in nature.

That's how I felt. Single-minded.

I was sitting high in a tree, back braced, sniper rifle in my hands, as I watched political luminaries assemble for Panama City's Independence Week ceremony.

It was 11:05 a.m., Wednesday, November 5th.

I was more than a hundred yards away. Even with my glasses clean, the crowd was a blur—people socializing and finding their seats on a stage decorated with bunting and flags. But when I pressed my eye to the rifle's scope, individual faces came into focus, filling the lens, as I moved the crosshairs from person to person searching for the assassin that Kal Wilson told me would be there.

He was not the only one expecting trouble. Security around the stage was intense. Panama's special assignment cops wear black. There were dozens moving through the crowd, using bomb-sniffing dogs and metal detectors at the two public entrances cordoned off by rope.

Political ceremonies attract political activists. There were several protests under way: clusters of people carrying signs, already chanting slogans. Elections were approaching. U.S. economic sanctions against Panama was a volatile subject, and so was Indonesia Shipping & Petroleum's control of the canal.

Some despised the *yanquis*. Some despised the IS&P. Discontent on other issues was scattered throughout. There were *many* issues because Panama is like no other country in the region.

Panama City was part of Colombia until the U.S. dug the canal, then protected its investment by backing independence. They named the new nation "Panama."

Panama was an invention of the Canal Zone, and the canal's construction spawned a population assembled from cultures around the world. It was not considered a

Latin country until the 1950s for the simple reason that its citizenry was so varied.

Kal Wilson had referred to Panama as an Ark. He had been stationed at nearby Albrook Air Base and he knew the people and the country well.

Once again, he was right.

The Apocalypse *could* start here.

I paid close attention to a large and vocal group of protesters to the north. Signs they carried identified them as members of Jemaah Islamiyah, an Indonesian faction devoted to creating an Islamic state in Southeast Asia and joining Middle Eastern Muslims in Holy War.

Ramadan had just ended, so there was a big turnout. Many wore traditional Muslim dress, loose robes, shawls, *kufis*. Women kept their faces covered with scarves, or *burqas*—a full-face veil with only a slit showing the eyes and bridge of the nose.

I moved the rifle's crosshairs from face to face.

Praxcedes Lourdes was a theatrical man. It was a costume he might enjoy.

I checked my watch: 11:10 a.m.

I expected to come face-to-face with Lourdes very soon.

WE HAD ARRIVED IN PANAMA CITY AT DAWN AND I had neither seen nor spoken to Kal Wilson. An hour after landing, I left Vue and Tomlinson in the lobby of the El Panama Hotel, so it was possible they had made contact. I didn't know. There was no reason for me to speculate.

Wilson had given me simple but specific verbal instructions plus the sealed envelope. I had not opened the envelope until I was alone in the suite we'd rented.

The president's note included a final, unexpected order. I felt numb as I read, then reread it. There was no mistaking what he wanted me to do. Question was, could I?

When I had read the card twice, I burned it and flushed the ashes.

I knew what was expected of me, even though I still didn't know what Kal Wilson had planned. The president shared information only on a need-to-know basis.

My only clue was what he had said on Cayo Costa: *Use a predator to lure a predator . . .*

But who was the barracuda? Who was the shark?

What I knew, apparently, was enough. I had orders. I would carry them out.

I knew how to view a parade ground or a motorcade route as a killing field and I knew how to reconnoiter that killing field. Where were the unavoidable intersections? The unobstructed walkways?

They were "X spots." Good places to kill.

A shooting post that would appeal to a skilled assassin would also appeal to me. I could identify those spots and secure them. More difficult was anticipating the scrambled behavior of an amateur.

I have done similar surveys other times in my life. It was the reason I had been in Colombia the day they fired a rocket at Wilson's motorcade.

I spent an hour jogging the area—joggers being as common as stray dogs and no longer drawing attention. I was already familiar with the Balboa and Quarry Heights sections because I'd spent a lot of time there with Zonian friends before the U.S. transferred control. By the time I was done jogging, I knew it better.

The Canal Administration Building, where the ceremony was to be held, is located at the base of Ancon Hill, a bunker-shaped mound that's forested, topped with radio towers and a giant Panamanian flag.

Five hundred feet below the Administration Building is an E-shaped fortress, separated by woods, canal housing, and gardens, all built on a steep incline. The Administration Building is museum sized, four stories high, built of rock, marble, and redwood, all from the U.S.—Teddy Roosevelt's way of marking this small country with his own spore.

The ceremony was to be held at the front of the building, where royal palms create a corridor connecting the massive entranceway with a stone monument and fountain, the Goethals Monument—a tribute to the canal's architect.

Panama is among the most beautiful countries in the world. This was the most beautiful section of Panama City.

The stage had been erected next to the fountain and monument. There was a podium with microphones screened with bulletproof plastic. There were four chairs to the left of the podium and two rows of chairs to the right.

The four highest-ranking people would be in the chairs to the left.

The back of the stage was tented so political luminaries would not be seen until they stepped out onto the stage—a security precaution.

I had no trouble finding a superb sniper post. While giving me instructions, Wilson had reminded me that on the east side of the Administration Building there was a trail called the "Orchid Walk." It zigzagged uphill, two hundred yards through rain forest. It was now overgrown, I discovered, but still passable.

I selected a tree at the edge of the trail that gave me a clear view of the stage and the adjoining park. I found branches that allowed me to brace my feet and back but weren't too far off the ground. Then I rigged a rope so I could get up and down quickly and spent a few minutes practicing both maneuvers.

The ceremony started at noon. It was now 11:20.

I took a last look through the sniperscope, then buckled rifle and sling to a limb that could not be seen from below.

I was expecting a visitor.

I WAS WEARING LEATHER GLOVES AND HAD THE rope coiled, ready to slide to the ground. I had a pistol and also the curve-bladed knife, the Indonesian *badek,* I'd taken from the bearded killer.

In ten minutes—11:30—I was expecting a man to come plodding up the steep trail. But people are sometimes early.

A hundred yards away, the stage was equipped with a sound system. A man was experimenting with the volume, his voice booming, *Testing . . . testing . . . one, two, three, one, two, three*, lyrical in Spanish, but I waited in silence of my own making, a silence that originated in a dark and single-minded space.

The inner ear bridges an ancient barrier between land and sea. Sound waves must be converted into waves of liquid before the brain reads them as electrical impulses. I was oblivious to the blaring speakers. But the sound of leaves stirring, then the pop of a branch broken underfoot, registered like gunshots.

I sat straighter, ears straining.

The night before, Shana Waters wasn't the only one who had used Tyner's satellite phone. I'd called my son in San Diego. The number was new—I hadn't had time to store it in my cell phone and forget it.

It was after midnight in San Diego but Laken was still awake doing research on his computer. Praxcedes Lourdes, I told him, was probably somewhere in Panama City doing exactly the same thing.

Maybe there is a paternal link between parent and child that alerts the brain's emergency circuitry. This is *important*. He did not argue or question when I told him to send Lourdes an e-mail.

"You want me to tell Prax that *I'm* in Panama City?" Laken had asked.

"Yes, and that you want to meet him."

There's an old trail called the Orchid Walk, I told my son. "He'll find it."

I gave him a time.

Ten yards downhill, around a bend, another limb cracked . . . then came the sound of a rock rolling free.

Lourdes had gotten my son's e-mail.

26

Praxcedes Lourdes was dressed as a woman . . . a Muslim woman, with traditional robes, a shawl, and a *burqa,* the full-face veil with only a horizontal slit for the eyes. The man was a freak for costumes.

I waited until he was beneath me, then jumped, using the rope to slow my fall. I crashed into him so hard he was launched tumbling into the bushes. His surprise registered as a girlish scream.

By the time he got to his feet, I had the knife out. I grabbed him by the shoulder, pulled him to me with unexpected ease, then looked into his eyes as I touched the blade to his neck.

Lourdes's burn scars are signatory. I expected to see one sleepy gray eye and one lidless blue eye. Instead, I was looking into eyes that were olive-brown, wide with terror.

I stepped back. It *was* a woman. She screamed—a high, warbling alert—as I slid the knife into my belt and stammered in Spanish, "I'm sorry . . . I've made a terrible mistake. I thought—"

I didn't finish. There was a rustling of bushes behind me, a *woof* of heavy breathing, and as I turned to look, a huge hand spun me as a knee hammered at my groin. I deflected all but the first kick, a glancing shot that buckled my knees with nauseating paralysis. The barrel of a gun, jammed under my chin, kept me on my feet.

Once again, I was looking at a figure cloaked in a *burqa*. This time, pale eyes stared back, one gray, one lidless blue.

"Ford, you meddling punk! I expected your spawn. A younger face. Softer. Skin I can *use*."

Praxcedes Lourdes swung his head at the woman, who was edging sideways down the trail. "Go, bitch! You've done your job."

The woman understood English. She lifted the hem of her robe from the ground and ran.

Lourdes had his left hand behind my neck, the gun in his right, and he pressed the barrel deep, rotating it as if burying a screw. He found the knife in my belt, then the pistol. As he tossed them away, I tried to spin away but gagged as he pushed harder and tried to knee me again. He stank of cigars, and also something fetid, like bugs I'd once left in a jar too long.

"I can't believe your son conned me. We were becoming such pals. Where is that sweet boy, California? I checked the IP address."

Lourdes the computer wizard.

My voice was hoarse as I nodded, "California. Yes."

Laughter. "What a fucking imbecile! You think reverse psychology works on me? So he *is* in California. I'll catch the next freighter. I'll bring scalpels and dry ice. Maybe there'll be a harvest moon."

As I brought my hands up to pry the gun away, his knee hammered me twice in the thigh. The body's most sensitive glands all seem linked to the gag reflex. My legs sagged once again and he collapsed with me onto the ground. He buried a knee in my stomach, then got to his feet and stood over me, a stainless steel revolver pointed at my head.

I told myself not to panic—*Breathe, the nausea will pass*—as he said, "Ford, I *knew* it was a con. I would have been on this trail waiting anyway. That's how stupid *you* are."

I took a chance and sat up. My pistol was only a few yards behind me, the knife next to it. I arched my back as if in pain, my right hand behind me. The first weapon I touched I would use.

"Keep your hands where I can see them!" Lourdes moved as if to kick me. I put my hands up to block him.

He stepped back. He motioned with the gun. I got slowly to my feet, expecting him to pull the trigger any moment.

"Your boy has such a beautiful face. Nothing at all like your slab of meat. I may boil you down for glue. Picture it before I put a bullet in your brain. How am I going to look wearing your brat's face?" He bowed and yanked the *burqa* off his head.

Praxcedes Lourdes resembled a human skull over which gray skin had been stretched too tight, then patched with melted wax. Tufts of blond hair grew out of white bone. He had the wild eyes of a horse that smelled smoke.

I had once sealed this man in a fifty-gallon drum, determined to roll him off a ship into the Gulf of Mexico. Wilson was right—I was a fool to have spared him.

Lourdes was reaching into the pocket of his robe as I said, "Plastic surgery can't disguise an asshole, Prax. It's been tried."

My lungs were working again, the adrenaline circulating. I took an angling step toward him as he pulled a lighter-sized butane torch from his pocket, then a plastic squirt bottle filled with some kind of gel.

I was watching the man's eyes. Excitement increases blood flow, eyes appear to glaze. With this freak, compulsion was pathology. He couldn't stop himself. He had to see me burn.

"You are so goddamn sure of yourself. You know what I'd like? I want to see you *run,* Ford!" Lourdes lunged at me with the bottle, squirting a stream of gel as he snapped the torch's flint trying to fire it.

It didn't light—and he also dropped his pistol.

I blocked some of the goop with my gloves as I sidestepped, then dove at him. I hit him just below the knees, knocking his legs from beneath him. Lourdes weighed close to three hundred pounds and he came crashing down on me. But he didn't let go of the torch, which still wouldn't start.

"Goddamn thing!"

We got to our feet at the same time and I waited for him to lunge. I dropped to one knee when he tried to club me, ducked under his huge hands, and came up behind with my left elbow cradling his throat, my left leg threaded between his legs so he couldn't move. I locked my fingers beneath his jaw, tilting his head back, and pinned my right knee against his spine. The gloves gave me a better grip.

Lourdes still had the butane torch and I snatched it from him. The gel was close enough for me to reach and I grabbed it.

"Ford . . . what are you doing?"

I was squirting a stream of gel down the back of his robe, *that's* what I was doing. The goop smelled of soap and petroleum.

"Are you insane? Stop that!"

Lourdes, the psychopath, was also claustrophobic. The last time we'd met, I had told him I would bury him alive if he threatened my son again. Fire, as it burns, can also entomb. It was close enough.

I had the man's head torqued so hard that he was looking over *my* shoulder. I could have broken his neck if I'd wanted. But I was furious . . . and he did not deserve a quick and painless ending that for me has become procedural.

Talking into his ear, I whispered, "Too bad, Prax, change of plans. *You've* got to run."

As I started flicking the butane torch, I watched the one lidless blue eye grow wider in that terrible face. Then, abruptly, he stopped struggling. He seemed to be focusing on something behind me.

"Ford! Let him go. No fires."

I waited until I heard, "Step away. That's an order," before I turned to confirm that the voice was familiar.

A man was coming down the hill toward me carrying a gun. It was Kal Wilson.

WILSON WAS WEARING A NAVY-ISSUE SWEATSUIT and ball cap pulled low on his head and pointing a pistol at Lourdes. It was the Russian silent pistol I'd seen earlier.

Vue was with him but several yards up the incline. The barrel of his submachine gun moved in synch with his eyes as he stood watch.

Lourdes appeared dazed. I felt the same. What was the president doing here?

"Step away," Wilson said again. He used the pistol to wave me back as he marched toward Lourdes. Instead of tinted glasses, he was wearing contacts. Even so, he paused to focus on the man's face. "Good God . . . I didn't believe the photos. You really are a monster. But you did it to yourself."

As I retrieved my pistol, then the revolver, I watched Lourdes touch his fingers to his face. "I didn't do this. I was trying to rescue my family when I was burned. I was a *child*."

Sociopaths perfect multiple personalities as camouflage. Lourdes *sounded* childlike.

I started to warn "Don't fall for it, Mr. President—" but Wilson silenced me with a look.

He took a step closer and studied the huge man's face. It was a patchwork of skin and stitching. Cheeks, jaw, and lips were made up of rectangles and squares of varying colors, flesh sewn together over years by quack surgeons. It was a mosaic of brown skin, white skin, black skin, and pieces that were jaundiced.

The sections had been harvested from people he had murdered, stolen like scalps, then worn as medals. Finding a new face, a whole face, was a recent obsession.

Lourdes's voice changed—now he was the good man wrongly accused. "You don't understand. Ford *attacked* a woman here just a few minutes ago. She ran away screaming. Call the police; they'll find her. I was just trying to protect her!"

Wilson's expression changed. It was the wrong thing to say.

I tossed Lourdes's revolver into the weeds as I pulled the semiautomatic from my belt. "Mr. President, I don't know how you got here but you should leave *now*. Sir? Mr. President?"

Wilson brushed past me. He didn't stop until he was a few feet from Lourdes. The pistol was pointed at the big man's chest. "On the island, in Nicaragua. Why did you set fire to the plane? You had to know I wasn't aboard. You murdered seven innocent people. *Why?*"

"Fire? I didn't—"

Wilson pulled the hammer back.

Lourdes made a quick personality change. "But it wasn't me! It wasn't me! I can tell you who did it, though. Ford—"

Lourdes must have recognized something familiar in Wilson's eyes—perhaps seen in a mirror—because he began to back away.

"Did you see my wife? Did you speak to my wife?"

Lourdes was nodding. "She was a nice lady. We talked! She got off the plane to stretch her legs and we talked. But the last time I saw her, or any of them people, she was getting back aboard. She turned, gave me a big smile and waved when she heard me yell good-bye. And then I left. And that's the God's truth."

The president snapped, "My wife was deaf, you son of a bitch," and backhanded him. He still had the fast hands of a Naval Academy boxer. The sound of skin hitting skin cracked like two boards slapping together.

Lourdes went into a rage if someone touched his face. The transformation was chemical and abrupt. His fingers explored the place where he'd been hit, eyes glowing. The monster resurfaced. "The bitch was *deaf*? Lucky *her*. Maybe she couldn't hear herself *scream*—"

Before he got the word out, Wilson shot him three times. The Russian pistol made a *plink-plink-plink* sound, no louder than the clicking of a telegraph key, or the refrain of a sonata.

THE PRESIDENT STOOD OVER LOURDES FOR A moment, his chest heaving. But then he took a long breath, back in control. He turned to Vue. "Let's go. I need to change."

He pulled off the sweatshirt as he started up the hill.

There was a white dress shirt beneath, the collar starched. As he handed the pistol to Vue, Vue handed him a gray suit coat from his shoulder pack, then a tie.

My brain was trying to assemble an explanation. "Mr. President? Did someone intercept my son's e-mail?"

"Your son? What's your son have to do with this?" Wilson was fitting the tie under his collar.

"How did you know I was here? That Lourdes would be here?"

Wilson said, "I knew because *I* told you about the Orchid Walk, remember? Lourdes knew because Rivera fed him the information." Wilson stared up at the tree canopy for a moment, took another deep breath, and released it. "Wray and I used to walk this trail every chance we got. She loved orchids." He paused as Vue knelt to retrieve something—the *badek* knife, short but balanced, with its curved blade. It was still on the ground.

Wilson recognized it. "Mind if I take that with me?"

"Of course. But why?"

"I have a speech to give."

I said, "President Wilson . . . do you have to go through with this? You killed Lourdes. Isn't that enough?"

Who was next? Thomas Farrish? Clerics? I hated the idea of him risking it. I nearly used the Panamanian cops with their metal detectors to dissuade him, but then I remembered that former presidents are not searched.

Wilson said, "No, it's *not* enough. There are all kinds of ways to destroy men and there's more at stake than you understand. Did you open the envelope I gave you?"

I nodded.

"Then follow your orders, Dr. Ford."

"I don't know if I can."

"You can, and you will."

As he started up the trail, I said, "Kal . . . are you *sure?*"

"Absolutely certain." Wilson took a last glance at the corpse of the man who had killed his wife, then caught my eye. He came as close as he could to smiling. "The shark and the barracuda," he said. "You make excellent bait."

27

At 1 p.m., I was sitting high in a tree, far from where Lourdes had died but close enough to hear the master of ceremonies announce, "Ladies and gentlemen, please welcome former president of the United States, Mr. Kal Wilson. He will speak in the absence of Ambassador Donna Riggs Johnson, who is unable to attend."

The military band played the first bars of "Hail to the Chief" as Wilson strode across the stage toward the podium. Through the sniperscope, his face filled the lens. He paused only to salute another unexpected guest, General Juan Rivera. Rivera was wearing a white formal uniform, medals and ribbons clustered on his chest.

Wilson pointedly did not stop to shake hands with the four men seated to the right of the podium. Among them was Thomas Farrish, who controlled the canal through his company IS&P, and his mentor, Altif Halibi, the Islamicist cleric who had issued the *fatwa* against Wilson and offered the million-dollar reward.

The two men wore similar expressions on their faces as Wilson stepped to the microphone—uneasiness and contempt.

In the months that followed, I would listen to the former president's speech many times, as did people around the world. Shana Waters, broadcasting live, got it all—so did New York. Via satellite. Digitally.

Wilson attached the microphone to his lapel, then spoke for less than five minutes. I expected him to talk about U.S. sanctions against Panama or instigators of the Apocalypse. Instead, he surprised everyone on stage, beginning: "I am not here in an official capacity. When I contacted the White House this morning, I was asked not to speak. Ambassador Johnson has also asked me not to speak. I am going to speak anyway. But the words and the opinions are mine alone."

As Wilson waited for his interpreter to translate, I used the telescopic sights to scan the stage, then the audience. Some listened, but gangs of protesters continued to chant slogans in the distance. From my post, forty feet above the ground, high on Ancon Hill, I could see other groups carrying signs, marching, near Balboa High School, and then Albrook Air Base just beyond, where Wilson had once been stationed.

The man really was revisiting places that had been important to him and his wife.

As Wilson resumed speaking, I returned my focus to the stage. I was using a tree branch to support the sniper rifle and I fixed the crosshairs on Wilson's chest. It was a strange and sickening sensation. Unreal. Like swimming from the light of a coral reef over a drop-off where the ocean plummets into the darkness of abyss.

On the card I had burned Wilson had written:

The presidency is sacred, and I will not risk disgracing the office because I have chosen to take a risk. If anyone attempts physical interference or restraint while I am on stage, shoot me. Shoot to kill.

Those were my orders. They came from a man who, I was aware, dreaded the humiliation of the disease consuming him but who also understood the power of symbols. If he allowed himself to be humiliated, the presidency would be debased.

Days ago, Vue had told me there must be wind and light when a great man dies, so the sky can take him. On this tropical afternoon in Panama, there were both.

I would carry out my orders.

AS WILSON SPOKE, THEN WAITED FOR HIS INTERpreter, a rhythm emerged that was subtle, inviting. During each pause, I used the sniperscope to observe the reactions of the audience, the Panamanian security police scattered through the crowd, and a half dozen men stationed behind Thomas Farrish and the cleric Altif Halibi.

Bodyguards.

If there was trouble, it would begin with them.

The interest in Wilson's words radiated gradually outward through several thousand people. One politician's truth is another politician's lie, but people recognize sincerity and they are attracted to it even when they don't agree.

What Wilson said was dangerous. They recognized that, too.

"A few months ago, an invitation was delivered to me in the form of a fire that killed seven people, including my wife. I am here to respond, and also point out that you, too, received an invitation. It was delivered on a Tuesday in September, in New York. Since then, it has been delivered many times around the world.

"There could be no better place to address this issue than Panama. Panama is at the crossroads of the world and your people represent every religion and race. The same is true of all the Americas, from Canada to Brazil.

"That is precisely why they hate us. We are joined by geography *and* our differences. It does not matter that some of us pray to a God they claim as their own. They say we lack courage, resolve, and morality. They say we are mongrel nations and unclean. They will not tolerate our tolerance.

"So they send these invitations—but from the shadows. The shadows are where intolerance and hatred and cowardice always hide."

For the first time, Wilson looked at Thomas Farrish and Altif Halibi sitting to his left. Farrish was dressed in a suit of white silk, the cleric was bearded and wore a turban and robes. Both sat stoically, refusing eye contact.

Wilson continued to look at them as he said, "Perhaps it would be good to explain who we really are and thereby remind ourselves exactly what our heritage demands of us.

"We are the sons and daughters of every race, all religions, joined between two oceans and by a passion for self-determination and freedom. We are not a perfect people. The inequities we suffer as neighbors, and inflict as neighbors, are many. But we do not hide in shadows.

"In us runs the blood of revolutionaries and explorers, of farmers, immigrants, and Aztec statesmen. In us runs the blood of train barons—and train robbers—and of individuals who, though chained in slave ships, refused to bow down as slaves.

"We are people who risked the gallows to create sanctuaries on earth that, for the first time, guaranteed religious freedom. In the years it took to build the Panama Canal, Muslims, Christians, Hindus, and Jews lived and worked and prayed here, side by side, and continue to do so.

"Our numbers include women brave enough to demand equality, and who continue to fight against the sickening control some attempt to impose on them. Are we a collection of mongrels? *Yes*.

"The same was said of us in another invitation. It was issued from Berlin in 1939.

"If you believe we lack courage and resolve, it may be because you have banned so many history books. Allow me to enlighten you.

"We are the fifty thousand who took our convictions

to earth at Gettysburg. We are the thousands of white crosses that rest where poppies grow at Flanders Fields— South Americans, Central Americans, and North Americans, all died in that war.

"We are Simón Bolívar's fearless charge against the Spanish, and a thousand Inca warriors, marching against the guns of Conquistadors. We are the Seventh Cavalry who perished at Little Bighorn. We are Apache warriors who refused to run and so stood awaiting death while chanting: 'Your bullets stand no chance against our prayers.'

"We are not an easy people. We love a winner and despise a coward. Courage is an immigrant's cornerstone, and our reverence for self-reliance has never been equaled nor will it ever be."

Once again, Wilson stared at Farrish and Halibi. "You can't possibly understand who we are. But our quandary is this: In any conflict, the boundaries of civilized behavior are defined by the party that cares least about morality.

"You have defined the boundaries and there are none. The lives of innocent women and children are meaningless. You hide weapon factories beneath day care centers. You hide collectively behind the caskets of innocents. You have no morality, no character, no conscience, while most people around the world are blessed—and burdened—by all three.

"Fascism has worn many costumes. Yours is religion. That makes it even more difficult, but we will find a way. Appeasement is suicide. The world is beginning to understand that." He paused, then pointed directly at them.

"Your cowardice only strengthens our resolve. Your hatred stands no chance against our prayers."

He returned his attention to the crowd. "Thank you. God bless you, and God bless Panama."

Wilson closed the leather folder and stepped back from the podium.

The crowd's applause was loud, much louder than when he'd been introduced, and Wilson paused to acknowledge it. He nodded to Juan Rivera. "Would you agree, General?"

Rivera marched to Wilson, gave him a bear hug, then exhorted the startled audience in Spanish, "You have just heard a *man* speak! Have you forgotten what it's like?"

The applause grew.

Wilson smiled. He looked happy; a man at peace, standing with his old enemy. It may be the happiest I had ever see him.

Then he turned and walked toward Thomas Farrish and Altif Halibi.

With the scope's crosshairs on the president's back, I moved my index finger to the trigger guard.

AS WILSON APPROACHED, FARRISH WAS LOOKING over his shoulder. He began gesturing to his bodyguards. The cleric Altif Halibi refused to make eye contact with the former president. It was more than disinterest; he radiated contempt. To acknowledge a *kuffar*—an "infidel cow"—was beneath him.

The crowd, I realized, had suddenly gone silent. The

Panamanian police watched with interest. Wilson was still wearing the microphone and they wanted to hear what he would say.

Wilson addressed the two men as if they were one. He said softly, "I accept your invitation. Here it is. Give me the money."

Farrish was snapping his fingers, trying to get security to intercede. I moved the crosshairs from the president's back to Farrish's head—*tempting*—as Farrish said, "What do you mean, 'It is here'? *What* is here? I have no idea of what you are saying." The man had spent his playboy years in the U.K.; the accent was British.

"You wanted my head. Here it is." Wilson tapped his temple. "You owe me a million dollars. I'm donating the money to Panama's orphanages."

Farrish laughed, but it was nervous laughter. The cleric stood, his hands folded into his robes, but he stopped when Wilson said, "What are you afraid of? I'll make it easy."

I watched Wilson reach inside his jacket . . . and I saw the fear in the cleric's eyes as he drew the curved knife— the *hadek,* an instrument made for killing infidels.

Someone in the audience screamed; everyone began moving then—Vue, Farrish's bodyguards, the police. But they stopped when Wilson tossed the knife at the cleric's feet. His voice was loud enough now to echo in the noon silence. "Go ahead. I've brought you my head, cut it off! Sunlight's a great disinfectant—for everyone but cowards."

Farrish stood. "I have had enough of this insanity!"

Wilson said, *"And so have I."* Then he slapped Farrish across the face, just as our seventh president, Andrew Jackson, had once done to a man who insulted his wife.

Rivera had placed himself between the bodyguards and the two men. The security police had closed ranks, but now more as admiring spectators.

Farrish was holding his cheek. His skin had the flushed, mottled look of a man who is frightened and in shock.

Wilson moved close enough to brush both Halibi and Farrish with his chest. "You offered a reward for my head. I want the money. *Now.* Or satisfaction. I'm challenging you to a duel. If you have the courage, *face* me."

Farrish looked at the cleric, the cleric looked at Farrish—then they both slid past Wilson, who remained solid as a statue.

The two walked swiftly toward the exit.

Epilogue

At noon, November 27th, a Thursday, Tomlinson and I boarded Amtrak's Silver Star in Tampa, kicked back in our respective sleeper cars, enjoying beverages and an elegant dinner. Eleven hours later, we disembarked beneath a blazing full moon in the village of Hamlet, North Carolina, population 6,018.

Hamlet's train station, with its Victorian Queen Anne gables, wood painted and polished bright, may be the most beautiful in America. Kal Wilson and blues icon John Coltrane were born nearby.

Tomlinson had stood by the tracks, in a circle of yellow light, watching our train pull out, gathering speed northbound toward Raleigh, Richmond, D.C., and Grand Central Station, New York.

"A time warp," he said.

The city's main street was deserted an hour before

midnight. No one else had gotten off the train, and the upstairs station windows were dark, save for one where the silhouette of a stocky man was hunched over a typewriter—or maybe a telegraph key.

"The moon's bright enough, we should've brought our ball gloves," I told him. We could have played in the middle of the street, no problem.

My arm felt good. Two weeks after returning from Panama, General Juan Rivera had met us at the Presidential Library in Minnesota. We'd gotten a sandlot ball game going with some local kids and Rivera had pitched three innings of shutout ball. Next day, we received VIP treatment, and a special tour of the Wilson Center.

The president himself had welcomed us into his office, then he took us next door to show us the First Lady's office. There was a concert grand piano, and Tomlinson had played "Moonlight Sonata" and "Clair de Lune" until a nurse noticed that Wilson was weakening. We pretended not to see the wheelchair she'd left around the corner.

The three of us said good-bye with the forced but courageous good humor that friends draw upon when they know they may never meet again.

BUT WE WOULD MEET AGAIN. TWO DAYS EARLIER, Vue had telephoned unexpectedly and invited us here, to Hamlet, saying, "He wants to see you."

As Tomlinson had once observed, it's impossible to say no to a man like Kal Wilson.

So we booked sleeper cars and took the train. We didn't

even consider flying commercial. We would have had to land in Charlotte, then there would have been a two-hour drive southeast.

Besides, we wouldn't have enjoyed flying commercial after the way we'd returned from Panama.

The White House was so delighted with Wilson's speech, and the reaction it had received worldwide, that the president had sent Air Force One as special thanks. He had insisted it be designated Air Force One, even though it carried a former president.

Shana Waters was aboard. She thought it was hilarious when, somewhere over the Caribbean, Tomlinson signaled for Wilson's attention and said, "Sam, I don't want to put you in an awkward spot, man, but"—Tomlinson had looked at Waters—"there are a couple adventurous types aboard who'd like to be the first to smoke a doobie aboard this fine aircraft."

Wilson had chuckled, but then said, seriously, "You'd need a time machine, I'm afraid. I'm *fairly* certain you wouldn't be the first."

Tomlinson liked that. "Wow," he said. "Radical."

Later, Waters came to me, stood on tiptoes, and whispered another adventurous suggestion. When I said, "I think we'd need a time machine to be first at that, too," she was not dissuaded.

Pulling me by the wrist, she countered, "I covered the White House for three years. You don't think *I* know that? But history's *supposed* to repeat itself."

In its way, Hamlet's train station was a time machine. Wilson had chosen this, his boyhood home, in which to spend Thanksgiving, and had decided to stay on until Christmas.

That's why we were standing in this North Carolina village, an hour before midnight, looking at a blazing moon.

It was a "hunter's moon," Tomlinson informed me. The first full moon in November.

"Yeah, man," he added, his tone introspective, "streets are empty, and it's bright enough to play. Next time, we bring our gloves."

But there would be no next time, as we both knew.

THE NEXT MORNING, WE STOOD ON A COUNTRY road, too small for the number of Lincoln Town Cars, unmarked Fords, and Secret Service SUVs parked in the sand, and watched Agent Wren touch an index finger to his ear before telling his partner, "He's countermanded my orders *again*. His doctor's, too. He says these two *gentlemen* should be escorted in immediately."

As Wren said "gentlemen," his eyes brushed past me with a variety of contempt reserved exclusively for rogue biologists who help rogue commanders in chief escape. Wren didn't like me, didn't trust me, and had contacted the head office in Maryland determined to keep Tomlinson and me out.

Finding several joints in Tomlinson's silver cigarette case, he believed, had finalized his case.

Instead, he had been overruled.

Wren's partner straightened his Ray-Bans and turned

toward two houses set back in a clearing of orange clay and pines. The area had been cordoned off with Secret Service agents, local law enforcement, and sophisticated electronic sensors.

Tomlinson asked Agent Wren, "Did his family own both these houses?" Each was tiny: white shingle exteriors, asphalt shingle roofs, and sand driveways.

Wren's partner answered, "No. The president and his family lived in the one on the right. The First Lady's family lived in the other. Their parents worked for the same textile mill, and they both moved to Minnesota at about the same time. That's where the Presidential Library's located. And the Wilson Center."

Tomlinson said we were aware of that as one of the agent's radios squelched, and I overheard, *"If Hunter wants privacy, that's what Hunter gets . . ."*

Not easily accomplished.

Overhead, two Blackhawk helicopters cauldroned like seabirds, maintaining secure airspace, keeping a half dozen TV news choppers at bay. There was a breaking story below. New York, Atlanta, and L.A. wanted a live feed when it happened.

Kerney Amos Levaugn Wilson lay dying in the house where he had been born.

LEUKEMIA DESTROYS RED BLOOD CELLS WITH A swarming indifference. Kal Wilson's face was the color of a mushroom, and he looked as frail.

He lay in a hospital bed, in the room that had been his

as a boy, surrounded by monitors and tubes but also family photos. The Boy Scout and the deaf girl, with this same white-shingled house in the background—there were several black-and-white shots in frames.

When Tomlinson and I entered the room, Vue gave us a quick hug, then shooed everyone else out. When he turned to close the door, I could see that he'd been crying. I don't know why I found that surprising but I did.

The president stuck his hand out. I shook it. His skin was cool but too loose over its fleshy scaffolding. He didn't object when Tomlinson leaned to pat his shoulder—a daring familiarity with this man.

"I'm glad you came," he said. "The holiday season's a busy time for everyone. But there's one last bit of business I'd like to dispose of before . . ." He had a mask that fed oxygen when he needed it and he fitted it over his face and took several breaths. He left the sentence unfinished.

"You received the envelopes containing your dossiers?"

Yes, we had. Tomlinson and I had not shared. Not everything, anyway. We all have done things in the past that we would prefer to remain in the past. That is certainly true of my life.

As the documents confirmed, Tomlinson had been recruited, tested, and then employed by a federal agency— the CIA, most likely—as "asymmetrical intelligence-gathering personnel."

"My God," he wailed when he told me, "I was a psychic spy. Like James Bond, man, only I never got to leave the damn room."

"You have nothing to be ashamed of," I told him.

I was referring not only to Stargate. Tomlinson had unwillingly participated in another CIA program, he discovered, that is not as well documented because files were ordered destroyed by Richard Helms, director of the CIA at the time.

According to information provided by Wilson,

The research project, code-named MKULTRA, was established to counter Soviet advances in brainwashing techniques. It was designed to study the use of biological and chemical materials in altering human behavior, and also human memory.

MKULTRA researchers demonstrated that human memory can be damaged or destroyed by electroshock treatments—Tomlinson was proof. But there was no way to *selectively* destroy memory, as Hollywood would have us believe.

Far easier, they discovered, was introducing specific, detailed memories of events that, in fact, never occurred. Give a subject a combination of drugs and shock treatments, for instance, show them a film of a murder scene over and over, and the subject would soon be convinced he was guilty.

"You had nothing to do with sending a bomb, or killing Naval personnel," the former president told Tomlinson. "You already know that. The information was in the documents I provided. But I wanted you to hear it from my own lips. Feel better?"

Tomlinson was looking at him affectionately. "You are

a good one, Sam. I wish you would've run for a second term. We need you, man."

According to polls taken after the stand he took in Panama, Kal Wilson could have won the presidency again—but the mention of a second term was still an unwelcome subject.

He pointed abruptly to the door and said to Tomlinson, "Give me a few minutes alone with Ford."

AFTER TOMLINSON EXITED, WILSON TOLD ME, "You never admitted that you are one of the thirteen plank members of the Negotiating and Systems Analysis Group. I want you to sit in on a little meeting I've arranged with three of those plank members. Right here. Are you willing?"

It seemed absurd to lie but I had to. "I still don't know what group you're talking about, sir."

He went on as if I hadn't spoken. "It's my understanding that members of your group trained and operated separately for security reasons. You've never met."

That wasn't exactly true. I was aware of the names of two fellow members. Hal Harrington, the software millionaire, and another who was a journalist.

I shrugged. "If you would like me to stay, I will."

"It is also my understanding that one of your members was supposed to destroy all documents relating to your group's activities. But he didn't."

That was my understanding, too, but I said nothing.

"Members of your group had quite a scare a few years

back when a *New York Times* reporter nearly came into possession of some of those documents. It was my last year in office."

I was beginning to feel uncomfortable. Even for a former president, Wilson knew way too much about the Negotiators.

"I really have no knowledge, sir—"

The door opened and I stopped in midsentence. It was Harrington, the intelligence guru Wilson said he no longer trusted. I no longer trusted him, either. Hal was the man who'd kept records that should have been destroyed.

Surprised, I looked from the president to Harrington. Typically, Harrington was wearing a tailored suit and tie. Atypically, he looked distressed.

Wilson took several breaths of oxygen, then said gruffly, "Tell him the truth."

Harrington cleared his throat. "I was using the stuff we had on your pal Tomlinson to keep you working for us. I don't apologize for that, damn it. We *need* assets like you, Ford.

"But now that you're both guaranteed a pardon"— Harrington grimaced at the former president—"I guess the only leverage I have is your sense of duty. I discussed it with President Wilson and we thought that if two plank members of the Negotiators asked you to keep working, you might reconsider."

I turned from Harrington to Wilson, then looked at the door. "I'm confused. You said a meeting of three plank members. Who's the third?"

President Kal Wilson was staring at me with his intense green farmer's eyes. He continued staring until a gradual and numbing awareness forced me to face him. He nodded. "That's why I couldn't risk running for a second term."

I sat back in my chair digesting this, remembering Wilson in my lab exactly one month ago saying, *"I ran across other globe-trotting Ph.D.s with backgrounds as murky as yours. Scientists, journalists . . . even . . . politicians."*

Wilson said, "I'm right about this, Ford. *Stay.*"

I RETURNED TO FLORIDA UNDECIDED.

We all accumulate past regrets and I began to fear my indecision would become another. Shortly after I got home, I sent the president a telegram—an anachronistic touch I thought he would appreciate.

RIGHT AGAIN STOP AS USUAL STOP AWAITING
INSTRUCTIONS STOP FORD

Two days later, I was beneath my stilt house, patching a hole in the shark pen, when I got word Kal Wilson had died.

I am still awaiting my instructions.